Troy Gree

Praise for

CARLA NEGGERS

"Carla Neggers is one of the most distinctive,
talented writers of our genre."
—Debbie Macomber

"Neggers keeps the reader guessing 'whodunit.'"
—*Publishers Weekly* on *The Widow*

"Suspense, romance and the rocky Maine coast—
what more could a reader ask?…Neggers writes a story so
vivid you can smell the salt air and feel the mist on your skin."
—Tess Gerritsen on *The Harbor*

"Neggers's brisk pacing and colorful characterizations sweep
the reader toward a dramatic and ultimately satisfying
denouement."
—*Publishers Weekly* on *The Cabin*

"When it comes to romance, adventure and suspense, nobody
delivers like Carla Neggers."
—Jayne Ann Krentz

"[Neggers's] skill at creating colorful characters and
deliciously twisted story lines makes this an addictive read."
—*Publishers Weekly* on *Stonebrook Cottage*

CARLA
NEGGERS

THE
WIDOW

MIRA®

MIRA

ISBN-13: 978-0-7783-2516-1
ISBN-10:   0-7783-2516-4

THE WIDOW

MIRA and the Star Colophon are trademarks used under license and registered
in Australia, New Zealand, Philippines, United States Patent and Trademark
Office and in other countries.

www.MIRABooks.com

Printed in U.S.A.

To my mother, and to the memory of my father

CHAPTER 1

Abigail Browning squirted charcoal lighter fluid on the mound of papers she'd torn up and piled into her backyard grill.

She had more pages to go. Another two spiral notebooks.

She set her lighter fluid on the little wooden shelf next to the grill and picked up the top notebook from the plastic chair behind her. When she opened the cover, she tried not to look at her scrawled handwriting, as pained as the words she'd written, or at the stains of long-spent tears that had smeared the ink as she'd forced herself to recount the tragic story of her honeymoon.

Each journal—there were fourteen, two for each year of loss—began with the same litany of facts, as if the re-telling itself might produce some new tidbit, some new insight she'd missed.

It's the fourth day of my Maine honeymoon, and I'm napping on the couch in the front room of the cottage my husband inherited from his grandfather.

Two loud noises awaken me. Tools clattering to the floor in the back room. A hammer. Perhaps a crowbar. I'm startled, but also amused, because I'd spent the morning helping Chris repair a leak.

As I get up to investigate the noises, I think it must be an unwritten rule—newlyweds aren't supposed to fix leaks on their honeymoon.

Abigail tore off that first page by itself and ripped it into quarters, setting them neatly atop her pile, the lighter fluid seeping into the cheap paper and old blue ink as if it were fresh tears.

Last night's anonymous call had changed everything. She needed a cover story to explain her actions—what she planned to do next.

She also needed clarity and objectivity.

Seven years of journals. Seven years, she thought, of trying to restore her emotional life.

I smell roses and ocean as I get up from the couch.
A window must be open.

Even now, at thirty-two, no longer a young bride, no longer a law student with a handsome FBI special agent husband, no longer inexperienced in matters of violent death, Abigail could feel herself walking into the back room, convinced the wind had knocked over tools she and Chris had left haphazardly that morning, when they gave up their leak-fixing to make love upstairs in their sun-filled bedroom.

She noticed the slight tremble in her hands and swore under her breath, tensing her fingers as she tore more pages and set them atop her pile. There was no wind, and the grass—what there was of it in her postage stamp of a backyard—was damp from an overnight rain. Adequate conditions for burning, although she was in a tank top and shorts. If her bare skin got hit with sparks, it'd serve her right.

As I step into the back room, I see not a cracked window but the door to the porch standing wide open, and for the first time I feel a jolt of real fear.

I didn't leave the door open.

"Chris?"

I call my husband's name just as I hear the floorboards creak behind me.

Just as the blow comes to the back of my head.

Her chest tightening, Abigail dropped the partially torn spiral notebook back onto the chair and quickly struck a wooden match, tossing it onto the pile of ripped pages.

Flames shot two feet into the hot, still air.

"Whoa, there. That's some fire you've got going."

She looked up at Bob O'Reilly trotting down the last of the steps from his top-floor apartment in the triple-decker they and Scoop Wisdom—all three of them detectives with the Boston Police Department—had bought together a year ago, pooling their resources to afford the city's sky-high real estate prices. Bob, a twice-divorced father of three, lived alone. Scoop, who worked in internal affairs and had a well-earned reputation with the women of Boston, occupied the middle floor. Abigail, a homicide detective and widow, had the first floor. She got along with Bob and Scoop partly because they understood she had no intention of sleeping with either of them.

"Outdoor burning's illegal," Bob said.

"I'm getting ready to throw some hot dogs on the grill."

"You don't eat hot dogs."

"Salmon, then."

At six-two, the veteran detective had nine inches on Abigail in height, and, although he was pushing fifty, he could run ten miles and still move the next day. He'd taught her how to use free weights properly, and he'd taught her crime scene investigation. She'd taught him what it was like to lose someone to violence.

She'd taught him that seven years was the blink of an eye.

A page, filled with bloodred ink, went up in flames.

As I regain consciousness, I feel the ice pack on the lump on the back of my head and almost vomit from the raging pain of my concussion.

"Don't move," my husband tells me quietly. "An ambulance is on the way."

I try to tell him that I'm fine, but I become very still as I notice the anger in his face. The knowledge. The awful sense of betrayal.

He knows who did this to me.

Bob pointed at the five-pound Folgers coffee can that she had set on the plastic chair, behind the stack of spiral notebooks. "What's that for?"

"The ashes."

"Come again?"

"I'm performing a cleansing ritual."

"A firebug I arrested ten years ago said the same thing."

"This is different," Abigail said, watching the pages blacken and burn. Once Bob left, she'd finish tearing up the last two notebooks, burn their pages, rid herself of their raw emotion.

Detective Bob O'Reilly of the BPD wouldn't understand cleansing rituals. He had pale skin and freckles and red hair that was graying gracefully; only his cornflower eyes suggested the work he'd done for almost thirty years ever got to him. His second wife had walked out on him two years ago, telling him he was an emotional basket case and recommending therapy. Instead, Bob got drunk with cop friends, packed up his stuff, and, swearing off marriage forever, moved out, eventually buying the triple-decker with Scoop and Abigail.

"Is that your handwriting? The purple ink?" he asked.

Abigail glanced at a scrap that had just caught fire. "I used different colored inks depending on my mood."

"How's a purple-ink mood different from, say, a blue-ink mood?"

"I don't know. It just is."

"What are these, journals or something?" He seemed to have to struggle to keep the disbelief out of his tone.

"I started keeping a journal after Chris died. My therapist suggested it."

"Oh."

"She said to write stream-of-consciousness, without thinking, but to try to use all five senses and the present tense. She wanted me to write about our time together…what happened when he died."

Bob scratched the back of his thick neck. "It helped?"

"I don't know. I guess. I haven't thrown myself off Cadillac Mountain."

She grabbed the partially torn notebook and opened it up to the middle, tearing a hunk of pages, trying not to look at the words.

Chris leaves me with the ambulance crew, who will take me to the emergency room at the hospital in Bar Harbor. He doesn't say where he's going. He doesn't promise to be back soon. He doesn't promise anything.

I have no premonition of anything bad about to happen.

I just don't want him to leave me.

Bob unhooked a pair of tongs from the side of the grill and stirred the blackened pages, rekindling the dying fire. "You never thought about killing yourself, Abigail," he said, not looking at her. "Only thing you thought about was finding out who killed your husband."

She flung more pages on the fire.

By nightfall, I'm worried. So are Doyle Alden, a local police officer, and Owen Garrison, Chris's rich neighbor. I can see it in their faces.

Chris should be back by now.

"Abigail? You're not breathing."

She made herself exhale and smiled at Bob, who, initially, hadn't even wanted her in the department, much less working at his side in homicide. Too much baggage, he'd told everyone, including her. It wasn't just her husband. It was quitting law school, it was her background. She'd had

to earn his trust. "I'm okay. I should have done this sooner.
It feels good."

"Why are you doing it now?"

"What?"

Bob wasn't one to miss anything.

Abigail tore more pages, tossed them whole onto the
fire, nearly smothering it.

I ignore warnings to stay inside—to rest—and instead put on my hiking boots and go off on my own
into the unfamiliar landscape. Unlike Doyle and
Owen and my husband, I don't know every rock,
every tree root, every snaking path through the woods
or along the shore.

I'm not from Mt. Desert Island.

Bob watched her squirt more charcoal lighter fluid on
her fire, the orange flames glowing in his face.

"The journals are emotional clutter—a drag on me."
Her words sounded okay to her, anyway. Plausible. "I'm
heading up to Maine in the morning."

"I see."

"I need to do some work on the house."

"Taking vacation time?"

"Some. Things are quiet right now. I have plenty of
time coming to me."

Bob poked at the fire with his tongs. He wasn't by
nature a patient man, but he had explained to Abigail,
equally impatient, how his experience had taught him the
value of strategic silence. She knew if she tried to fill the
void, he'd have her.

The combination of the lighter fluid, the flames, the

heat and the emotion had her eyes stinging. But she didn't cry.

She'd never cried in front of Bob or Scoop, any of her fellow police officers.

I see Owen Garrison down on the rocks, near the waterline, below the skeletal remains of the original Garrison house, burned in the great Mt. Desert fire of 1947.

I can taste the ocean on the air and smell the acidic odor of the damp, peat-laden earth.

My mind doesn't want to take in what I'm seeing.

The body of a man.

Owen tries to stop me from running. "Don't, Abigail…"

She picked up the spiral notebook on the bottom of her pile. The last one to burn, and the first one she'd filled, the handwriting oversized and thick, a pen difficult for her to hold in those initial, terrible weeks of rage, shock and grief.

With a sharp breath, she ripped out too many pages at once and distorted the metal spiral, ended up tearing sheets on an angle. She threw what she had onto the fire and pulled off the bits that had stayed behind, then grabbed another fistful and yanked those pages free.

Bob O'Reilly continued to watch her.

"I'm taking the ashes with me to Maine. As many as I can fit in the coffee can. I'm going to dump them in Frenchman Bay. It's part of the ritual."

"Should be pretty up there," he said.

I keep running. I don't slip on the rocks or hesitate, even as Owen grabs me by the waist. "Chris was shot, Abigail. He's dead. I'm sorry. There's nothing you can do now."

Owen won't let me go to my husband. He won't let me contaminate the crime scene when there's no hope.

All we can do now, he says, is find the killer.

Bob hooked the tongs back onto the side of the grill. "Forget it, Detective Browning. You're not fooling me. You're not even coming close. Cleansing rituals. Emotional clutter." He snorted. "Bullshit."

Abigail tilted her head back and gave him a lofty look. She could feel her tank top sticking to her back. Her hair, short and dark, had twisted itself into corkscrews. Bob didn't wilt under her scrutiny, and finally she sighed. "I have no idea what you're talking about."

His cornflower Irish eyes leveled on her. "You haven't given up, Abigail. You won't toss in the towel on finding your husband's killer, ever."

"If you were in my position, would you give up?"

"We're not talking about me." He leaned in toward her. "Something's happened. Something's changed. What?"

Abigail turned away from him. "Bob…"

He grunted, silencing her. "If you can't tell me what's really going on, you can't tell me. Just don't give me cleansing rituals."

"Okay, but the part about fixing up the house—"

"That's a little better, as cover stories go."

"It's not a cover story—"

"Abigail."

She decided not to push her luck, and Bob didn't press her further, scowling once more before heading back up to his third-floor apartment. Abigail watched her fire die out, here and there bits of unburned paper amid the ashes. She peeled the lid off her coffee can and noticed that she'd started to cry, almost as if she were someone else.

Using a long-handled spatula, she scooped ashes into the Folgers can.

Not all the ashes fit.

She stirred those left in the grill. All she needed to do was start a fire with two of Boston's most respected detectives on the premises. She'd been a detective for just two years. By Bob O'Reilly and Scoop Wisdom's standards— by her own standards—she was still a novice.

They believed in her, and she proved herself one day at a time, but she'd decided, even before she'd formed her own plan of action, not to tell them about last night's call.

An anonymous tip.

It wasn't the first in seven years, and it wasn't the craziest—but she didn't need two trusted colleagues, two unwavering friends, to talk her out of following up on it.

Her spatula struck a half-burned page pasted to the bottom of the grill, the words jumping out of the ashes at her in thick, black marker, as if somehow she needed reminding.

I am a widow.

CHAPTER 2

The tip had come to her the night before in theatrical fashion.

It was the second Saturday in July, the day Abigail and Chris had chosen for their wedding seven years ago. She had spent the day alone. She always did, despite her friends and family who would call and invite her to barbecues and dinners, a movie, a Red Sox game.

Once, her mother, a corporate attorney with a high-powered husband, a woman who'd learned how to relax, had offered to book Abigail a spa day. *"Get a massage. Get your toes done. You'll feel better."*

Only her mother, Abigail had thought. But Kathryn March had made her widowed daughter smile with that gesture—mission accomplished.

Her father was a different story. He never tried to make his only daughter smile on her anniversary. He knew he couldn't. Abigail had told him he couldn't.

"Was Chris killed because of you?"

"Abigail...don't..."

"Was he?"

"I was the father of the bride on your wedding day. That's all."

"Did you put him up to something on his honeymoon? You've seen the file on his murder. What's in it? What aren't you telling me?"

The truth was, there was nothing in Chris's file. Otherwise his murder wouldn't have remained unsolved. Investigators wouldn't release certain details to a family member—in their place, Abigail wouldn't, either. But the Maine State Police and the FBI weren't hiding anything from her. Although he was a director of the Federal Bureau of Investigation, a hard-driving, self-made man, a former Boston cop himself, John March had no advantage when it came to his son-in-law's murder.

He couldn't produce a killer any more than she could. The evidence just wasn't there. He couldn't even console his daughter.

Not that she needed consolation. Not anymore. What she needed was resolution.

Answers.

But on the second Saturday in July, Abigail thought only of the man she'd loved and their time together. She didn't think of Chris as the FBI special agent brutally murdered on his honeymoon, nor did she let her mind wander to the stack of materials she'd collected herself for her own investigative file on his death.

She'd landed at their favorite restaurant on Newbury Street and asked to sit by the window, where she could see the outdoor tables, crowded with diners enjoying the warm July evening, and passersby, young lovers holding hands, older couples out for an evening, perhaps celebrating their own wedding day.

Abigail wasn't celebrating, but she wasn't mourning, either.

"I love you, Abigail. I'll always love you."

She wanted to crawl back in time and tell him…*don't! Don't love me! Love someone else. Live, Chris. Live.*

But, because she couldn't, she ordered a glass of Pinot Noir and thought of her wedding flowers—hydrangeas, roses—and that sparkling Maine afternoon, and how handsome Christopher Browning was as he'd waited for her to walk up the aisle on the lawn of the quaint seaside inn where they were married.

"Excuse me—ma'am? Are you Detective Browning?"

Her waiter's words yanked her out of her memories and dropped her back into the real world. "Why—"

"You have a phone call."

A call? Why not reach her on her pager or cell phone? She eyed the waiter. He was young, unfamiliar. "Who is it?"

"I don't know. I just—" He gestured back toward the bar. "Someone gave me the phone and said it was for you."

"All right. Don't go far, okay? I might want to talk to you."

He nodded, retreating fast.

Abigail held the phone to her ear. "Yes?"

"I'm sorry to disturb your dinner." The voice was unrecognizable, barely a whisper. She couldn't even tell if it was a man or a woman speaking. "Are you having your husband's favorite wine?"

"Who is this?"

"Pinot Noir, correct?"

Damn. She pushed back the emotion of the evening and called on her law-enforcement training and experience. *Keep whoever it is talking.* "That's right. Are you here? Join me."

"Another time, perhaps."

"Did you know my husband?"

"Shh. Shh. Just listen. Your husband turned over too many rocks. Bad things crawled out. He was eliminated." The static whisper made the words seem even creepier, more menacing. "His death wasn't a random act of violence."

"I need you to be more specific—"

"You need to *listen.*" It was the first time the caller had put emphasis on any one word. "Things are happening on Mt. Desert. Again."

"Is someone else in danger?"

"You're the only person the killer fears."

"Are you suggesting I'm in danger?"

"I'm suggesting you're the one who can find the answers. *Detective.*" A brief pause. "You've gained experience over the past seven years. You haven't lost your determination to solve your husband's murder. The killer knows you won't stop until you do."

A cold finger of emotion penetrated her cloak of professionalism. "How do you know what the killer knows?"

"I have to go."

"Wait—you said 'things' are happening. What kind of things?"

"No more."

"What about the rocks Chris turned over—what crawled out? Give me an idea. Otherwise, once I hang up, I drink my wine, have a nice dinner and dismiss this as another crank call. I've had several over the years, you know."

"This is the call you've been waiting for. You know it is."

"Don't—"

Click.

It was done. The call was over. Abigail set the phone on the table and dug her detective's notebook out of her handbag and tugged off the Bic pen she kept attached to it. The waiter, who must have been watching, wandered back to her table, but she held up a hand, silencing him as she wrote down every word the caller had said to her.

When she finished, she flipped the pad shut and sat back, eyeing the waiter. A kid, really. "What's your name?" she asked him.

"Trevor—Trevor Baynor."

She took down his address and phone number, learned that he worked at the restaurant twenty hours a week—the rest of the time, he studied jazz at the Berklee College of Music. Piano.

"I need to get back to work," he said.

"Sure. First tell me who took the call I just received. The bartender?"

He nodded. "Her name's Lori."

"What did she say to you when she handed you the phone?"

"She said—I don't remember."

"Try."

He shoved a hand through his tufts of thick blond hair. "She said to give you the phone. That you had a call."

"She knew my name? How?"

"The caller, I guess."

"There are a hundred people in this restaurant, Trevor. How did Lori know I was Detective Browning?"

"Oh. Yeah." He grinned a little. "I didn't think about that. She gave me your table number, said, 'I think that's her.' It's not like she knows you."

"Did you see anyone else on a phone while I was taking my call?"

Trevor's eyes widened in surprise or possibly fear. "No—I mean, I didn't notice. I wasn't looking. People talk on cell phones all the time."

"Okay, Trevor. Thanks." Abigail got to her feet. "I'll go talk to Lori. Don't throw my wine away. I haven't given up on dinner yet."

Lori, a sleek, black-clad woman in her early forties, didn't know much more than Trevor did. The caller had spoken to her in a whisper, too. "I just figured it was someone with a voice problem—throat cancer, laryngitis, whatever."

"Man, woman?"

"Could be either. Why, don't you know?" She frowned, her black eyeliner giving her a dramatic but raccoonish look. "Maybe I should get the manager."

"Sure. That'd be fine. In a sec, though, okay? While your memory's fresh, tell me exactly what the caller said to you."

"Exactly? Well—I picked up and said hello. I'm informal. And the person on the other end said, 'I'd like to speak to Abigail Browning. Detective Browning.' That's you, right?"

"Just go on, please."

"I said, are you sure you have the right number, and the caller said, 'She's dining alone. She has short dark hair.'" Lori shrugged, easing back from the shiny dark-wood bar. "I looked around, and bingo. There you were."

"Then what?"

"I told the caller I spotted you and gave the phone to Trevor."

The manager, a middle-aged man in an overly formal black suit, appeared and asked what was going on, and

Abigail let Lori fill him in, watched both of them for any indication either one had been part of the setup. But they seemed as caught off guard by the call as she was. They didn't know the caller. They hadn't agreed—for money, for grins, for love—to tip off him or her when Abigail arrived at the restaurant.

And the restaurant didn't have Caller ID, either.

Abigail called her partner, Lucas Jones, because he was experienced—if not as experienced as Bob O'Reilly and Scoop Wisdom—and because he didn't live above her. While she waited for him, she pushed her wine aside and ate half a piece of warm bread, staring out at a young couple walking hand in hand down Newbury Street, the woman's wedding ring glinting in the streetlight.

Abigail wanted to tap her on the shoulder and ask her what she would do if the man she loved was murdered four days into their honeymoon, if, after seven years, his murder remained unsolved, his killer at large?

Would she lie awake nights, worrying whether or not the killer no one could catch had killed, would kill, again?

Would she read about murders in the paper, hear about them on television, and wonder if they were the work of her husband's killer—if she'd done enough, worked hard enough, fought hard enough, prayed hard enough, to find the killer?

Or would she put her husband's death behind her and try to lead a normal life?

But the couple wandered out of sight, just as Lucas arrived. Lucas was in his late thirties—not particularly handsome. He had a wife in law enforcement, and a young son—a normal life. He sat across from her. "Abigail, what is it?"

"Probably nothing," she said, and told him about the call.

The next day she burned her journals and made plans to go to Maine.

After she'd burned her journals and scooped their ashes into her coffee can, Abigail drove out to the gold-domed Massachusetts State House and parked in front of a brick townhouse across from Boston Common. She could still smell lighter fluid on her fingers. The elegant house had black shutters and a brass-trimmed glossy burgundy-painted front door, with just enough room on either side of its front steps for a rhododendron and a few evergreen shrubs.

Above the single doorbell was a discreet plaque. The Dorothy Garrison Foundation. Since it was Sunday, the offices were closed.

"Doe," as her family called her, had drowned in Maine when she was fourteen. Owen Garrison had been just eleven and witnessed his sister's drowning, helpless to save her when she slipped and fell off the cliffs, not far from where he found Chris's body eighteen years later.

Abigail eyed the tall, spotless windows with their sheer curtains and heavy drapes, the old-Boston formality of the place a contrast to the physical, unrelenting, unforgiving work that Owen did as a specialist in disaster response. Three years ago, he founded Fast Rescue, a nonprofit organization that fielded highly trained, volunteer search-and-rescue teams prepared and equipped to arrive within twenty-four hours of any disaster, manmade or natural, anywhere in the world.

They weren't spontaneous volunteers, and they didn't respond to situations that could be handled by local organizations. They were part of an intricate network of national and international emergency responders. Hurricanes, earthquakes, tsunamis, floods, fires, tornadoes, mudslides, bombings—if people were missing, trapped, swept away or otherwise in need of being found and rescued, Owen and his teams would be there.

Abigail ran her fingertips along the cool black-iron fence. When Edgar Garrison had bought his Boston dream house a century ago, had he imagined his great-grandson dangling from a helicopter to pluck desperate survivors of massive flooding from rooftops, or digging through the rubble of a collapsed building, working his way to a trapped six-year-old?

Hard to say. The Garrisons were an unpredictable lot, as far as Abigail could tell. But the men were all handsome. *Very* handsome, in fact. She'd seen pictures of old Edgar, the money-maker, an avid outdoorsman who'd teamed up with the Rockefellers and other wealthy summer residents to turn much of Mt. Desert Island, Maine, into a national park. Quite attractive, if a little stuffy. The good looks of his son, Brennan, were softer, more refined. He'd surprised his family by marrying a boar-shooting Texas beauty twenty years his junior.

Now eighty-two, Polly Garrison still could grab headlines. Their son, also named Edgar, was the quiet one, although just as startlingly handsome, in his own way, as his father and grandfather. He and his wife had established the foundation in their daughter's memory and donated their Boston house for its headquarters not long after her accidental death. They moved to Texas and raised Owen there.

Owen wasn't soft or refined or even what Abigail would call traditionally handsome. But he was certainly good-looking.

And he was the only Garrison who still had a presence in Maine.

His family sold their house on Mt. Desert Island to Jason Cooper, who also owned a beautiful estate on Somes Sound. His younger half brother, a prominent Washington consultant, spent five months a year at the old Garrison house. Also a well-known amateur landscaper, Ellis Cooper had converted the yard into impressive gardens. He'd held a party there the day Abigail was attacked and, later that night, Chris was killed. They'd been invited but didn't go.

After the break-in, when she was on her way to get checked out at the local hospital, Chris had stopped briefly at the party. Abigail knew he was looking for her attacker. But the party had broken up, and somehow—for reasons she still didn't understand—he'd ended up down on the rock-bound waterfront below Ellis's delphinium and roses, where, early the next morning, Owen Garrison had found his body.

The Garrisons and the Coopers presented a complicated set of problems for Abigail. They'd known Chris and his grandfather far longer than she had. They'd had both a direct and indirect impact on the lives of the two Browning men. Will Browning, Chris's grandfather, had moved into the former Garrison caretaker cottage after he'd helped stop the fire that had destroyed their original house, the first Edgar's pride and joy. Police believed Chris's killer had hidden in its skeletal remains.

And Abigail had long believed that Doe Garrison's tragic death and the helplessness Chris, only fifteen himself, had felt at the loss of his friend and neighbor had helped propel him into the FBI.

To find out what happened to him and why—who killed him—Abigail had become increasingly convinced that she needed to better understand Chris's relationship with his wealthy friends and neighbors on Mt. Desert.

Polly Garrison, Owen's colorful grandmother, seldom turned up there anymore. Five years ago, Abigail had found her way to Polly's home in Austin, Texas, on a hot July weekend. She remembered her surprise at how simple and classic the house was, and the smell of the shade and the gentle spray of a sprinkler that reached just to her ankles.

Polly answered the door herself, silver-haired, striking.

"Abigail? I didn't realize you were in Austin."

"I'm sorry to disturb you, Mrs. Garrison. May I have a minute? I'd like to talk to you about your family's relationship with the Coopers."

Her lovely gray eyes settled on Abigail. "Why?"

"Curiosity."

The older woman smiled. "That's what makes you a good police officer. Your curiosity. You'll be a detective one day, I do believe."

"Maybe. It's hot here. Are you ever tempted to spend the summer in Maine?"

"I'm often tempted, but the memories..." She took a small breath. "I sometimes visit my grandson there. It's not easy for me, but Owen—he embraces adversity."

No surprise there. "You're not from Austin."

"West Texas. My husband and I moved here after we were married. We kept houses in Maine and Boston for many years. Our son eventually took over the Boston house. But he lives here now, too."

"Because of your granddaughter."

Polly Garrison's eyes misted. "Yes. Because of Doe."

"The Coopers bought your house on Mt. Desert Island after she drowned."

"That's right."

"*But you kept land there, and eventually Owen built his own place there.*"

"*Owen couldn't bear for us to leave Maine altogether. It was as if to do so would be to betray Doe. He was only eleven when we lost her.*"

"*I can't imagine.*"

"*None of us can.*"

"*But Austin's home for him?*"

"*I'm not sure anywhere's home for him. Abigail…*" The older woman extended a hand. "*My dear, we all understand your need for answers, but don't you think Chris would want you to be happy?*"

"*I am happy. But I want to know who killed my husband.*"

As a line of cars passed behind her on Beacon Street and children squealed on Boston Common, Abigail realized her throat had tightened with the onslaught of memories, the July heat, the awareness of what she meant to do.

After her chat with Polly Garrison, who had revealed little about her family's relationship with the Coopers, Abigail had returned to her modest Austin motel. She took a shower. Her hair had been long then, dripping into her clingy camisole top when Owen turned up at her door.

Just out of the army, he was rugged and hard-edged and not very pleased with her.

"*You're out of your jurisdiction, Officer Browning. And you're not a detective.*"

"*Astute of you.*"

"*Next time you want to come down here and ask my grandmother about her dead granddaughter—don't. Deal with me instead.*"

Abigail didn't defend herself. She simply pointed to the

two-inch scar under his eye. "Where did you get that scar—a search-and-rescue mission?"

"Bar fight."

On his way out, he paid for her motel stay. She didn't know until she packed up the next day for Boston. It wasn't kindness on Owen's part. It was his way of telling her she was on his turf, and out of her league.

Except she didn't give a damn. Then or now.

"Things are happening on Mt. Desert. Again."

If so, were the Garrisons and the Coopers involved? Abigail had no idea, but she meant to find out.

When she got back to her triple-decker, she pulled a six-pack of Otter Creek Pale Ale out of the refrigerator, microwaved a bag of popcorn, sharpened three pencils, unwrapped three fresh yellow legal pads and put everything out on her little kitchen table.

Then she phoned her upstairs neighbors, and they came.

Scoop Wisdom had a shaved head and a ferocious, unbridled demeanor, but he'd adopted two stray cats. Abigail didn't believe anyone who had cats could be all that scary.

The cheerful blues and yellows of her kitchen—even the beer and popcorn—had no apparent effect on either man.

"I need your help," she told them.

Scoop's dark eyes narrowed on her. Bob just scowled.

She raked a hand through her short curls. "I got a call last night."

Bob snorted. "About goddamn time you came clean."

"What? Lucas told you? When?"

Scoop grabbed a beer, opened it and took a long drink. "He called me on his way to meet you at the restaurant. I called Bob."

"And none of you said anything? Lucas, you two—"

"We don't butt into other people's business," Bob said.

Abigail had to laugh. "You're detectives. You butt into other people's business all the time." But not hers, she realized. "All right. I should have told you myself. I needed today to get my head together. Burning my journals helped."

Scoop frowned at her. "You burned your journals?"

"They weren't evidence." She shrugged. "They're where I dumped my emotions."

"Oh. Okay, then." Obviously not wanting more details, Scoop pointed with his beer at the stack of files. "These your files on your husband's murder?"

"My notes, newspaper articles, photographs, sketches. Everything I could pull together on my own, without stepping on toes."

Bob grabbed a beer for himself. "You tell the Maine police about the call?"

"Yes."

"And?"

"Unimpressed but investigating."

"What about Daddy?"

She looked at the stack of files. She'd never asked her father to go through them with her. He'd never offered. He wouldn't want to encourage her to investigate Chris's death on her own. "No. I haven't talked to him."

Scoop took a seat at the table and lifted a file from the pile.

Abigail swallowed. "It's been a long time. It's a very cold case."

"Then let's heat it up and see what happens."

"Guys…are you sure?"

Bob slung an arm over her shoulder. "That's the thing you still have to get through your head, kid." He winked at her. "You're not alone."

CHAPTER 3

Owen Garrison wasn't one for suntan lotion and picnic baskets and lazy days on a beach. After forty-five minutes on Sand Beach, he was restless. The horseshoe-shaped beach was a rare stretch of sand carved out of Mt. Desert Island's granite coastline, the water turquoise on the sunny early July afternoon.

Compared to Maine's more expansive beaches to the south—York, Ogunquit, Wells—it wasn't crowded at all.

But Owen paced in the sand, which clung to everything, as he kept an eye on Sean and Ian Alden, eleven and nine, towheaded boys who'd known no other home but the fourteen-mile-wide island. Their father was the local police chief. Owen had complicated Doyle and the boys' lives when he'd asked Katie Alden to head up the proposed Fast Rescue field academy in Bar Harbor. He wanted it up and running by fall, and Katie, a paramedic and search-and-rescue specialist, had taken on the challenge. She'd left for six weeks of training in London two days ago. The boys were doing fine, but Doyle was still sulking about not having her around for most of the summer.

Owen was just off a two-week operation in South Asia following a 7.5-magnitude earthquake and figured the least he could do was help watch the boys once in a while.

A kid—maybe Sean or Ian—squealed. Before Owen realized what was happening, he was jerked back into the past, remembering his sister on this same beach, running into the water and out again, squealing in delight, flapping her arms against the power of the waves and the shock of the cold water.

"Come on, Owen. Don't be a chicken! You get used to the cold."

But you didn't, he knew. You might not feel it, but the cold would wear on your body, weaken it.

The day his sister drowned, the water temperature was fifty-five degrees. Early-stage hypothermia had tired her more quickly, shortening the time she could tread water amid the waves and wait for rescue.

Owen, helpless to save her, had watched Doe slip under the water.

Enough.

He snatched up two towels from the heap of stuff the Alden boys had insisted on carting down to the beach. He waved to them. "Time to warm up."

They didn't argue, although Owen had no idea whether they cooperated because of something they heard in his tone or because they'd had their fill of waves. Unlike most of their fellow beachgoers, Sean and Ian were wet from head to toe—and they were blue-lipped and shivering.

Owen draped towels over them and opened up a blanket, spreading it out on the sticky sand.

"Sit. Wrap up good. Give yourselves a chance to warm up."

Ian, the younger boy, skinnier than his brother, sat on the blanket and tucked his knees up under him, encasing his entire body in the oversized towel.

"Do you boys know what to do if you get stuck out in cold water?" Owen asked. He was in jeans and a polo shirt. Nice and dry.

Sean, his teeth chattering, sat cross-legged on the blanket. "Yell for help?"

"You should have a whistle with you if you're out in the woods or on the water, kayaking, canoeing, whatever. If you get into trouble, you blow the whistle to alert people you need help. You should also have a life vest when you're in any kind of boat. You almost never want to try swimming to shore."

"Why not?" Sean asked.

"Swimming uses up your body's heat faster. You want to conserve heat."

Ian frowned. "Why?"

"So you don't get hypothermia. That's when your body temperature drops. At first you get blue lips and start shivering. But it gets worse—you get confused, you slur your words, your muscles get weak. You end up in a world of hurt."

"Oh, right." Sean nodded knowledgeably. "Mom told us. She says people don't dress right on a hike, and they end up dying of the cold. Even in summer."

"And in water, your body loses heat even faster. Try to keep as much of your body out of water as you can. If you can reach an overturned boat, hang on to it. If you can't, keep your head out of water and stay as still as possible.

Tread water if you're in a life vest, get into the 'heat escape lessening position' or H.E.L.P.—you cross your arms high up on your chest and draw your legs up toward your groin. Huddle with other people in the water."

"Have you ever been stuck in cold water?" Sean asked.

"No."

"Have you ever rescued anyone who had hypo—" Ian frowned. "What is it?"

"Hypothermia. Yes. I've rescued lots of people with hypothermia."

And he'd recovered bodies of people who'd died of it, too.

Both boys' color had improved, and they'd stopped shivering. Owen knew they'd warm up fast, but he probably shouldn't have let them stay out in the chilly Maine water that long. Their father, though, wouldn't care—Doyle had grown up on Mt. Desert Island and had a healthy respect for the elements, but he wasn't afraid of them. And he wouldn't want his boys to be afraid.

Sean and Ian pulled on sweatshirts and sweatpants but balked at wearing shoes because of the sand stuck between their toes. They ran ahead of Owen up to the parking lot and his truck. He wrapped the extra stuff in the blanket—untouched chocolate bars and water, sunscreen, bug spray, shoes, extra towels—and followed the boys. He could still feel the adrenaline that had sustained him through the past two weeks of nonstop work. It'd be a while before he could relax.

This had been a long year of disasters. He knew he needed to rest.

He tossed the blanket in the back of his truck. He had a full range of emergency supplies and equipment there. If anything had happened down on the beach, he'd have been prepared.

He liked being back on Mt. Desert. A third of the island's 82,000 acres formed the bulk of Acadia National Park, protecting its glacial landscape of pink granite mountains, finger-shaped ponds, evergreen forests and rockbound coast. Owen was a part-time resident, often away for long stretches, but he knew a part of his soul would always remain there.

The boys had fallen asleep by the time Owen reached the private drive off Route 3 where his great-grandfather, a visionary and an eccentric, had built a stunning "cottage" in 1919 that burned in the great fires of 1947. The mammoth conflagration consumed thousands of acres and hundreds of summer mansions, its path still marked by younger deciduous forests. After the fire, Owen's grandparents built a smaller house on the ledge behind the original site, above the Atlantic. Now it was eccentric Ellis Cooper's summer home. But when his family sold their Mt. Desert property after Doe's death, Owen had talked his grandmother into saving a chunk of waterfront for him. It was where he'd built his own Maine place, working on it on and off over the past ten years.

He turned down the narrow gravel road that led to his house and, up the headland, the Browning house. Will Browning had often helped Owen work on his house. When he was home, Chris would pitch in. He'd lost his parents to the sea as a toddler, and his grandfather, a solitary man, had raised him.

Originally, the Browning house had been a guest cottage, but Owen's great-grandfather had sold it to Will after he'd worked tirelessly, for days, trying to save the island during the great fires.

Now, the house belonged to Chris's widow.

Abigail.

Owen pushed her out of his mind and parked at his house. The boys, re-energized from their car nap, ran down to the rocks to investigate what the outgoing tide had left behind in the quiet pools of periwinkles, mussels, lichens and seaweed. But the temperature was even cooler out on his granite point, and Owen filled up the woodbox and rummaged in the cupboards for something hot for the boys to have for dinner.

No one believed he'd last the summer in Maine. If a disaster didn't call him away, Owen would usually find something that did.

Doyle Alden arrived at dusk to collect his sons. A big, fair-haired man, he and Owen had become friends as boys, when they'd go off hiking and fishing together, when where they were from and who their families were didn't matter. Sometimes, Chris Browning would join him and Doyle. Chris had always been driven, determined not to live the life his father and grandfather had. As much as Owen knew he respected his family, Chris didn't want to be a lobsterman or a handyman, and he'd worked hard to have a different future. He'd gone to law school and become an FBI agent, and he'd married the daughter of a man everyone had known would become the next director of the FBI.

And if Chris had chosen another spot for their honeymoon, he might still be alive. Instead, he'd taken his bride home to Mt. Desert Island.

Doyle had been Chris's best man. Sean had been the ring-bearer.

Owen had arrived in Maine on a two-week leave from the army three days after the wedding.

In time to find Chris's body.

Doyle's voice brought Owen back to the present.

"Katie e-mailed me," Doyle said, staring out the French doors at the water. The boys, finished with dinner, had gone back out. "She says she's settling in. Says the flowers in England are beautiful right now."

"She'd notice," Owen said.

"The six weeks will be up before we know it."

Owen could hear the struggle in Doyle's tone to hide his resentment. He'd put the decision to do this training in Katie's hands, saying it was hers, not his, to make. She'd pleaded with him to discuss his feelings with her, but he'd refused. And now he was irritated, because deep down he'd wanted her to stay.

It was all more complicated than Owen could get his head around, but Doyle and Katie had been together since they were teenagers. As ornery as Doyle could be, he would know that if his wife didn't need his permission to go to England, she at least deserved his support.

"Summer's my busiest season," he said. "Katie could have picked a better time to learn how to save the world."

"She didn't pick the time. I did."

Doyle gave him a faint smile. "Yeah? Well, screw you."

The boys pounded onto the deck and burst inside with a frenzied energy that seemed to lift their father's mood. Ian's fingers were blue-red, a sign he'd been into the tide pools. He had his mother's curiosity and affection for living things. Sean got more pleasure from scrambling over granite boulders.

"What's going on?" Doyle asked at their obvious excitement.

"Nothing," Sean said, his cheeks reddening as he warmed his hands in front of the woodstove, the fire glowing behind the screen.

"Nothing's got you all excited, huh?"

Ian started to speak, but Sean shot him a warning look. "Dad, can we stay here tonight?"

"Not tonight. Let's wait until a night I have a meeting, if that's okay with Owen."

Owen shrugged. "That'd be fine." But he could see that Sean and Ian had something they were keeping from their father. "Did you notice the fog on the horizon?"

"Uh-huh." Ian nodded, but he was watching his older brother, presumably for another warning look if he strayed too close to spilling whatever it was they were hiding. "It's coming closer. Sean calls it The Blob. We pretend it's a monster."

Ian roared and stretched out his arms, pretending he was The Blob. Sean rolled his eyes. Owen followed them and their father out to the car. Sean said he wanted the front seat, Ian said it was his turn—the fight was on. Doyle settled it by making them both sit in back.

"They don't fight that much," he told Owen, then gave a tight smile as he opened the car door. "Katie's doing. They're more likely to act up around me."

In the back seat, his window open, Sean had grown pensive. "Dad, do you believe in ghosts?"

Doyle didn't hesitate. "No. Why? You boys think you saw a ghost?"

Ian's eyes widened, and he elbowed his brother. "Sean, Dad'll know what to do."

Sean snapped his seat belt. "We didn't see nothing."

"Anything," Doyle said. "You didn't see anything."

"That's what I said."

Doyle started the car. "Forget it." He looked exhausted, overwhelmed without Katie at his side.

"Wouldn't surprise me if you saw a ghost out here. It's been that kind of day."

But as Doyle backed out of the driveway, Owen noticed Ian in the back seat, pale, his blue eyes unblinking, and felt his stomach twist.

They know about Chris Browning.

Owen knew Doyle avoided mentioning his childhood friend in front of Sean and Ian and never discussed the details of a long-unsolved murder that had deeply affected him. Their father's silence had created a void that the boys, apparently, had filled on their own.

But what had made them think they'd seen a ghost?

Doyle Alden pulled into the short driveway of the little house he and Katie had bought six weeks before Sean was born and fixed up themselves. It was on a side street near the police station, a few miles from Owen's place. Bar Harbor, where the Fast Rescue Field Academy would be located, was about twelve miles up and across the island, a picturesque drive that his wife would have to start making every morning once the construction was finished.

An unmarked Maine State Police car eased in behind him. Doyle recognized Lieutenant Lou Beeler behind the wheel, and knew it couldn't be good news.

"Go on inside, guys," Doyle told his sons. "I'll be a couple minutes."

In the glare of the front-door light, Lou looked thin and tired, his hair grayer. He planned to retire in the fall after thirty years on the job, fifteen of them in the Criminal Investigative Division. He was a decent guy with an extraordinary record, one of the most respected detectives in Maine. But riding off into the sunset with Christopher

Browning's murder unsolved grated on him. An FBI agent married to John March's daughter, a man beloved on Mt. Desert Island—shot on his honeymoon within shouting distance of his boyhood home, left to bleed to death amid the rocks, seaweed, salt water and gulls.

Who wouldn't want to find Chris's killer?

"What can I do for you, Lou?" Doyle asked.

Lou rubbed his lower back. He'd have driven to Bar Harbor from his home hear Bangor. "Fog's rolling in. I can smell it."

"I hadn't noticed."

"I don't like driving in it. My eyes aren't what they used to be. How's Katie?"

"Fine. She's in England."

"I heard. Working with Owen Garrison's outfit now?"

"Yeah." Doyle knew Lou was just being friendly, but he hadn't had much patience for the past few days and wanted the older man to state his business. "The boys and I are on our own for a few weeks. They're inside now, waiting for me."

"Sure, sure. I'll get to the point. Has Abigail Browning been in touch?"

Hell. Doyle shook his head.

"She got a call last night. I thought you should know," Lou said in a professional tone that belied his personal interest in the case. He then gave Doyle details on the call. "I doubt it'll amount to anything, but—I don't know. It doesn't feel right."

"Is Abigail on her way here?"

Lou sighed. "I didn't ask, and she didn't say. But what do you think?"

"I wouldn't be surprised if she's here now."

Lou kept his steady gaze on Doyle. "I don't know about

you, but I never thought I'd still be hunting Chris Browning's killer after seven years."

"Didn't you? Here's how I see it. A burglar targeted the island seven years ago and stole a lot of jewelry from rich summer residents. He landed at the Browning house, thinking it was a guest cottage for the Garrisons or the Coopers, and Abigail surprised him. She was assaulted, and Chris took matters into his own hands. The burglar killed him and took off, never to return."

"That's one scenario."

"It's the only one that makes sense and fits the facts. If Abigail thinks she's going to come up here and find answers, she's wrong."

"She's thought that for seven years—"

"And she's been wrong for seven years. She just stirs people up for no good reason."

Lou sank back against the hood of his car. "The caller said things were happening here."

"It's a busy island that gets three million tourists every year," Doyle said. "Of *course* things are happening here. You can cherry-pick a dozen possibilities without breaking into a sweat or thinking hard."

"What about things happening among the Garrisons and the Coopers?"

Doyle scoffed. "Something's always going on with them. Owen's starting up this field academy. He just got back from digging for earthquake survivors."

"The Coopers?"

"Grace Cooper's up for a big State Department appointment. Her father's doing some complicated business deal. Her uncle's designed a new garden for one of his rich friends. Her brother's here this summer. He made it through a whole year of college." Doyle narrowed his eyes on his fellow, more experienced law enforcement officer. "But you know all that, don't you, Lou?"

"Yeah. I do. Well…" He smiled. "I hadn't heard about Linc Cooper not getting kicked out of another college. You'll call me when Abigail turns up?"

"I'll call. Thanks for stopping by. By the way, did you stop by the Browning house just now?"

Lou shook his head. "No, why?"

Doyle decided not to tell him about the boys and their ghost. "Just curious. Sure you don't want to come in?"

"I should get back. Say hi to the boys for me."

After Lou left, Doyle locked up his car and headed inside. The house wasn't the same without Katie. He didn't know how he'd manage for six weeks without her. The place needed vacuuming. He had to take out the trash, clean the bathrooms, mop the kitchen floor. Normally he and Katie and the boys split the housework, but he could see now he hadn't been doing his fair share.

He didn't need to deal with Abigail right now. She had a way of getting on his last nerve.

With a little luck, she'd get assigned to a hot case in Boston and forget about the anonymous call. Let the state and local police investigate. Stay out of it.

Doyle snorted, noticing he'd left the coffeepot on that morning.

What was he thinking?

Luck just never seemed to be on his side.

CHAPTER 4

Abigail left Boston early Monday morning, and by the time she took Route 3 over the Trenton Bridge onto Mt. Desert Island, she ran into a wall of fog. Not pretty fog, either. It was slit-your-throat depressing fog. She had her coffee can of journal ashes on the front seat next to her. She'd almost dumped them at a rest stop between Augusta and Bangor, just to be rid of them. It was as if every memory of her life with Chris was in there, condensed, trying to pull her inside with them and draw her into the past, keep her there forever and never, ever let her go.

She stopped in Bar Harbor at a streetside deli-restaurant and bought containers of clam chowder, lobster salad and crab salad, and two huge peanut butter cookies. Droopy-eyed tourists griped about the fog. *"It could last for days."*

Well, Abigail thought, climbing back into her car, it could.

When she arrived at her house on the southern end of the island, the fog, if possible, was even thicker, encasing the tall spruce and pine trees in gray, obscuring any view. Water, rocks and sky were indistinguishable.

The front steps were slick with condensation, and the air tasted of salt and wet pine needles.

Her 1920s house was too small, too simple, for today's coastal living standards. If she put it on the market, it would sell for its location. A new owner would almost certainly bulldoze it and build from scratch.

Perhaps just as well.

She unlocked the door and, with the damp air, had to push hard to get it open. Inside, her house felt like a tomb. Cold, dark, still. Midafternoon, and it might have been dusk.

Flipping on a light in the entry, Abigail walked into the kitchen and dropped her keys on the counter, the silence not comforting, only making her feel more alone.

The ashes called to her.

She could hear Chris's voice.

"It's not a palace, but I wouldn't give up this place for the world. I love it here, Abigail. I don't want to live here. But I don't ever want to sell it."

He'd wanted her to fall in love with his boyhood home— not the house so much as the island, its breathtaking beauty, its simplest pleasures. She didn't need to have the same memories he had, he'd said.

"We'll make our own memories."

She spun on her toes and ran back outside, slipping on the steps and the stone walk, sinking into the soft gravel of the driveway as she went around to the passenger side of her car. She ripped open the door and grabbed the coffee can.

"We'll raise our kids out here."

Without thinking, she ducked under the dripping

branches of a pine tree on the side of the house, emerging on the strip of grass that passed for a yard.

She made her way through the gloom along a footpath worn into the damp grass and rocky dirt, following it to the tangle of rugosa roses and the tumble of granite boulders that marked the water's edge. No marshes and bogs here, no gentle easing from land to ocean. Two centuries ago, the Brownings had parked themselves on the rockbound island and carved out a living for themselves amid Mt. Desert's gales, salt spray, acidic soil, impenetrable granite and incredible, austere beauty.

Abigail tucked her coffee can under one arm. Beneath her, the Atlantic was gray and glassy, barely visible in the fog. She heard seagulls but couldn't tell how far away they were. Sucking in a breath, she plunged down the rocks, careful with her footing on steep, potentially slippery sections. As her familiarity with her stretch of coast kicked in, she moved faster.

The tide was out, and she dropped down from a rectangular boulder onto smaller rocks covered in seaweed and barnacles, cold, gray water seeping over them. She could feel the dampness in her bones now. When she'd packed up for Boston last night, after Scoop and Bob had left her with her notes and files and mess to clean up, she'd imagined dumping her ashes on a crisp, clear Maine afternoon.

She crept out to the edge of a rock slab—the water was deeper here, deep enough for the ashes. Holding the coffee can in front of her, she peeled off the plastic lid.

"Abigail?"

"Oh, my God!"

Startled, she spun around at the voice, real or imagined, and the coffee can went flying, ashes spilling over her, the rock, the water. The can banged off granite and into the gray ocean.

"Chris?"

She shook herself. What was wrong with her, calling out to her dead husband?

Squatting down, she reached for the coffee can, but it floated farther away. Determined, she lurched forward—too far forward. She dropped her left hand onto the rock at her side to regain her balance, but a cluster of sharp barnacles dug into her palm. She jerked her hand back and started to jump up, but slipped, tipping over into the water.

She shuddered at the shock of cold water and scrambled right back up onto her rock. She was soaked, cursing. *Freezing.* But as she climbed up onto a boulder above the tideline, she slipped again, banging her knee.

A man materialized out of the fog above her and lowered his hand to her. "You're wearing the wrong shoes."

"The wrong—" She looked up at Owen Garrison, handsome as ever, dry. "I nearly drown, and you're worried about my shoes?"

"Now that you didn't drown, yes. You're going to slip and slide all the way back up to your house in those shoes."

They were five-dollar slip-on sneakers she'd picked up for the summer. Bright red. Fun. Not intended for tramping through the wilds of Maine.

She took Owen's hand, noticed the warmth of his firm grip as he helped her up onto his boulder. If she didn't accept his help, she'd only land up in a worse predicament. Maybe break an ankle.

She had to be practical.

"You startled me," she said. "That's why I fell."

He shrugged. "Sorry. Did you cut yourself on the rocks?"

"I scraped my hand. It's no big deal. The cold's numbed it."

She was shivering. She hadn't expected the ash-dumping to turn into an ordeal, and she still had on her shorts and T-shirt from her trip. Even without the dunking, she'd have been cold in the relentless fog.

Owen wore jeans and a lightweight fleece the color of the fog—and, she noticed, of his eyes.

"Want me to fetch whatever it is you dropped?" he asked.

"It's just a coffee can of ashes."

"From your woodstove?"

She shook her head. "I brought them up here with me—"

"Abigail…"

"Oh—no, no. They're not *human* ashes." But Abigail had no intention of telling him they were ashes of seven years' worth of journals she'd burned yesterday in a grill. "They're just from something I burned. I can fetch the can later."

Owen, however, had already jumped lightly down to the wet slab below the tideline. He scooped up the coffee can and, in two long strides, was back up on the dry boulder with her—not breathing hard, not wet. She did notice he'd gotten a glob of ashes on his hand and fleece.

"Thanks," she said, taking the can from him. "I should go back and put on some dry clothes. That water's damn cold."

"About fifty-five degrees."

She winced. "Now I'm *really* freezing. What're you doing out here?"

"I heard you and decided to investigate."

"But you didn't know it was me," she said.

"No, I didn't."

He wasn't explaining any further, obviously. Abigail started past him, slipped, cursed and felt him clamp a hand on to her upper arm. She gritted her teeth. "I see what you mean about my shoes."

"Hikers fall all the time because they underestimate how slippery wet rock can be."

"I'm not a hiker. I was just out here doing a cleansing ritual—never mind." She sighed at him. "You're going to hold my arm until I reach grass, aren't you?"

"Unless you want to keep falling."

"Or I could take my shoes off. Except then I'd be even colder." She smiled. "I have tender feet."

He hadn't released her arm. She wasn't wearing her weapon, thankfully. It was locked up in her car. All the panic and urgency she'd felt about getting rid of the ashes had dissipated with the shock of the cold water and her sexy Maine neighbor. Now, she just wanted warm clothes and a bowl of hot chowder.

Because her shoes were less than useless wet, Owen ended up half-carrying her up the rocks.

"I've dripped on you," she said when they reached the path.

"Not a problem. When did you get here?"

"An hour ago." *If that.*

He nodded to her Folgers can. "And you had to dump your ashes right away?"

"I need the can for paint. I'm going to be working on the house."

"Ah."

She ignored his skepticism. "I didn't realize you were in Maine."

"I've only been here a few days. Fast Rescue is opening a field academy in Bar Harbor. We hope to have it up and running this fall."

Abigail remembered her caller's words.

"Things are happening on Mt. Desert."

Owen Garrison and his nonprofit outfit starting a field academy was something that was happening. Had her caller read about it in the paper, on the Internet? Heard about it from a friend?

And what possible difference could Owen's presence and a new training facility make in the investigation into Chris's murder?

"Why Maine?" she asked.

"Makes sense. Katie Alden is perfect to be the director." He touched Abigail's shoulder. "You should get into those dry clothes."

The combination of his tone and her surroundings—her fatigue, her raw emotions, the fog—had his words curling up her spine. She backed away from him, sliding in the grass. She finally kicked off her shoes, scooped them up and continued on barefoot, turning when she reached the bottom step of her porch. "Thank you for your help."

"Anytime."

"I'll be more careful about my choice of shoes next time."

She ran inside, not stopping until she reached her one bathroom upstairs. She grabbed a towel and started to dry off, but caught her reflection in the mirror.

Her forehead and cheeks were smeared with soot.

So much for playing the experienced, confident Boston homicide detective.

As she dried her face, she burst into laughter.

On his way back along the rocks from Abigail Browning's house, Owen watched a seagull plunge into the fog and disappear, and he thought of his long-dead sister.

Doe had wanted to become an ornithologist.

"Don't you love that word, Owen? Say it. Ornithologist."

Although her given name was Dorothy, their grand-mother—the inimitable Polly Garrison—had nicknamed her Doe because she was nimble and had hair the color of a deer's coat.

And innocent eyes, Owen thought.

Such innocent eyes.

When she fell into the Atlantic, slipping on the wet cliffs through the woods on the other side of the Browning house, farther up the headland, her deer-colored hair had swirled in the waves like seaweed.

Owen had been about twenty yards behind her, and when he ran to the edge of the rock, the tide had pulled Doe farther out. Helpless to save her, Owen had tried to scream for his parents, anyone, but no sound came out. He'd had no whistle. Doe had run down from their summer house, crying, and he'd followed her, hoping to console her so that she'd pull herself together in time to go hiking with him after lunch.

Help had arrived in the form of the Brownings in their lobster boat. But they were too late. Everyone was too late.

Forcing himself to exhale, Owen pulled off his fleece. His skin was clammy, and the closeness of the fog was making him claustrophobic. It was his one weakness in the work he did—he didn't like feeling closed in. He'd learned to control his reaction and focus on the job at hand.

That's the problem, he thought. He didn't have enough to do. His mind was free to go off on tangents.

And being around Abigail Browning always got to him.

He stood on a coarse granite slab above the water, above the narrow crevice where he had found Chris Browning on a cold, clear July dawn, the sky streaked with shades of lavender and pink.

Owen had found the shell casings first—up at the remains of his family's original house. Even now, in the impenetrable fog, he could see the silhouette of its skeletal chimney, sunken and crumbled but, still, partially intact. The perfect spot for Chris's shooter to hide.

Retreating back through the woods to the private drive would have been easy. A car concealed in the woods. A bicycle. A friend on the way. Who'd have noticed?

Chris was an FBI agent. He knew the island better than most.

For too long, no one had considered he might be in trouble.

His dark-eyed wife, a bump on her head, her legs unsteady, had been drawn to the spot of her husband's murder as if by instinct, as if Chris, settled now in death, had called her there to end her uncertainty.

"I'm going to find out who killed my husband."

Owen had never doubted Abigail's words. Even as she'd dug her fingers into his arms, as he'd held her back from going to her husband, further contaminating the crime scene, he'd believed her determination and conviction were for real.

She wouldn't stop. Not Abigail March Browning.

Now, she was back on the island.

He wasn't fooled by her soot-smeared face and slippery shoes or her dunk in the ocean.

Abigail was a tight-jawed, hard-assed detective.

She wasn't in Maine to fix up her house and dump ashes. She was there for the same reason she was always there—for the same reason she hadn't sold her house in the past seven years and put Mt. Desert Island behind her altogether.

To find Chris's killer.

Owen turned away from the water and walked up to the path that would take him back to his house. In the shifting fog, spruce branches and the old foundation above created eerie, unnatural shapes.

No wonder the Alden boys thought they'd seen a ghost out here.

Maine was full of ghosts. Owen just had no intention of letting them run him off.

CHAPTER 5

I can see his eyes as I pull the trigger.

I thought he'd be too far away, but I can see them. Wide open. Defiant.

Knowing.

He says his wife's name, but only I am close enough to hear him above the waves and wind.

"Abigail."

He calls her name because he loves her. Not because he believes she's the one who has just shot him.

He knows it's me.

That bothers me sometimes, still.

Other times, I'm glad.

Yes, it was me, you arrogant bastard.

As I pull the trigger a second time, I think only that finally I am free, finally I am safe, finally I have done what I needed to do.

I don't think that his wife will hound me forever.

I don't think by pulling the trigger I have sentenced myself to another kind of prison and torture.

Seven years.

Abigail will never quit. I could hear it in her voice the other night, on the phone. While she was having dinner alone on her wedding anniversary. Those solitary annual dinners are her tradition.

I picked that night to call on purpose.

I'm not a monster. I don't kill indiscriminately.

I kill to solve problems that cannot be solved another way.

I kill because I'm left no other option.

I kill without pleasure.

But I also kill without remorse.

Abigail.

He loved her.

She loved him.

What did Chris know of love?

What does Abigail know?

She will know of love in the end.

That I promise.

CHAPTER 6

"Listen up, Linc. I'm giving you this one chance. That's it."

Linc Cooper looked through the tall spruces at the Atlantic Ocean below him, the sun chasing away the last of the fog on the bright, cool morning. He was on a vertical zigzag of stone steps that Edgar Garrison had carved into the granite hillside behind his summer house almost a hundred years ago. They used to lead to an old-fashioned teahouse. Now the steps led to the house the Garrisons had built after fire had destroyed their original "cottage" down on the waterfront.

The new house, with its blue-gray clapboards and black shutters, was supposedly smaller and more restrained, but Linc, who'd never even seen pictures of the Garrison's original Maine home, had never liked it.

He had always loved playing on the steps as a little kid, if only because no one noticed him out there. His uncle Ellis considered the house his own, but, in reality, the deed belonged to Linc's father, Jason Cooper.

Everything, Linc thought, was in his father's name. His father was clever, responsible and ruthless. His younger half brother, Ellis, was passive by nature and gentle in temperament, not unambitious but more measured in his wants and needs.

"I don't give second chances. Don't make the mistake of thinking I do."

Chris's voice. When he had jumped out of the dark and clamped a hand on Linc's shoulder, Linc had wet his pants. Chris hadn't relented.

Thirteen years old, and Linc had never felt such shame as when he looked into his idol's eyes and saw that he knew everything.

"You have nothing to prove to anyone, Linc. Not to me. Not to your father or to your sister."

He'd wanted to be like Chris Browning. It didn't matter that Chris was so much older. Linc wanted to be self-reliant, capable. Chris had no family money to fall back on. His parents had died when he was a baby. He'd made his own way in the world.

"What kind of man do you want to be?"

Linc sat on a stone bench on a narrow landing on the steep steps. How many times had he thought about finding Abigail Browning and telling her everything he knew about the night before she was attacked, before her husband was killed?

Telling her what he'd done seven years ago as a stupid kid.

He heard footsteps above him on the steps and looked up just as Mattie Young came into view. Chris's friend, the Coopers' yardman, the local drunk. *A creep.*

Mattie jumped the last two steps onto the landing. "Hey, Linc, my boy." He grinned, smug, sarcastic. "Fancy meeting you here."

There wasn't any "fancy" to it, and Mattie knew it—he'd provided the when, where, the why. And the consequences of not showing up.

Deliberately, just to rub Mattie's nose in the disparities between them, Linc had put on an expensive sweater and khakis for their little meeting, and he'd shaved. Mattie had come down the steps from working in Ellis's gardens, but he would have been a mess, regardless. He'd tied his stringy, greasy hair into a ponytail and wore a stained T-shirt and torn, frayed jeans that sagged on his scrawny frame.

He pulled a pack of cigarettes from his back pocket and tapped one out. "Your crazy uncle has me moving a rhododendron. He doesn't think it's thriving where it is. It looks fine to me." He stuck the cigarette between his lips. "What the hell about me? I'd like to thrive."

"Then stop smoking. That'd help."

"Sarcastic little shit, aren't you, considering the spot you're in?"

Linc felt his jaw set hard. "I hate your guts."

Mattie laughed. "Feeling's mutual, kid. You got my best friend killed—"

"Your best friend? You didn't even go to his wedding. You were in a ditch somewhere sleeping off a couple bottles of cheap booze."

"So I was." Using a small disposable lighter, Mattie lit his cigarette, inhaling deeply before returning lighter and pack to his pocket. "Do you have my money?"

"A thousand. I can't get my hands on ten grand at once without drawing attention to myself. I told you—"

"Show me the thousand."

Linc reached into his day pack, dropped at his feet, and withdrew a sealed envelope. His stomach rolled over. Sweat erupted on his back. He couldn't believe what he was doing, but what choice did he have? Especially now, with his sister Grace's State Department appointment in the works.

He handed the envelope to Mattie. "Go ahead and count it if you want. It's all there."

"I don't need to count it. If you're lying, I know where you live, don't I?"

"You're scum. I don't know what the Brownings ever saw in you. They were good guys. You're a piece of shit."

Mattie didn't react with his usual anger and defensiveness. "Chris and his grandfather looked past my mistakes. They saw the real me. I'm getting back into my photography." He folded the bulging envelope, squeezing it into the palm of his hand as if it held all his answers—as if it wasn't just money. "Your money's going for a good cause. Think of it as your penance and my new beginning."

Linc snorted. "The real you is a bottom-feeding lowlife. It always has been. It always will be."

"I never stole from the people who cared about me."

Shame rippled through Linc, and his legs weakened under him. "If you're so good, why don't you tell the police what you know? About me. The burglaries. Why blackmail me?"

"A guy like me doesn't get many second chances."

"Why did you wait until now?"

"I wasn't going to put the squeeze on a teenager. And now—the timing's right. You're not going to the police, not with your sister's big appointment hanging in the balance." Mattie grinned, the sarcasm—the pleasure he took in what he was doing—back. "What do you think Grace would say if she could see her baby brother now?"

Linc couldn't bear to think about Grace's disappointment. Eighteen years older, more like an aunt than a sister, she was the only child of their father and his first wife, a marriage that had ended the summer Doe Garrison had drowned. He and Grace had no other siblings. It was just the two of them.

Mattie blew cigarette smoke out of his nose. "Relax, kid. I'm not greedy. Once I have my ten grand, we're square."

He was forty-two but looked older. Grace said she remembered when he was a talented, promising photographer. But Mattie Young had hit the self-destruct button a long time ago.

"I returned all the items I stole," Linc said, hating the meekness in his voice. "Why punish me?"

"Why shouldn't I?" Mattie gave him a knowing look. "Don't you punish yourself?"

Linc didn't answer.

"And you didn't return everything, did you? Abigail's necklace is still missing."

"I told you. I didn't steal it. I didn't attack her. I didn't kill Chris."

"Who'll believe you without proof of who did steal the necklace and attack her, of who did kill Chris?" Mattie dropped his half-smoked cigarette onto the stone and crushed it under his cheap work boot. "I need to get back to your uncle's rhodie. Work on the rest of my money. I want it within the next few days. All of it."

"I'll get it just to watch you piss it away."

"All that anger. It'll eat you alive if you let it."

"I hope you choke on your own vomit."

Mattie shrugged. "You're not alone." He squatted down, picked up the crushed cigarette and tucked it into a front pocket as he rose. "Best to cover my tracks. Your uncle doesn't let me smoke on the grounds. If he or your father or sister finds out about the money, what will you tell them? Do you remember your cover story?"

Linc didn't want to argue with him anymore. "I'll tell them I bought some of your old photographs."

"Very good," Mattie said, then smiled. "See you soon."

After his blackmailer left, Linc turned and faced the water, looking down at the near-vertical hillside. Juts of exposed granite ledge, moss, bare roots of trees—spruce, pine, fir, a few beeches and birches—clung to its thin, acidic soil.

"I'm on my honeymoon, Linc. You and your shenanigans aren't even on the list of things I want to be thinking about this week."

Linc gulped in a shallow breath. He felt hollowed out, a shell of everything he wanted to become. He was twenty now, and he hadn't succeeded at anything yet—except video games and getting kicked out of schools.

And begging his father's forgiveness.

Avoiding his sister's disappointment.

What would the scandal of what he'd done seven years ago—of what he was doing now, paying off a blackmailer—do to Grace's appointment? The FBI was running a background check on her. It could take several months. She'd already begged Linc to behave, which was part of the reason he was on Mt. Desert for the summer.

But Mattie Young had approached Linc three days ago and demanded ten thousand dollars in exchange for his silence, changing everything.

"I believe in you. Don't disappoint me."

Countless times, at his lowest depths, Linc had used Chris's words to give himself courage—to try again after yet another failure.

Linc knew what his dead friend would have him do.

Tell everything. Confess.

Not let Mattie confuse and manipulate him.

But Linc also knew he wouldn't come clean.

He couldn't tell anyone about the blackmail—or what he had done that had gotten him into this mess.

CHAPTER 7

Grace Cooper stepped carefully in the lush grass of her uncle's backyard, as if she didn't want to leave footprints. "Ellis has worked very hard to make these gardens look natural. It seems contradictory, doesn't it?"

Abigail smiled, enjoying her tour of the award-winning gardens. "Everything's so beautiful. I'm lucky if I can keep a pot of geraniums alive."

"I know how you feel," Grace said with a laugh.

Ellis was transplanting a bush with Mattie Young and had left his niece to deal with his unexpected guest, suggesting a quick garden tour. At thirty-eight, Grace was striking with her fine blond hair and strong features. Her eyes, a clear, pale blue, were her best feature. She was gracious and politely reserved.

The mix of perennials and annuals, their colors and textures contrasting here, complementing there, sparkled and glistened in the clear and crisp morning air. Abigail had walked up from her house, yesterday afternoon's escapade on the rocks with her journal ashes and Owen Garrison behind her.

Grace leaned over and brushed her fingertips over a perfect dark pink foxglove. "These gardens are Ellis's pride and joy. It won't be easy for him to give them up."

"Give them up?"

"Oh. I assumed you'd heard. We're selling the property."

"This place?" Abigail didn't hide her surprise. "No, I hadn't heard."

And Grace would know she hadn't heard. It was just her way of reminding Abigail that she didn't know everything about the Coopers. Abigail had no illusions about her relationship with them. It wasn't unfriendly, but they were aware she kept track of them—and that she did so because of their connections to Chris. They'd known him all his life. Ellis had held a garden party here the day she was attacked and robbed and Chris was killed. Someone had burglarized them and a handful of their friends that summer, although whether it was the same person who attacked her and stole her necklace remained an open question.

"The timing's right," Grace continued. "Linc and I aren't children anymore. My father can only get away for a few weeks in the summer. Keeping two houses here just doesn't make as much sense these days."

"Why not sell your place on Somes Sound?"

She shrugged, moving past sprays of coral bells and painted daisies. "It's right on the water, and it's really the family place more than this is. Ellis agrees. I think he wants to buy his own place. He's so much younger than my father—he didn't have the money when my father bought this property from the Garrisons."

"Won't Ellis miss his gardens, especially?"

"I imagine so, but he's become quite the amateur land-scape designer—I'm sure he'd love to get his fingers into something new. And there's not much more he can do here."

"But it wasn't his idea to put the home on the market?"

"He trusts my father on these matters." Grace paused, then smiled as she moved on to a sun-filled garden "room" of peonies. "We all trust my father."

"He's a smart man," Abigail said.

"That he is. And you—why are you here?"

"In Maine? I'm painting." She and Lou Beeler had agreed to limit the number of people they told about the anonymous call. "I've already been to the hardware store this morning."

"Good for you. I hope you'll join us for lunch one day while you're here. I'm sure my father would love to see you. And Linc's here—"

"I saw him on the steps while Mattie had a cigarette."

Grace rolled her eyes. "Mattie knows Ellis doesn't allow smoking on the grounds. Well, Linc won't tell."

"Neither will I. I'm not here to stir up trouble."

"Aren't you?" But she added quickly, "I have to go. I have calls to make. Take all the time you want looking at the gardens. Ellis will be flattered."

"Congratulations on your appointment."

She brightened. "Thank you. I'm thrilled. It's a tremen-dous honor, and I look forward to the work." She started back to her uncle's house, then stopped and glanced back. "It's good to see you, Abigail. I mean that."

With Grace's departure, Abigail walked over to a small garden shed at the far end of the yard. Mature herbs and tall wildflowers grew to its small, four-paned windows. As a young bride, new to Maine, new to Garrison wealth, Polly Garrison supposedly had insisted on keeping chickens.

Abigail peeked behind the shed—sure enough, there was a boarded-up, chicken-sized door.

Mattie Young dragged a hose toward the shed. "Hey, Abigail, how's it going?"

"Great. Beautiful day. You?"

"Paying the bills."

"I was just talking to Grace. I hadn't realized the Coopers were putting this place on the market."

"Not the Coopers. Daddy Jason."

"But Ellis—"

"He goes along. Can't afford to piss off big brother, you know?" Mattie coiled the hose into a heap under a water line at a corner of the shed. "Makes no difference to me. New owners will need a yardman."

Abigail didn't respond. She'd lost patience with Mattie's chronic bitterness and cynicism a long time ago. Even Chris, who'd stood by his childhood friend through one self-indulgent, self-destructive screwup after another, had finally written Mattie off after he didn't show up for their wedding.

"I hadn't realized Linc was up here," she said. "I saw you two talking—"

"We're allowed to talk." He caught himself, stepping back from the house. "Sorry. It's just—you're a cop. Every time you ask a question, I think I'm being interrogated."

"That's understandable," she said, neutral.

He picked at a mosquito bite on his wrist. "Linc's at a loose end this summer. I think he's bummed about his dad selling this place. He's never known a time when it wasn't in his family. He doesn't remember when the Garrisons owned it."

"I hadn't thought of it that way. But the Coopers' house on Somes Sound is even bigger and fancier—"

"Don't I know it?" Mattie grinned, but he didn't manage to take any of the edge off his put-upon attitude. "I mow their yard every week."

Portly Ellis Cooper joined them. He was neatly dressed in khakis and a bright blue golf shirt, a retractable walking stick tucked under one arm. His favorite pastime was to wander in his five acres of gardens. His property also backed up onto woodland trails that led into Acadia and down the steps and across the private drive, included the cliffs where Doe Garrison had drowned. Ellis could roam to his heart's content.

"Abigail—my apologies for not greeting you sooner. I wanted to finish in the garden and wash up before saying hello." He put out a hand and shook hers warmly. "Wonderful to see you."

"You, too, Ellis. I don't think I've ever seen your gardens this gorgeous."

"We had a cool spring. Everything seems to have blossomed at once. Did Grace give you the grand tour?"

"She did. I should let you all get back to your day. Is Linc still here? I haven't had a chance to say hello—"

"He took off a few minutes ago," Mattie said.

Ellis seemed faintly irritated at his yardman's interruption, but he hooked his arm into Abigail's, smiling at her. "I'll walk with you. You came up the steps, didn't you? I was worried the fog would settle in for a few days, but it blew out almost as fast as it blew in."

When they reached the front of the house, he unhooked his arm from Abigail's, and she grinned at him. "You'd have made a good bouncer in another life."

He laughed. "I'm just a political consultant and gardener."

"I don't know how good a consultant you are, but you're obviously quite the gardener."

"Grace told you we're selling the place? I could continue here forever, but I have to admit I'm excited about the prospect of a fresh start somewhere. Keeping up five acres of gardens is a huge responsibility. I've naturalized more and more in recent years, but it's still a lot of work."

"You and Mattie manage everything yourselves?"

"I bring in specialists from time to time. Mattie—well, you know what he's like. He's just reliable enough and just hardworking enough that I can't fire him. I don't think he's drinking, not right now. The truth is, I feel sorry for him." Ellis's expression softened. "Chris's death shattered him. He's never been the same."

"He'd started drinking again before Chris was killed."

"True, but he was starting to turn himself around that summer—or so most of us thought. Hard to believe it's been seven years. Jason thinks it's been long enough not to affect prospective buyers. Even if Chris wasn't killed on the property, it was close—" He stopped himself, looked stricken. "Oh, Abigail. I'm so sorry. I know it must seem like yesterday to you. I didn't mean—"

"It's okay, Ellis. Forget it."

Abigail was accustomed to people getting tongue-tied around her. She wondered if it'd be different if she'd re-married, if she'd been older when she was widowed.

She said goodbye to Ellis and followed a shaded stone path surrounded by thyme to the steps. Abigail imagined Owen's eccentric great-grandfather taking the time, the money and the energy to have the steps carved into the granite hillside—all to get to a teahouse. He wasn't in the same league as his superrich Maine neighbors like the Rockefellers, but he'd had vision and optimism, a trait most people said his great-grandson shared, although Abigail doubted Edgar Garrison'd had a two-inch scar under his eye from a bar fight.

As she descended the zigzag of steps, a slight breeze stirring, Abigail wondered if she should give serious thought to selling her own Mt. Desert Island house. With Lou Beeler's retirement in the fall, would the dozens of state and local detectives who'd worked on her husband's seven-year-old murder continue? Who would have his dedication, his interest?

Was it time to give up Maine?

She pushed back the thought, jumping down the last stone step to the narrow, well-kept private road. Owen and the Coopers paid for upkeep. They'd never sent her a bill for so much as a dime. They could afford not to rent out their houses. Abigail couldn't. Without the money from renting to cop friends, she wouldn't have been able to afford the taxes, utilities, the occasional repair job.

Chris had never cared about money or social status. Before his death, everyone knew her father was slated to become the next director of the FBI. It hadn't fazed Chris—he just didn't think that way.

But other people did, and she'd often wondered if his part-time neighbors on Mt. Desert Island had accepted him in the same way he did them.

"You're the only person the killer fears."

Had the killer feared Chris?

Abigail crossed the quiet, isolated road to the driveway entrance she shared with Owen, then turned onto her own driveway, feeling the wind pick up as she got closer to the water.

She'd come up here with questions and something of a mission, but no plan.

What she needed was a plan.

She'd paint, and she'd come up with one.

Linc Cooper pounded onto Owen's deck in a state, pacing, starting to speak then stopping again. Owen tried to remember when he'd last seen him. Two years, at least. At the time, Linc had just dropped out—or, more plausibly, had just been kicked out—of Brown. He was smart, and most people expected him to get himself together one of these days.

Lincoln James Cooper had everything—except, Owen thought, what any kid needed most, which was a family who believed in him and considered him more than an afterthought. Linc was supposed to reflect his father's and his sister's successes and dreams. Whether he had any of his own didn't seem to matter. It wasn't necessarily what anyone intended or wanted. It was just the way the Cooper family worked.

Owen's own family was more straightforward. *"Just don't get killed,"* they'd tell him.

Finally, Linc plopped down on a wooden chair and looked up at Owen without meeting his eye. "I want you to teach me what you know. Show me how to do search-and-rescue. Take me on. You're not doing anything this summer—that's what I hear, anyway."

"Linc—"

"I'd pay you. You're the best, Owen. I want to learn from you."

"It's not about the money. Why don't you apply for a spot in the field academy? We'll be doing a full range of training."

The kid shook his head, not even considering the idea. "That'd never work. My family would never let me take time off from school to do SAR training."

"Don't put words in their mouths. Besides, you're over eighteen—"

"You think that matters?" Linc slumped in his chair and kicked out his legs, looking defeated. "My family's not like yours. I can't just go my own way."

"You are going your own way. You're choosing your own course now."

He snorted. "Whatever."

Owen smiled at the twenty-year-old. "Don't give up so easily. If you disagree with me, fight for your position—"

"I don't want to fight for anything." His eyes teared up unexpectedly, and he shot to his feet, turning his back to Owen and looking out at the water. "I'm just tired of being a weak-kneed loser."

"Get your stuff together." Owen glanced at his watch. "Meet me here at one o'clock. We'll go on a hike. Take things from there."

"You don't have to—"

"If you're not here at one, I leave without you."

Linc shifted back to him and nodded. "I'll be here."

He jumped down from the deck and ran back to his rattletrap of a car with more energy, his foul mood and unfocused irritability and defeatism at bay. Owen remembered being twenty. He'd gone against his family's expectations, but they'd supported his need to figure out his own life.

He watched a cormorant dive into the water just off his rocky point. He had no idea where he'd take Linc, but he liked the idea of getting out on the island. Seeing Abigail yesterday—knowing she was barely a quarter mile up the rocks from him—had thrown him off.

Nothing about her was uncomplicated.

Except, he thought, her determination to find her husband's killer. That was straightforward, clear and unchanging.

And it was why she was on Mt. Desert.

It was always why she was there.

CHAPTER 8

Abigail dropped onto the wooden bench in a booth across from Lou Beeler, who'd arrived at the tiny harbor restaurant ahead of her. He already had a mug of black coffee in front of him. "Thanks for coming," he said.

"I'm glad you called. I'd just finished trimming the entry."

"Painting?"

She nodded. "Helps me think."

"Keeps you out of trouble, too."

There was that. A waitress with the face of a heavy smoker came for Abigail's order. "I'll have whatever Lou here's having," she said.

The woman raised her eyebrows. "The fisherman's platter?"

Abigail looked at the older detective. "How do you stay so thin eating a fisherman's platter, ever?" She shifted back to the waitress. "A shrimp roll with fries and iced tea will do it. Thanks."

The waitress retreated without a word, and Lou sat back, eyeing Abigail with a frankness she'd learned to expect from him. Major crimes outside the cities of Portland and Bangor fell under the jurisdiction of the Maine State Police Criminal Investigative Division. Lou Beeler had been dedicated to his job almost as long as she'd been alive, and he knew what he was doing. They got along. He was sympathetic to her position as the widow of a murder victim and respectful of her expertise as a homicide detective—neither of which meant he would open his file on Chris for her.

She doubted Lou had held back much. Ballistics—he'd never give up what he had on the murder weapon. In his place, Abigail wouldn't, either. But she had a fair idea that the killer had used a handgun, not an assault rifle, despite the distance and the accuracy of the shot.

The two crimes that day seven years ago—the break-in and Chris's murder—had always created a discordant note for her. Whacking her on the head, stealing her necklace. Shooting a man after lying in wait for him. They didn't seem to go together. And yet how could they not?

If nothing changed, Lou Beeler would retire with the murder of Mt. Desert Island native and FBI Special Agent Christopher Browning unresolved.

That fact couldn't sit well with him, and Abigail hoped that she could play into his potential desire to tie up loose ends this summer.

"I don't have anything to report on your call," Lou said.

"I'm not surprised. Whoever it was went to some trouble to cover his tracks. Or hers. I still can't even tell you if it was a man or a woman."

The waitress returned with a glass of tea and a pot of coffee, refilling Lou's mug. Abigail added a packet of sugar to her tea, which looked strong and not particularly fresh. "I've been here for less than a day and already have heard about a million things going on around here. Owen Garrison's on the island. His organization, Fast Rescue, is opening up a field academy in Bar Harbor. Grace Cooper's been appointed to a high-level State Department position, pending an FBI background check. Linc Cooper's here. Jason Cooper's selling his brother's house out from under him."

"You've been busy," Lou said.

"Actually, I've just taken a couple walks and said hello to the neighbors."

"If you want a green light to look into this call of yours, you've got it. You know what lines you can and can't cross."

Their lunches arrived, Lou's plate of fried seafood so full, a shrimp fell off onto the table. He stabbed it with his fork, coated it in homemade tartar sauce and popped it into his mouth. "Unbelievable. You can't fry seafood this way at home."

"Just as well, don't you think? We don't need any more temptation." Her own shrimp roll was decadent enough, a once-a-year treat. "Is Doyle Alden up to speed on the call?"

"Yes, ma'am. He'll be here any minute. I should warn you—he's not in the best mood."

"When has Doyle ever been in a good mood? What's it this time?"

"Katie's out of town. Fast Rescue hired her as director of the new academy. She's in England for six weeks of training."

"Good for her," Abigail said. "I know it's Doyle's busy season, but he'll survive."

"Here he is now." Lou nodded toward the door. "He doesn't think your call's going to amount to anything, either. If there was something specific to go on—"

"I know. There's nothing but mush."

Lou scooted over, and Doyle sat on the bench next to him and shook his head at the two plates of fried seafood, never mind that Abigail's was smaller. "I can't eat that stuff anymore. Gives me heartburn."

"Good," Lou said with a grin. "I was afraid I was going to have to share."

Doyle settled his gaze on Abigail. "I haven't seen you since last summer. You're looking good."

"You, too, Chief."

"You got here yesterday?"

"In the fog. I'm painting my entry lupine-blue. So far as I know, it's always been white."

Doyle scoffed. "You're not up here to paint."

"Well, no. Finding out who interrupted my wedding anniversary dinner the other night would be more important than painting. I assume Lou told you about the call."

"We're looking into it," Doyle said. "If we learn anything, we'll let you know in due course."

Abigail bit into her shrimp roll, just to keep herself from throwing a few piping hot native Maine shrimp at Alden. She wouldn't be getting any green light from him to poke around his town.

Lou tackled a big piece of fried haddock. "You two. Come on. We're all on the same page here."

Doyle kept his gaze pinned on Abigail, who was seated across from him. "I don't know about that, Lou. You and I know the call's most likely bullshit. Abigail does, too, but she doesn't care—she'll use it to stir people up. Doesn't matter who gets caught in the crossfire. Chris's killer could be long gone and maybe hasn't stepped foot in Maine in seven years, but she can't deal with that. She wants it to be one of us."

"There are too many secrets among your husband's friends and neighbors."

Chris hadn't had a better friend than Doyle Alden, and yet, Abigail thought, she'd gotten on Doyle's nerves right from the start—because marrying her meant Chris was never coming back to Mt. Desert to live.

Lou started to speak, his anger and shock at Doyle's bluntness obvious, but Abigail reached across the table and touched her fellow detective's hand. "It's okay. Doyle has a point. I haven't given anyone here a moment's rest since Chris died. To say I want Chris's killer to be someone from the area isn't fair. I don't."

"But you believe it is," Doyle said.

"I'm keeping an open mind. So should you."

Before Doyle could launch himself across the table and go for her throat, Lou dipped a fry into his little tub of ketchup and handed it over to him. "Eat up, Doyle. If one fry gives you heartburn, see a doctor. If *I* get heartburn from listening to you two, I'm going to knock both your heads together before I go for the Rolaids. Got it?"

Abigail didn't doubt that Lou Beeler could, and would, do exactly what he promised. "I understand your wife's in England, Chief," she said. "My caller said things were happening up here—"

"Leave my wife out of your guessing."

"It's not a guess. It's a fact that she's not here."

"It's also a fact that a lobsterman up on Beals Island caught a blue lobster last week."

"No kidding? What did he do with it?"

Lou picked up his coffee mug. "I should have ordered a beer when I had the chance. He donated the lobster to the Mt. Desert Harbor Oceanarium. I read about it in the paper.

Abigail, we're on your side—all of us. Doyle, me, the entire Maine State Police. We all want to solve your husband's murder as much now as we did the day it happened. We'll pursue any and all leads with vigor."

Abigail tried to put herself in Lou's shoes as the lead investigator on a seven-year-old case, but she couldn't. She'd only been a detective two years. The cold cases in the BPD's files weren't ones she'd worked on. The family members weren't people she'd come to know from year after year of them pushing, prodding, demanding answers—pleading for resolution. From wanting to give them those answers.

"I know you will," she said curtly. "But neither of you believes the call will amount to anything."

"It's the fifty-seventh phone tip we've received over the years."

"The first in two years," Abigail said. "The first I've received in Boston, at dinner, on my wedding anniversary."

Doyle, sneaking a fried scallop from Lou's plate, seemed calmer, less antagonistic. "You're high profile. John March's daughter, a Boston homicide detective. I don't need to tell you that complicates matters, makes it harder to separate bullshit from something real."

She pushed aside her plate, no longer hungry. "The call may be bullshit, but it was real."

"Yeah." Doyle got heavily to his feet. "You've got the station number and my home phone and pager numbers. Feel free to call anytime."

"I will. Thanks."

He left, the door banging shut behind him, and Lou scowled across the table at her. "You had to goad him?"

"Me? What'd I do?" But she sighed, shaking her head. "He's never liked me."

"That's a two-way street, sister."

"It's not—"

"He knew Chris for a lot longer than you did. Do you think you might be just a little bit jealous of Chief Alden?"

Abigail sat back against the scarred wood of the booth and studied the man across the table from her. "You know how to play hardball, don't you, Lou?"

"It doesn't come naturally, if that's any consolation."

"Not much. What're you going to do when you retire?"

"My wife and I bought a used camper. We're tearing it apart and plan to put it on the road and take off for three months. Then, who knows?"

"Think you'll miss the work?"

"I've loved my job, but I'm looking forward to whatever comes next. What about you?" He set his mug down but kept his eyes on her. "You see yourself on the job for another twenty, twenty-five years?"

"You mean will I quit when I find Chris's killer?"

"I mean will you quit either way. Can you see yourself investigating homicides twenty years from now when your husband's is still unsolved?"

"I don't think that far into the future."

"Maybe you should," Lou said, but he didn't take the thought further, and nodded at her plate. "You taking that shrimp home with you?"

"No. Take them, Lou. Enjoy."

He grinned at her. "I will."

CHAPTER 9

By dusk, Abigail had put a second coat of her perky lupine-blue paint on the entry walls and was up on her stepladder, an unsteady relic from Chris's grandfather, dipping her brush into her coffee can.

She'd poured about two inches of paint into it. If it fell off the ladder, there'd be less to clean up. A few touch-ups, and she'd be finished. Then came the cleanup. Brush, tray, rollers. Herself. She'd splattered paint on herself from head to toe.

Bob or Scoop or any of the guys she rented the house to would have gladly painted with her or for her, and they wouldn't have cared about getting a break on rent—they knew she could have charged twice as much. She didn't care about making a profit.

But doing the work, the steady rhythm of it, the kind of concentration it required, helped anchor her mind just enough for her to think productively, not an easy concept to explain but one that worked for her.

Not that she'd produced any great insights since she'd first dipped her brush into the blue paint.

She'd opened up all her windows and could hear gulls and the wash of the tide, passing boats, the occasional rustle of leaves and branches in the wind. Peaceful sounds that somehow made her feel less isolated.

She thought of Owen and wondered if he ever felt isolated, or if he would have preferred to have their quiet waterfront all to himself.

A different sound caught her attention. She paused, paintbrush in midair, to hear better.

There it was again.

A whisper, she decided. Someone was outside.

She laid her brush across the top of her coffee can and dismounted the ladder, then fetched her gun from the small safe in the front room. She slipped on the belt holster. If not for the call the other night, she wouldn't have bothered.

She stepped into the back room, listening through the open back door.

A whiny whisper. A sharp one in response.

Kids.

Tucking her weapon into her holster, Abigail walked outside, the evening air cool, almost cold, the navy blue sky dotted with the first stars of the night.

"Shh." Another whisper. "Be quiet."

"I am being quiet. *You're* the one."

The voices came from a trio of pine trees to Abigail's right. She walked down the porch steps. "You can come out of the trees. The mosquitoes must be eating you alive."

"You won't tell our dad?"

The Alden boys, she thought. Had to be. Doyle and Owen had developed a tight, if unexpected, friendship, especially in the years since Chris's death.

"Come on, guys. Sean and Ian, right? It's getting dark."

The two boys stepped out from behind the smallest of the pines into the yard. The older boy, Sean, looked more defiant than embarrassed or fearful. Ian stayed a half step behind his brother.

"You remember me, don't you? Abigail—Abigail Browning."

They nodded simultaneously but said nothing.

"Are you and your dad visiting Owen?"

"Just us," Sean said. "Dad's at a meeting."

"Is Owen behind you?"

Ian gasped, but Sean shook his head. "We're on a mission," he said in a serious tone.

Abigail didn't want to make light of whatever they were up to. "What kind of mission?"

"*Sean.*" Ian tugged on his brother's arm. "We can't tell her. Dad'll kill us."

Sean was silent a moment, then said, "Ian and me are just practicing our nighttime navigation skills."

"That's your mission?" she asked.

Both boys nodded.

"How did you end up here? Was that part of your mission?"

Ian took a step forward, and in the light from her house, Abigail saw that he was pale and nervous. Because of her? She could see tears forming in his eyes.

"Boys," she said gently, "what's going on?"

Before they could answer—or lie—pine branches

moved behind them, creating shadows on the grass, and Sean and Ian shot toward Abigail, ducking behind her with a terror that was both immediate and real.

"It's just me," Owen said, ducking out into the open. "Sorry if I startled everyone."

Given his experience, stealth would come almost naturally to him at this point. Abigail slipped her arms over the boys' shoulders as they stood on either side of her. "Why don't we all go inside for a minute? You can inspect my paint job while I make hot chocolate. Then you can warm up before you go on your way."

Owen eyed the boys, unamused. "You two told me you were going upstairs to read."

"We did," Sean said. "We just—"

"I can't have you stay with me if you're going to sneak out." Owen shifted to Abigail, easing up slightly. "They went out a window on a bedsheet. I was lighting a fire in the woodstove. I never heard a thing."

"They told me they were practicing their nighttime navigation skills," she said, not bothering to hide her skepticism. She gave their shoulders a quick squeeze. "But I think there's more to their story, right, guys?"

Ian broke away from her and appealed to Owen. "I told Sean—"

"You're responsible for your own decisions."

"But he made me!"

Sean snorted. "I didn't make you do anything. You wanted to go."

"I didn't think the ghost was real." Ian had a panicked note in his voice now. "I thought—I thought—"

"Whoa, slow down," Owen said.

Abigail turned Sean to face her and bent down so that

she had eye contact with him. "Tell me about the ghost, okay? Everything you can think of."

His face had gone deathly white, his lower lip trembling, but he didn't respond.

"We heard it," Ian said, crying now. "We heard the ghost!"

Abigail didn't shift her gaze from Sean, who nodded. "We heard it breathing."

"Where?" she asked.

"In the ruins."

"The ruins?"

"The old foundation," Owen said. "That's where you heard someone the other night, too, isn't it, boys?"

"Yes," Sean said.

"Might it have been an animal?" Abigail asked. "A fox or a squirrel maybe?"

The older boy, his color only marginally improved, shook his head. "It was human. It was…we think it was…"

Chris, she thought.

She put a hand on Sean's shoulder. "Do you boys think you heard my husband's ghost?"

A tear dribbled down his cheek. "We had to be sure. The other night—we were pretty sure that's who it was. Now—" He wiped his tear with the back of his hand, took a quick breath. "It has to be."

Abigail straightened and glanced at Owen, who looked pained, not only for the frightened boys in his charge, she thought, but for her. "I'm sorry. They have active imaginations."

"Maybe," she said, "but they heard something out here."

"Yes, but it wasn't a ghost."

She didn't care. "Wait in the house. I'll go take a look. Then I can drive you all back to your place."

"That's not necessary," Owen said quietly. "The boys and I can investigate on our way back."

Abigail shook her head. "I don't think so."

"Then we'll go together."

She could see he was as determined as she was. The tension between them seemed to have helped steady the boys. She sighed. "All right. Let me get a flashlight." She smiled at him. "Don't worry—I've got on the right shoes."

Nature was slowly, but inexorably, reclaiming the land where Owen's great-grandfather had built his summer place almost a hundred years ago, no doubt never imagining that a killer would one day hide in its remains and lie in wait in order to commit murder. Most of the charred rubble was long removed. Now, trees and brush grew in the sunken chunks of foundation, and only parts of the original stonework could be distinguished from the surrounding landscape.

Owen kept the boys close to him. Their talk of a ghost had kicked the cop in Abigail into gear. He watched her push ahead on the path through low-growing wild blueberry bushes and junipers.

Feet-flat-on-the-floor Abigail Browning didn't seem the type to believe in ghosts. So, what did she think she'd find out here?

Obviously she had something on her mind, Owen thought as she squeezed between a fir tree and a six-foot section of chimney that had broken off its base. She stabbed her flashlight beam into the dark.

"What does she see?" Ian asked, taking Owen's hand.

"I don't know. Abigail?"

She visibly relaxed. "Well, well. I like to keep an open mind, but I'll bet ghosts don't smoke cigarettes and drink beer." She shifted her flashlight, taking in more corners of the little hideout and then pointed the beam back at Owen and the boys. "Come see."

Owen let Sean break off from him and run ahead. Ian looked up at him for a cue, and he nodded, the younger boy immediately pulling his hand free and scooting after his brother.

Using her flashlight as a pointer, Abigail explained the scene to the boys. "Someone used that rock over there as an ashtray," she said. "See the cigarette butts? And there. A squished empty pack of Marlboros."

"I can still smell the cigarettes," Ian said.

"Did you smell smoke when you were out here?" she asked.

Sean shook his head. "No. Look at those beer cans. How many of them are there?"

"Let's count them. One, two, three—"

"Eight," Ian said. "There are eight!"

Owen walked on the dark path behind them, shifting into a steady rhythm. He'd hiked in Acadia with Linc Cooper earlier that day, but Linc had gone inside himself, trudging along a mountain trail, preoccupied and unwilling—perhaps unable—to explain what was on his mind. To be twenty and that caught up in his own demons didn't seem right to Owen. But if he'd skipped the hike, he might have been less preoccupied and caught the boys sneaking out the window, sparing Abigail a trek out to investigate a ghost.

He stood behind her, noticing the shape of her back, hips. She kept herself in good physical condition. He said, "Seems someone had himself a party out here."

"More than one party, I'd say." She gestured into the

shadows with her flashlight. "There are more butts and beer cans over there."

"That's what we heard?" Sean snorted in disgust. "Some *drunk?*"

"We don't know whoever it was got drunk," Abigail said. "It's tempting to jump to conclusions, but we don't have all the facts. Anyone you know smoke Marlboros and drink Budweiser?"

Mattie Young.

Owen could see Abigail had already considered Mattie as a possibility, if not a likelihood. The boys shook their heads. They knew Mattie, who'd grown up with their parents, as well as anyone, but they wouldn't pay attention to what he smoked and drank.

Without warning, Abigail put her hand on Owen's upper arm and smiled at him. "I'm not taking any chances of falling in front of you again," she said as she stepped back from the chimney, then jumped lightly back onto the path, in no more need of a steadying hand than he was. She returned her focus to the boys. "What night did you first think you heard this ghost of yours?"

Owen answered, coming up behind her. "It was Sunday night."

She nodded. "Do you think whoever was out here heard you? Were you talking to each other, making noise playing on the rocks or anything?"

"Oh," Sean said, as if just figuring out what she was asking. "Well—yeah, we made noise. But when we heard someone up here, we tried to be quiet."

"What about tonight? Do you think our partier realized you were out here? Were you trying to be quiet and sneak up on him?"

"We were trying, but it didn't work."

Sean was calmer, Abigail's steady, pragmatic questions having what Owen suspected was their intended effect—to get information and, at the same time, to help the boys to see the scene from her point of view.

"Maybe whoever it was just didn't want to be seen," Abigail continued. "Even if it was someone you know."

"Like who?" Sean asked.

"Talk to your dad. See what he says." She brushed at a mosquito in front of her face. "This is a beautiful spot, but I'd bring my bug spray next time."

"The mosquitoes are bothering me, too," Ian said.

"I'm finished here. You guys need me to walk you back? You can borrow my flashlight—"

"I have one," Owen said, producing a small flashlight from his back pocket.

She grinned at him. "Always prepared."

"Let us walk you back. You're the one out here alone."

"That's not necessary." But she tilted her head back, studying him in the near-darkness. "All right. You guys can all walk me home. Let's get moving before I lose another pint of blood to these mosquitoes."

Since she was the one with the gun, Owen wasn't sure who was escorting whom, but his flashlight was more efficient than hers, and he knew the rocks better than she did.

She let them take her as far as the pine trees where she'd caught Sean and Ian hiding.

"We're sorry, Mrs. Browning," Sean mumbled, not waiting to be asked.

"Sorry for what? I like having company. Next time you'll definitely have to come in for hot chocolate. And it's Abigail. Not Ab, either. Or Abbie. Just Abigail." She winked at both boys, adding in a conspiratorial whisper, "But you might want to apologize to Owen about the bedsheet thing."

They'd all but forgotten that one and turned to him, wide-eyed. "Are you going to tell Dad?" Ian asked.

Owen grinned. "Depends how much work I can get out of you two before he shows up. Of course, you could always read those books—"

"We'll read," Sean said.

His brother nodded. "We'll read all night!"

Abigail laughed, and as she started into the trees, Owen called to her, "If you need us, give a yell."

"I will." She glanced back at him. "And the same here. If you need me, give a yell."

They were, after all, neighbors.

On the way back across the rocks to his place, Sean and Ian peppered Owen with questions about Abigail and what she was doing out here by herself, and why wasn't she married—and why was she a detective?

"Sorry, guys," Owen said. "I don't know all that much about Abigail."

A true statement, as far as it went. And as long as he was being honest with himself, he admitted he'd like to change that.

The boys ran up onto the deck and back into the house.

Owen lingered out in the cool night air. He did want to know his neighbor across the rocks better.

He had for a long time.

CHAPTER 10

Mattie Young jammed his shovel into a two-foot hole he'd dug and hit rock. He laid the shovel next to him and got down on his hands and knees, digging into the hole with one hand, but he couldn't find the edges of whatever he'd just struck.

"It's ledge," he said.

Ellis Cooper peered into the hole. "That's not ledge. That's just a rock. Dig it up. The hole's not deep enough."

Mattie wanted to take the shovel to Ellis's head, except Ellis had always treated him well. Mattie knew his nerves were frayed, and he hadn't been sleeping well. Drinking too much, smoking too much. And Linc. The money. The tension of whether the kid would crumple under the pressure and tell someone about the blackmail.

I should have demanded the ten grand all at once.

For the Coopers, ten thousand dollars was a minuscule amount. Even Linc could manage to scare up that much without drawing too much attention to himself—if he tried. He just needed the right motivation.

For Mattie, ten thousand dollars was a fresh start.

A new life.

"We need at least another eight inches," Ellis said, pulling on his doeskin work gloves, not that he'd be doing any of the work. "You'll try, won't you?"

Mattie nodded, rancid-smelling sweat pouring down his face and back, dampening his armpits. He could taste the booze and cigarettes from last night. He'd scared the hell out of Doyle's sons, but what the hell was he supposed to do? Even half in the bag, he'd known he didn't want Sean and Ian to see him. They'd tell their father—and Owen. Possibly Abigail, too. He didn't need anyone's scrutiny right now.

Let them think he was a ghost.

He'd only brought enough beer to keep himself from de-hydrating after a long day digging and hauling and snipping for the Coopers. He knew his limits, never mind what anyone else said. He'd hoped the cigarettes would help with the mosquitoes. He didn't like the smell of bug repellant.

Angling the blade of his shovel, he jabbed it into the hole and carved around the edges of what turned out to be a rock, not ledge. But it was a big damn rock. Mattie dropped the shovel again and dug both hands into the hole, trying to get his fingers around one end of the rock. He didn't wear gloves. His hands were so callused that new nicks and scratches didn't bother him.

Ellis leaned over him. "Use your shovel for leverage."

Ignoring him, Mattie got his hands under an edge of the rock and squatted down, putting his legs into it as he pulled hard, grunting. That end of the rock came loose, but it was too big for him to just pry it up out of the hole. He sat back on his butt, catching his breath.

Ellis was still hovering. Mattie wiped his mouth with the back of his dirt-encrusted hand. "You can go do something else," he said. "This is going to take a while."

"That's all right. I'll stay here in case you need me. I don't mind."

Mattie almost burst out laughing. Ellis, help him? The guy liked to work in his gardens, but he only did jobs that amused him. Digging up rocks wasn't one of them.

Getting back up onto his knees, Mattie grabbed his shovel and stabbed it onto the other end of the rock, dislodging it, too. Using both hands and shovel, he managed to get hold of the entire hunk of granite and heave it out of the hole and onto the pristine grass.

"That's a good-looking rock." Ellis rolled it over with his foot. "Clean it up. I might find a use for it."

How 'bout I bash you over the head with it?

But Mattie coughed, nodding, then sat on the grass, his muscles jittery, his head pounding. Maybe he'd had one more beer than he should have last night.

"The hole's deep enough now," Ellis said. "We need to get that hydrangea into the ground as soon as possible. It's late in the season for transplanting shrubs. I don't want the roots to dry out in this sun."

What would you do, boss man, if I barfed into your hydrangea hole?

"I'm on it," Mattie said.

Ellis nodded, satisfied. "Don't strain yourself."

The guy meant well, Mattie reminded himself as he dug back into the hole. Ellis provided steady work and often made up stuff for Mattie to do on slow days, just to be sure he had a paycheck. That he was a perfectionist came with the territory. Occasionally, Mattie fitted in small jobs at other places on the island, but he'd never encountered anyone more dedicated, more passionate about his gardens than Ellis Cooper. That he could give them up without a whimper was hard to believe.

On the other hand, Ellis would never let anyone know if he was displeased with his big brother Jason.

He might not even be able to admit his displeasure to himself.

Jason had the power, the reputation, the charisma, the money. Ellis had the talent, the vision, the discretion, the empathy for others. He had done well. He was a trusted Washington consultant—he'd advised his niece on her rise to power within very tough circles. He'd never married, but he was sociable, always on everyone's guest list. In Maine, he liked showing off his gardens.

If Linc confided in anyone, it wouldn't be his father—it'd be his uncle or his sister.

Grace.

Mattie reached for the hydrangea, whose roots were in no danger of drying out. He couldn't think about Grace Cooper. Not now, not ever again.

He thought about his money instead, and his new life.

Think what you could do with twenty grand.

Linc could get another ten, easy. And he would pay it, given the right leverage.

Abigail…

Mattie dropped the hydrangea into the hole, which, because of the size of the rock he'd just dragged out of it, was actually too big. If Ellis noticed, he was keeping his mouth shut.

And that's what you should do, Mattie thought. Keep your mouth shut. Mind your own business.

"I'll get the hose," Ellis said.

Mattie nodded. "Thanks."

He gulped in air as he shoved dirt into the hole and patted it around and under the hydrangea roots. If he didn't get control of himself, someone would be shoving dirt around his dead body, burying him in the cold, rocky ground.

Who the hell would miss him?

Not a soul. And for damn good reason.

Abigail took the last three steps of her porch in a single leap and ran into the back room to grab the phone. "Hello—"

Dial tone.

She was too late.

She slammed the receiver onto the old base and cursed herself for not having bought a portable phone by now. There was no cell service out here, but she could have had a portable phone on the porch and reached it before whoever was calling hung up. Instead, she'd adopted the "if-it-ain't-broke-don't-fix-it" mentality of the Browning men and hadn't replaced the working phone that came with the place.

Nor had she added an answering machine. How often was she here to need one? And vacationers didn't want one. They came to Mt. Desert Island to escape such trappings. Even Bob O'Reilly and Scoop Wisdom.

Maybe it was Bob who'd just tried to reach her.

She debated calling him to tell him about the Alden boys' "ghost" and the cigarette butts and beer cans.

If Sean and Ian hadn't told their father about last night,

Owen would have, and Doyle, if he was any kind of police chief, any kind of friend, would talk to Mattie and confront him about what he was doing on Garrison property. What he was doing drinking.

Abigail locked her back door and went out the front door, locking it, too. She'd tucked her gun back into her safe. She'd gone out to the old Garrison foundation that morning. Nothing had changed. The beer cans and cigarette butts were still there. In daylight, she hadn't found any other evidence of interest. Someone—in all likelihood, Mattie Young—had been smoking and drinking out there.

And, perhaps, spying on her or Owen, or both.

Abigail jumped in her car and took off up the driveway, rolling down the windows, hot all of a sudden. And it wasn't because of the missed call and thinking about Mattie Young.

It was because of Owen Garrison.

Thinking about him.

She'd spotted him out on the rocks in his jeans and untucked, weathered polo and could almost feel his desire to be alone, his burnout and fatigue after a grueling year of responding to one disaster after another.

Had Doyle told him about the anonymous call?

Her reaction to Owen, Abigail knew, wasn't just neighborly—and it had nothing whatsoever to do with her being a detective, her vow to find Chris's killer. It was far more elemental than that.

The guy was sexy as hell, and she'd have had to be a rock not to notice.

She drove through picturesque Northeast Harbor, relatively quiet for such a beautiful summer day, and out to Somes Sound, the only fjord on the east coast. Its finger of salt water almost cut the island in two. Thirty years ago, Jason Cooper, then a young tech entrepreneur, bought a modest house on a coveted stretch of the sound. He'd added to it over the years, transformed it into one of the most stunning properties on Mt. Desert.

The security gate was open. Abigail drove down the paved driveway to the stone-and-clapboard house, secluded among tall evergreens and mature maples. Its understated landscaping soothed more than awed, and as she parked behind Grace's silver Mercedes, she noticed bright turquoise and orange kayaks leaned up against the garage. The Coopers owned a yacht as well as a smaller sailboat and speedboat. Jason, if not his two children, loved to be out on the water.

As she got out of her car, Abigail smelled roses in the warm early afternoon air. She followed a stone path around to the front porch, a small white poodle running down the steps to greet her. "Hey, girl," she said, bending down to pet the dog. "Cindy, right?"

"Actually, it's Sis. We had to have Cindy put down over the winter."

Abigail looked up at Jason Cooper as he walked down from the porch. "I'm sorry. I didn't know."

"She was eighteen. It was time."

He snapped his fingers at the little dog, who immediately scurried to his side and sat, panting as she watched Abigail, as if jealous of her freedom to ignore Jason Cooper. He smiled, reminding her of Grace. He looked younger than sixty-two—too young, certainly, to have a thirty-eight-year-old daughter.

"How are you, Abigail?" he asked.

"Doing just fine, thanks. And you?"

"Enjoying the beautiful day." He nodded at her. "You look as if you've been painting."

She glanced at her paint-spattered shirt. Her shoes were covered, too. Fortunately, they were the cheap ones. Jason, of course, was casually but impeccably dressed, not a thread out of place in his dark slacks and golf shirt. She grinned at him. "I did get some on the walls. I painted the entry. Now everything else looks shabby."

"That's often the way it is with any kind of renovation."

"I imagine so. I just got here on Monday. How long have you been here?"

"A little over a week. Grace and Linc came up on the weekend." He scooped up Sis, cupping her in one arm as he straightened. "Is this a social visit, or are you investigating something?"

"Not my jurisdiction." She gestured toward the stone urns of well-behaved plants. "Everything looks so beautiful. I was up at Ellis's yesterday. I've never seen his gardens this perfect. I understand you're putting his place on the market?"

"It's not his place any more than this is my place."

"You're co-owners?"

"We're a family." Jason gave her an indulgent smile. "Ask all the questions you want, Abigail. I know any change in our lives up here puts you on alert."

Especially, she thought, when coupled with a weird phone call. She ignored the edge in his tone, and how he'd avoided a direct answer to her question. "Why sell now? I'm curious, that's all."

"It's just a matter of timing. Would you care to come inside?"

The invitation was his way of ending the conversation.

She was supposed to recognize it as such and leave, but she was tempted to call his bluff and accept. Instead, she chose not to give him a direct answer. "You all must be thrilled about Grace's appointment. Does it make for any additional scrutiny?"

"Not really. She has to go through the background check, of course, but that's of no concern. Abigail—"

"FBI turn up yet?"

His expression turned cool. "Not that I know of."

"They'll want to talk to me, Jason. Because of Chris."

"And because of who your father is."

Abigail said nothing.

Sis fidgeted, and Jason finally set her back on the walk, snapping his fingers again. The little dog shot up the stairs onto the porch without a backward glance at her master. He watched her, as if he thought she might do something unexpected, out of control.

"It's hard to believe it's been seven years," he said finally. "Grace and Chris met when they were eight years old. His death was a terrible tragedy. The lingering questions—" He broke off, shifting back to Abigail. "I'm sorry Grace's situation has to stir up the past for you, but it's out of our hands."

"Until I know who killed Chris, the past is always stirred up for me."

"Even after seven years? Abigail." He seemed genuinely distressed. "You have to live your life."

"I am living my life."

"Maybe that's what you believe, but if you were, you'd have sold your house a long time ago. You don't belong here." His tone wasn't unkind. "You only keep that house because of Chris. Because of the past."

She wasn't digging into her soul with Jason Cooper. She regretted having gone as far as she had with him. "You could be right, but painting's got to be a good sign, don't you think?" She didn't give him a chance to answer. "Is Mattie Young here by any chance?"

"He's working up at Ellis's all day. He'll be here tomorrow."

"What's he driving these days?" she asked, thinking of his party out in the old foundation. What had he done with his car? Had anyone seen it? Had he driven home under the influence?

"A bicycle," Jason said. "Mattie lost his license over the winter."

"DUI?"

He nodded. "Unfortunately. The dark winters and isolation got to him. He goes to meetings. He's making an effort."

Not a consistent one, Abigail thought, picturing the beer cans. Unless they weren't Mattie's. She had no real evidence they were. "He's still living in the same place?"

"He rents a house around the corner from Doyle Alden. That's how he got caught drinking and driving—Doyle saw him scream past his house. Why?"

"Just curious."

Jason smiled, but his eyes remained cool. "Always curious, aren't you, Abigail?"

"It's a March family trait."

The reminder of her father obviously didn't sit well with Jason Cooper. "I suppose it is. If you won't come in—"

"No, thanks. I should get back. Nice to see you."

"Likewise."

Before she could get out another word, he was walking onto the porch, snapping his fingers at his little dog.

***

When she arrived at her house, Abigail pulled on shorts, a T-shirt and her good running shoes and jogged up the private drive and out onto the main road, finding her pace, telling herself she needed stay in shape. But she could feel her restlessness building into frustration, questions and threads of conversations, new possibilities, coming at her all at once.

And memories. They jumped at her with every stride—and not just her own memories, of her short-lived marriage, of her widowhood, filled with seven years of prodding and pushing for answers to her husband's unsolved murder. Chris's memories came at her, too. The stories he'd told of his childhood on the island that had taken shape in her mind over the years, until they were as real to her as the images of her own past.

Chris and Doyle Alden…Mattie Young…the three of them going off on a lobster boat with Chris's grandfather, the old man teaching them what he knew about tides, currents, hidden dangers, good stewardship of the land and sea that had sustained their families for generations.

Abigail could picture them on Will Browning's lobster boat when they'd realized a girl was in the water. Doe Garrison, a wealthy summer resident. A pretty girl, by all accounts. Happy. A nature lover like her great-grandfather.

The local boys were just teenagers themselves. At seventeen, Mattie was the oldest. Doyle, fifteen. Chris was fourteen, like Doe.

They'd pulled her out of the water, but it was too late.

"I could see her brother up on the cliffs watching us try to save her. I'll never forget his face, Abigail. Never."

Will Browning raced to the harbor, an ambulance waiting.

"The Garrisons and the Coopers were on the dock. Polly

Garrison, Doe's parents, Owen. They were in shock. They knew that she was gone. Jason Cooper, Ellis. They tried to stay out of the way. But Grace—she was thirteen years old, and her best friend had just drowned."

As she maintained her steady pace, Abigail pictured the horror of that beautiful summer afternoon and wondered how much of it Owen remembered.

Every second, probably.

She could understand how he could keep coming to Maine, build a house a few hundred yards from where his sister had drowned. It wasn't just out of a stubborn need to appreciate what Doe had loved but out of a knowledge that, in order to be whole, he had to embrace that loss and make it a part of him, not run from it, cut it out of him or drag it behind him.

But was she really thinking about Owen's behavior… or her own? What, really, did she understand about Owen Garrison?

When she trotted back up her driveway, Abigail was almost relieved to find a black government car and a well-dressed, straight-backed man and woman knocking on her front door.

FBI agents.

They introduced themselves as Special Agent Ray Capozza and Special Agent Mary Steele and declined Abigail's invitation to go inside, instead joining her on the driveway. Capozza, a compact, no-nonsense man, insisted on showing her his credentials. "We're here on routine business, Mrs. Browning."

"You're running a background check on Grace Cooper, yes, I know. And, please, call me Abigail. Did my father tell you I was here?"

"No." Capozza wasn't going any further.

Steele, a sharp-featured brunette who looked as if she expected a bear to jump out of the trees, nodded vaguely out toward the water. "Pretty spot. I can see now why you hung on to this place. Your husband—" She broke off, looking awkward, then plunged ahead. "We're aware of what happened to him, Mrs. Browning—Abigail. No one's forgotten. No one will forget."

Capozza nodded in agreement, even if he wasn't ready to be that frank. "We're not here to investigate his murder, but we're in close touch with Maine CID. If we learn anything new, we'll let them know."

"Of course. Thanks." A courtesy call, Abigail realized. That was what this visit was. "Thanks for stopping by."

"We'll want to talk to you about your relationship with Grace Cooper at some point," Capozza said.

And Chris's relationship with her, no doubt. He and Grace had known each other most of their lives. If he'd died of natural causes seven years ago, he'd be a footnote, if that, in the two FBI agents' investigation. Now, they'd be prepared for anything—they'd hope, if not expect, to run across some new, telling tidbit. Abigail could see it in Capozza's and Steele's faces. They would love to stumble on the one missed fact that would solve the cold case of Chris's murder and turn their routine background investigation into something more.

"Anytime," she said. "I'll be here for the rest of the week and through the weekend, at least."

Special Agent Steele opened up the driver's door of their car and glanced back at Abigail. "Why are you up here this week? Vacation?"

Capozza toed a loose rock in the driveway. "Funny coincidence, isn't it?"

"You've talked to Lieutenant Beeler and Chief Alden," Abigail said.

They nodded. Leaning against the open car door, Steele said, "We know about the call."

"You want me to take you through it?"

"You don't mind?"

"Not at all." Abigail smiled, watching her fellow law enforcement officers slap at mosquitoes at almost the exact same moment. "Now would you care to come inside?"

Abigail sank into the old leather chair in her catch-all back room and felt the cold air off the water blow in through the open door. The wind had picked up with the incoming tide. She liked the sound of it, the taste of the ocean on it, but she'd have to get up and close the door eventually. The temperature was supposed to drop down into the forties overnight.

Would Mattie sneak into the old foundation tonight for a secret party?

The FBI agents had listened carefully to her story about the call. They'd asked the same follow-up questions that Lucas, Bob, Scoop and Lou had also asked—that she'd asked herself. She'd half hoped answering them again would bring new insight, but it hadn't.

After Capozza and Steele left, Abigail had gone into the musty cellar and dragged tools up to the back room and laid them out on the floor. A set of screwdrivers and a set of wrenches, two different kinds of hammers, chisels, scrapers, level, a crowbar, a utility knife, a drywall saw, a sledgehammer.

The Browning men had taken good care of their tools.

She'd left the electric drill and saw in the cellar, and other tools that were either unfamiliar to her or looked dubious. Chris and his grandfather weren't big on throwing things away. They'd recycle broken bits of one thing and use them to fix something else.

The back room needed more than a fresh coat of paint. It needed gutting. New wallboard, new wiring, new flooring. Abigail had collected do-it-yourself books over the years. Surely there was a chapter on gutting a room. How hard could it be? She just had to be careful not to drop anything on her head or electrocute herself.

The wind picked up, gusting through the open door. A light plastic chair scraped across the porch floor and fell over backward, landing with a bang that, although she'd seen it coming, startled her.

She shot out of her chair and grabbed the sledgehammer, lifting it with both hands, remembering Chris grinning at her as he'd held it himself so long ago. What had he been doing? She couldn't even remember.

She saw the section of wall where they'd fixed the leak on their last morning together. The job had never been finished properly. She could see the edges of tape and dried spackling, and the paint over the repair work didn't match the white of the rest of the wall.

Abigail could do the work herself, or ask friends, or hire it out, but she simply hadn't gotten around to it.

"Oh, Chris."

Her voice caught on the wind and seemed to echo out on the darkening rocks.

She drew the sledgehammer back and, on an exhale, smashed it not into the haphazardly repaired wall, but the narrower wall next to the porch door.

The plaster cracked. White dust puffed out from where the sledgehammer had struck.

She smashed the wall again. This time, the head of the massive hammer broke through the plaster.

Tears mixed with plaster dust in her eyes.

"I owe you, my friend."

Seven years…

"I owe you all I am."

CHAPTER 11

The acidic smells of evergreen and peat mixed with the smells of low tide, filling the cool night air. Owen stood out on his deck, listening as he angled his flashlight beam up onto the rocks. He'd been drawn outside by voices, a sharp exchange near the old foundation.

Mattie Young stepped out of the shadows and crooked an arm in front of his face. "You're blinding me."

"What're you doing out here, Mattie?"

"Running from Abigail. She's armed—I thought she was going to kill me."

"I wasn't going to kill you." Abigail jumped lightly off a boulder and landed behind Mattie, who flinched. "I'm still not, but I wouldn't throw another beer can at me if I were you."

Her voice was calm, coplike.

Owen lowered his flashlight, pointing the beam at the

ground and lighting the way for the two of them. "Come on over here. We can sort this out."

"Not me," Mattie said. "I'm going home."

"How?" Abigail asked him. "Are you going to ride your bike in the dark?"

"Yeah. I do it all the time. You don't like it, call Doyle. I'll tell him you threatened to shoot me."

She sighed. "I didn't threaten to shoot you, Mattie."

"You're armed—"

"Damn right I'm armed. Were you spying on me?"

"Why would I spy on you?"

"That's not an answer. You were out here Sunday night—before I got here. Did you know I was on my way?"

"Of course not. How would I?"

Abigail paused for a half beat. "You know you can't drink safely, don't you?"

Mattie didn't answer. Neither of them, Owen noticed, had started back toward his deck, his warm fire, a chance to talk.

"Get yourself to a meeting," Abigail said. "No more jaunts out here in the dark with a six-pack. Right, Mattie? Makes sense?"

"Go fuck yourself, Abigail. You're not a detective here."

Mattie spun around and marched out to Owen's driveway, oblivious to the dark.

"Where's your bike?" Abigail called.

"Up on the road. Don't worry about it."

"Did you hide it?"

"Go to hell."

"At least your language is improving. If you hid your bike—"

"I'm not hiding anything." He stopped abruptly, turning back to her. "I just don't bow down to you. I knew Chris's parents. I knew his grandfather. I knew them before you were even born. You think you're the only one who cares about what happened to Chris? You think you're the only one who wants his killer found?"

"Mattie," Owen said. "That's enough. Go home. Get some rest."

"Sleep it off, you mean? I'm not drunk."

But he tripped as he reached the driveway, swearing, then held up one hand, his middle finger clearly visible in the light from the house. He continued on around a bend in the driveway, disappearing into the blackness.

Abigail had gone silent. Owen raised his flashlight to her, catching the hard set of her mouth. She had on a sweatshirt, but she had to be cold.

"Come inside," he said. "Warm up."

"Thanks." She climbed up on the deck, glancing up the driveway. "He has a point. You all knew Chris longer than I did."

"He was just trying to get under your skin."

"Maybe. Chris didn't make excuses for him, but he didn't judge him, either, even after he knew he had to detach from him. He believed in Mattie. He has such talent."

"Talent's not a lot of use if you don't make something of it."

"Chris always said Mattie never had a sense of his own limitations. One of those good thing, bad thing deals. The good thing—it allowed him to take risks with his photography. The bad thing—he doesn't save money, he doesn't set realistic goals. He basically thinks the rules don't apply to him."

"That's part of why he keeps drinking."

"Alcoholics Anonymous is for other people. Not for

him." She sighed. "It's such a difficult disease. If he could make that breakthrough—"

"Only he can. No one else can do it for him."

"I said pretty much the same thing to Chris. But he knew without me having to tell him. We all know."

Owen could feel the cold now. He'd shot outside in his T-shirt. "Mattie's used Chris's death as an excuse not to deal with his problems."

"Maybe." Abigail's expression hardened again. "But Mattie has had his own agenda long before Chris was killed."

Owen stepped closer to her, flicking a fat mosquito off her forehead.

She waved at one in front of her. "I should have put on bug spray."

She followed him inside. She wasn't winded from chasing Mattie out on the rocks in the dark. She was in good shape. As a cop, she would need to be, but she also seemed to enjoy physical activity—a thought that twisted itself into an image that Owen suspected she'd shoot him for having in his head.

"I have a bottle of Chianti I've been saving."

"Saving for what?"

"Now, I guess. I've had a long year, and I don't like to drink alone."

She smiled, sitting on a chair in front of the woodstove. "Open it up, then. What did you do today?"

"Linc Cooper stopped by. He wants me to teach him everything I know in two weeks or less." He grabbed a wine bottle off the rack in his kitchen. "I remember that feeling. Linc's got a big set of issues. He thinks learning to jump out of a helicopter is going to help solve them."

"Did it help you?"

He opened the wine. "I had a different set of issues."

The fire had gotten hotter than he'd meant it to, Abigail's cheeks reddening in the warmth. The hard look was gone now, her dark curls softly framing her face. "You've got white dust in your hair," Owen said, setting two glasses on the counter and pouring the wine.

"I've been knocking out walls."

"Cathartic?"

"I don't know. I suppose it is. It's just one of those things that needs to be done."

"Did you stake out Mattie just now, or did you hear him and investigate?" Owen walked over to her with the two glasses and handed her one. "I'm guessing you laid in wait for him."

"You're guessing wrong. I was curious, and just took a walk over there—"

"In the dark."

"Correct."

"Without a flashlight?"

"I didn't need one, really, out in the open on the rocks, with the stars and the moonlight. Once my eyes adjusted, I was fine. There was one short stretch of woods that was a little tricky."

Owen sat on the chair opposite her. "And a flashlight would have warned Mattie you were on the way."

She tasted the wine. "So it would have."

"Are you ever off?"

She frowned at him. "What do you mean, 'off'? Crazy? Out of control?"

"I mean, do you ever turn off your inner detective?"

"Ah. That 'off.' I have no jurisdiction here. Why?"

"I'd just like to know when I'm talking to Abigail, my

pretty dark-eyed neighbor, and when I'm talking to Detective Browning, my pretty dark-eyed cop neighbor."

"They're one and the same." She drank more of her wine. "So, how did Linc do on your hike?"

"Fine. He's in better shape than he thinks he is. He asked about you—why you're here, that sort of thing."

"That's understandable. Whenever I'm here people get stirred up. I remind them of a lot of unanswered questions. And Linc." She shifted, staring at the fire. "Chris's death was hard on him. He was just thirteen. He idolized Chris."

"I remember."

"Think you can help him?"

"Traipsing Linc Cooper up and down mountains wasn't exactly what I had planned for the summer."

"What did you have planned?"

Her voice held none of the suspicion and frustration it had when she was out on the rocks with Mattie, and her eyes shone in the glow of the orange flames. Owen could see the plaster dust on her hands, in her hair, and thought of her alone in her dead husband's house, knocking out walls.

"I don't know what I had planned," he said.

"That could be just what you need—to have a few weeks with no plan."

He smiled. "My grandmother would say that describes my whole life. She says I'm a tumbleweed at heart."

"Maybe that's why you like Maine. All the granite around here isn't going anywhere. It gives you a sense of permanence that you don't have in your life right now."

"So philosophical."

She laughed. "Now you're scaring me." She got to her feet, took another sip of the Chianti before setting the glass down on a side table. "I don't want to keep you. Thanks for the wine."

Something about his tone—his expression, whatever—had spooked her, made her self-conscious, aware. Owen rose, setting his wineglass next to hers. "Linc thinks you're going to end up selling your place, too. I told him it wouldn't feel right not having a Browning out on these rocks."

"The real Brownings are all gone now. Too many of them died young. Chris, his parents. God knows how many ancestors. I swear his grandfather lived to ninety-five just to spite the odds."

Owen touched a finger to her jaw. He felt the heat of the fire on one side of him and, on the other side, the cool night air coming through the partially open door. Her skin was warm, soft. "Abigail."

She took an audible breath. "I'll never have that kind of love again. A first love. I know that." She seemed to make herself look at him, her gaze clear, unwavering. "But don't think I haven't loved again. Or that I can't."

"What about falling in love again?"

"I haven't—not in the way you mean. I have a good life. I have wonderful friends and colleagues, a great family, rewarding work. That's a lot."

"Enough?"

"I don't live in the past, if that's what you mean. I want answers to Chris's death. I want justice for him. But that's not the only thing that gets me up in the morning."

With the tip of his finger, Owen traced the outline of her mouth, saw her shut her eyes for a split second longer than a normal blink, telling him she wasn't unaffected by his touch.

"What about you?" she asked. "You haven't married."

"Not yet, no."

"Then it's something you think about—something you want."

But he took a step closer to her, easing his hand behind her neck, breaking her concentration. He couldn't pinpoint when he'd first become attracted to her. Maybe he'd always been attracted to her, but she'd seemed so untouchable, so remote. Chris Browning's widow. But over the years—a glimpse here and there on the rocks, a friendly chat from time to time when they'd run into each other on a walk, at the hardware store, in the post office. He'd never expected to act on his attraction. And, yet, here he was.

His mouth found hers for a whisper of a kiss, but he knew he was holding back—he knew he had to put a hard brake on how far he wanted to go with her. She sank the fingers of one hand into his upper arm, not to balance herself, he realized, but to communicate that he'd gotten to her. Her lips opened to the kiss, and he responded, his tongue mingling with hers, her grasp on his arm tightening.

He lowered his arms around her middle and lifted her slightly off her feet, drawing her against him. How easy it would be to slide her pants over her slim hips and take her right here, in front of the fire.

Slipping his hands inside her waistband, he splayed his fingers against her firm, warm flesh.

"Damn, Owen," she said, taking her mouth from his and throwing her arms around his neck. Her breathing was ragged, her eyes were shining, and under her shirt, her nipples were clearly visible. She pressed herself against him and found his mouth again. *"Damn."*

"Tell me what you want." He slid his hands deeper into her shorts, the flesh hotter, wetter. How had they come this far, this fast? One quick move on his part, and she'd be fully exposed. "Tell me, Abigail."

She smiled. "I think it's obvious what we both want." She settled her feet back onto the floor and dropped her arms from his neck. "You do like to live dangerously, don't you?"

"And you don't?"

"Well…" She seemed to realize she had nowhere to go with that one. "That's not the point. Or maybe it is."

But they both knew when to give in to an impulse, and this wasn't the time—if only, Owen thought, because they both also knew it was more than an impulse. Something real was going on between them and had been for a long time.

He stepped back from her. "Another glass of wine?"

She smiled. "That would be wonderful."

Linc heard the clatter of a bicycle on the driveway outside, in the dark, and knew it was Mattie Young.

Who else would it be?

His father looked up from his book and frowned. "What was that?"

"I think it's one of my friends," Linc said, already on his feet. They were in the front den, pretending they were a normal family. Him, his father, his sister. "We're supposed to make arrangements to hike the Bubbles tomorrow."

"Oh. Wonderful."

Linc had known his father would like that one. The thought of his one-and-only son doing something physical, besides playing video games, would appeal to him. He wouldn't risk inadvertently dissuading Linc by interfering—which Linc counted on. He'd seen how his father had reacted when he'd told him about hiking with Owen. The restrained approval, as if going overboard would turn Linc right back to being a couch potato.

Grace, however, quietly put down the book she was reading and followed her brother onto the front porch. "Linc, it's Mattie, isn't it?"

"I think so. I suspect he's drunk."

"My God. I'd hoped he'd stopped for good this time." She kept her voice to a whisper and showed no sign of wanting to see Mattie herself. "Please, do what you can to make sure he doesn't hurt himself or anyone else."

"Like you, Grace?"

Even in the dim light, he could see her flush. "The FBI's here on the island, checking up on me, my past. We all know that. But that's not what I was thinking—"

"I know it wasn't. I'm sorry." He nodded in the direction of the front door. "Go back in. Keep Dad occupied. He's not going to give Mattie many more chances."

Linc waited a few seconds to give Grace a chance to get back inside, then took the porch steps in two leaps and ran out to the driveway.

Mattie kicked his bike. "Fucking piece of shit."

"Mind your language here," Linc said. "You know what my father's like."

"He swears. I've heard him."

"He doesn't always live by the same rules he expects the rest of us to live by."

"Especially the hired help?" Mattie half tripped over the bike, standing close to Linc, his eyes wild, furious. But he wasn't drunk. "I want my money."

"Not here—"

"All of it. Every goddamn dime."

"Mattie, I *can't.*"

"Linc, you *can*. Your daddy has that much stuffed in his mattress. Get it, before I demand another ten."

Linc's stomach rolled over. He thought he'd throw up right there on the driveway, but saw the futility of arguing with Mattie. He just wanted to get rid of him without attracting his father's attention. "All right, all right. I'll see what I can do. Can you give me a couple days?"

"Tomorrow."

Linc nodded. "Okay. No promises, though—"

"Get. Me. My. Money."

"I will."

Mattie sucked in a breath, mollified, then coughed, half sobbing. "I'll do good with it. I'm getting back into my photography. I don't care if you think I'm scum. People will see the real me."

The real Mattie? Linc checked his disgust. "I hope so, Mattie."

"You wait. You wait and see."

"I will. Everyone's always said you have an incredible talent for photography."

"It's not just talent. It's skill. There's a lot more to photography than just pointing a camera and pressing a button."

"You know more about it than I do."

"Damn right."

For a moment, Linc almost felt sorry for Mattie— wanted him to get back on his feet. The guy who was blackmailing him. "Look, why don't I give you a ride back to your house? It's dark as hell out here, and it's cold—"

Mattie shook his head. "I'll ride my damn bike. When I get my license back—" He sniffled, picking up the bike. "No more, you understand? No more. I'll show everyone."

"I bet you will."

After two tries, Mattie got his bike rolling, and he pedaled smoothly off into the night. Linc walked out to the end of the driveway and shut and locked the security gate, knowing it was what his father would expect. And he needed the time to pull himself together.

The backs of his legs ached from hiking with Owen. He had to be crazy to think he could do search-and-rescue—he wasn't in Owen's league. The guy climbed up mountains as if he was on a stroll. He was strong, sure-footed, in top shape.

His father was right, Linc thought. *Everyone* was right. He was soft.

And now he was in serious trouble, too. He was letting Mattie blackmail him and had just come down close to rooting for the guy.

He started back down the dark driveway, wishing he'd just trip and break his neck and die on the spot. He was useless. *Worse* than useless. He was an albatross around his family's neck.

He brushed at his tears with his forearm.

Mattie had no honor, no boundaries, no rational thought process. He was unreliable, contradictory, volatile. Linc could let himself get sucked into Mattie's twisted thinking. He couldn't trust him.

Linc swallowed a sob. Where was he going to get nine thousand dollars by tomorrow—hell, by next week, even? What would Mattie do if he didn't come up with the money?

Tears ran down his face. What he couldn't stand, far more than the fear of not getting Mattie the money, was the thought that anyone—even that drunk—would think he'd killed Chris Browning.

But why shouldn't they think it?

Chris is dead because of you.

Stumbling, Linc cut past the garage and across the yard, knowing he had to compose himself before he saw his father and sister.

He could see the silhouette of the mountains across the sound, against the starlit sky. "I got you killed, Chris," he whispered. "Please forgive me. *Please.*"

Owen Garrison had found a way to thrive in spite of the guilt he had to feel over his sister's death. But Linc didn't have Owen's strength.

"Linc?" His sister walked down from the stone terrace, casting a long, black shadow under the night sky. "Is everything okay? Dad's getting worried."

"Everything's fine. I was just on my way in."

She stood next to him. "Mattie?"

"He's gone. He wasn't drunk. He just—he wanted to check about coming out here tomorrow. I don't know." Linc gave a fake laugh. "Mattie goes his own way."

"That he does." Her voice was subdued, and her color was off—it wasn't just the light. She shivered, wrapping her baggy sweater more tightly around her. "We should go in."

"Grace—" Linc stopped himself. "Never mind. You're right, we should go in. It's cold out here." He sniffled. "That's why my nose is red and running."

"Is it? I hadn't noticed."

That was his sister, Linc thought. Always so decent. He wanted to tell her about the blackmail and get her advice. But how could he? She had enough on her mind. She might feel obligated to tell the FBI. Would that screw up her appointment?

But if she didn't tell them and they found out, then what?

No, Linc thought, following her through the cool grass, he had to figure out this one on his own.

Get Mattie the rest of his money. Hope it'd be enough.
Only for guys like Mattie Young, there was never enough.

He'd be back once he had the ten grand. He wouldn't
be able to resist.

CHAPTER 12

The boys started bickering five minutes after Doyle picked them up at camp and hadn't stopped since. For two cents, he'd put them on a plane to London. Let their mother deal with them.

"Why can't we stay with Owen?" Sean asked, a demanding note in his tone.

"Because you went out his window."

"Nothing happened. We didn't get hurt. He didn't mind. Come on, Dad, it was no big deal."

"*I* mind. What if it hadn't been Mattie up in the old foundation? What if it *had* been a ghost? Then what, huh?" He glared at Sean, then shifted to Ian. "There. You don't have an answer, do you? You didn't think this one through. You just got a bee up your behinds and out the window you went—"

They sputtered into giggles.

"What're you laughing at?"

"'Bee up your behinds,'" Ian said. "That's funny, Dad."

He sat back, grinning at his two sons. "What am I going to do with you? Did you tell your mother you went out Owen's window on a bedsheet when she called?"

"No," Sean said.

Ian nodded. "She'd worry."

"What about me? Don't you care if I worry?"

That just drew more laughter.

At least, Doyle thought, the rascals weren't fighting with each other. If he heard one more squawk, whine, fake cry or whispered threat, he'd shove them both upstairs and sit and watch television by himself.

Someone pounded on the door—not a normal knock, and it was past nine o'clock. Doyle got out of his chair, pointing at the boys. "Stay put. Understood?"

He flipped on the outside light and peeked out the window, seeing Mattie Young shifting from one foot to the other on the front stoop. Doyle felt a prick of irritation. He'd resisted tracking down Mattie today and asking him about the beer and cigarettes in the old Garrison foundation—why he'd let Sean and Ian think he was a ghost. He'd had to calm down first. And it wasn't anything that couldn't wait a day, never mind how Abigail Browning would have handled it.

"It's Mattie," Doyle called to the boys. "I'll be just a minute."

"Okay, Dad," Sean said, as if he were the boss. "Take your time."

Doyle pulled open the door and stepped outside, Mattie automatically backing up, hunching his shoulders in that guilty way he had. He looked gaunt and cold, his hair hanging down his back in a greasy ponytail, his skin pocked with mosquito bites.

"What's up, Mattie?" Doyle asked him.

"This isn't an official visit. I mean—I'm not here on police business. You don't have to log me in somewhere."

"I guess that depends on what you want."

Mattie shivered, not meeting Doyle's eye. "I want you to tell Abigail Browning to stay away from me."

"Why? What'd she do to you?"

"Nothing—not yet."

"Then on what grounds?"

"You don't need grounds. I told you, I'm not here because you're a cop. I'm here because you're my friend. She'll listen to you."

"When did you last see her?"

Mattie licked his lips and looked behind him, as if he expected to find Abigail standing there. "Just now."

"Damn it, Mattie, are you going to make me pry it out of you? Just tell me what happened."

"She scared the hell out of me." Mattie turned back to Doyle, the light hitting the burst blood vessels in his face. "I was minding my own business—"

"Where?"

"That doesn't matter."

Doyle rocked back on his heels. "She caught you drinking out at the old Garrison foundation."

Mattie's mouth dropped open. "She told you?"

"No, Mattie, she didn't tell me."

"But you—" He stopped himself, gave a little laugh. "Did the boys see me out there? I tried not to let them see me. I figured—you know. I didn't want them getting the wrong idea."

"What wrong idea would that be, Mattie? That you were drinking beer and smoking cigarettes by yourself in the dark?"

"Just one beer. Honest."

"It's never one beer with you, Mattie. You're a drunk. You know damn well what alcohol does to you—"

"Yeah. I know. That's why I stay away from it."

"Drinking beer isn't staying away from it." Doyle realized he wasn't even angry. He was just sick of Mattie and his problems. "You know the deal. Alcoholism is a disease. It's not here today and gone tomorrow. It's here to stay. Stop running from it. Face it."

"I have faced it. I can drink one beer. Not everyone has to go cold turkey. One beer, and that's it."

"No, Mattie, you can't drink one beer and that's it."

He rubbed his nose with his fingers and stared down at his feet, not out of shame, Doyle knew, but irritation. Mattie liked to think he knew better.

He lifted his head. "I wasn't on Abigail's property."

"No, you were on Garrison property. Did Owen see you?"

"I shouldn't have bothered coming here. I thought you were my friend."

"You don't treat your friends well, Mattie. You're a chronic liar and a disappointment to everyone who's ever cared about you. What do you expect me to do? As a friend?"

"Nothing. Not one damn thing. Just forget I even came here."

"If Abigail crossed the line—"

"What would you do?"

"I'd do my job."

Mattie snorted. "Yeah. Right. The detective daughter of the FBI director. Chris's widow. You wouldn't do anything if she knocked me on the head and I was in the E.R. for stitches."

"Go home. Sleep off your self-absorbed rage. Stay off Owen Garrison's property and don't provoke Abigail."

Doyle regarded Mattie with a resignation he'd come to terms with a long time ago, a disappointment so deep, he couldn't even feel it anymore. "That's my advice."

Mattie stepped forward abruptly, grabbing Doyle's upper arm. "Something's going on with Abigail." He dug his fingers into Doyle's arm, then let go, flipping his ponytail over his shoulder. "I'm attuned to people. I see everything. I see things other people don't. It's why I keep drinking."

"You keep drinking because you're an alcoholic and you won't take responsibility for your own recovery."

"I'm not being paranoid. Abigail wants to find Chris's killer. I don't even think she cares if she gets the right person anymore. She just wants it over. The wondering, the hunting."

"Mattie, come on. You're not making any sense." Doyle felt the familiar sense of desperation that being around Mattie, his wasted life, often brought out in him. "Why would she push for answers if she doesn't care if she gets the right answers?"

A veil of denial fell over him. Doyle had seen Mattie go into this mode before, shutting down, pretending he didn't care what happened to him—to anyone. "Whatever. I just wanted you to know the score. You don't want to tell her to stay away from me, fine. Your call. Say hi to the boys for me, okay? They should ride their bikes over to my place some afternoon."

"Mattie—"

He'd already started down the steps and waved a hand to Doyle without looking back. "See you around, Chief. I need to be up early to help Ellis. Real estate agents are going to come check out the place soon. Everything's got to be perfect."

"Yeah," Doyle said. "That's Ellis. Hey, Mattie—"

But he was done. He walked out to the road and picked up his bicycle, walking it a few steps before climbing on. Doyle didn't stop him. Years ago, he'd watched Mattie Young throw away his potential as a photographer and slip deeper and deeper into self-destruction, bitterness and entitlement. No one could help him if he didn't want to help himself—if he didn't even admit to the damn problem.

In the months before Chris's death, they'd all seen a glimmer of hope. Mattie was cleaned up, working hard, doing his photography. Happy. Making plans for the future. Taking responsibility for his own recovery and making the needed changes in his life.

He'd started to slip before Chris's wedding. And two days after Owen had found Chris's body—before their friend was even laid to rest—Mattie turned up on Doyle's doorstep, drunk.

He'd had fits and starts of sobriety in the seven years since, but he'd always find a reason to go back into the bottle. Now, it seemed to be because he'd convinced himself he could manage one beer.

Except, from the description Owen had given, Doyle knew damn well Mattie wasn't stopping his solitary parties after just one beer.

He shut the door and went back inside, wishing Katie was there to talk to. She'd known Mattie as long as he had, but she had more distance than Doyle did.

He was just wrung out.

"What did Mattie want?" Sean asked.

"Not much. You boys ready for bed?"

For a change, they didn't argue with him or pick a fight with each other. Doyle followed them upstairs. If he had his way, Katie would be home this summer, and Abigail

Browning would be investigating homicides in Boston, not sticking her thumb in everyone's eye up here.

But when the hell did he ever get his way?

Mattie got off his bike thirty yards from his house and walked it to his driveway. His butt hurt from the hard seat. He wanted to get one of those gel seats.

What he *really* wanted was to have his license back.

Doyle had refused to pull any strings to help him or look the other way. He could have—Mattie hadn't run over anyone or anything. His blood-alcohol level had been just over the legal limit. What harm would it have done for Doyle to give him one more chance?

As he dropped his bike onto the grass in front of his crummy rented house, someone darted out of the dark shadows. He jumped back, almost screaming.

Grace Cooper put a finger to her perfect lips. "Shh. It's just me."

"Grace—man, you almost gave me a heart attack."

"I'm sorry. I don't want anyone to see me."

Of course not. He nodded like a fool. "I understand. I'll be at your place tomorrow to mow the lawn. Why didn't you just wait—"

"This can't wait." She spoke in a controlled voice just above a whisper. "Mattie, the FBI's here, on the island."

He pulled a pack of cigarettes from the front pocket of his denim jacket and tapped one out, noticing that his hands were surprisingly steady. "They are, huh? Daddy March knows them?"

"There are a lot of FBI agents. Abigail's father can't possibly know them all."

"Bet he knows the ones sent here to check up on you."

"They're not checking up on me. They're conducting a routine background investigation."

She had on a long, shapeless sweater, its ice-blue color and the harsh light from the nearby houses washing out her face more. She wasn't as plain as she thought she was, and she could be passionate. Mattie remembered just how passionate.

He knew she didn't want to remember anything about their time together.

She crossed her arms over her chest, as if she knew what he was thinking. "Long day today?"

"They're all long days this time of year. What're you doing, besides worrying about what people are going to tell the FBI?"

"My father and I took the boat out today. The little one." She licked her lips, looking away from him. "It's a good time to be away from Washington for a few days. Things are quiet."

"I'd like a nice lazy day."

"We used to have days like that. Remember?" She turned back to him, a spark of affection in her eyes, surprising him. "You'd keep a camera with you at all times. You had such hope."

"So did you," he said.

"I still do. This appointment means a lot to me."

"And to your father?"

"Of course. He's very supportive. Mattie—I'd never ask you to lie…" She trailed off. When he didn't speak, she shook her head. "Never mind. I shouldn't have come."

"The FBI doesn't know about our affair."

She lowered her eyes. "No. I didn't tell them."

"It'd come back to haunt you, wouldn't it? An affair with

the town drunk. The yardman. A murdered FBI's no-account friend." Mattie couldn't believe the bitterness in his tone, how fast it had infected him. "I'm the guy you had because you couldn't have him."

She gasped. "That's not true! That was never true."

"No?"

"Of course not. Mattie, don't say such a thing."

But he knew it was true. He'd known it seven and a half years ago, when he'd had five months of bliss—pure heaven—with Grace Cooper. He'd had such high hopes. She'd planned to rescue him from himself, clean him up, show him off as her brilliant photographer lover, her salt-of-the-earth Mainer.

And when her eyes were closed, she could pretend he was the man she couldn't have.

By unspoken agreement, Mattie had never said aloud that she was in love with Christopher Browning. But she had been, and for all he knew, she still was.

"Who knows about us?" he asked.

She winced visibly. "No one."

"What about your brother? He's a sneaky little shit. He knows everything that goes on around here."

"Linc doesn't know. We did nothing wrong. I just don't want to expose you to unnecessary scrutiny."

He grinned at her. "That's your story, huh?"

She stiffened, dropping her arms to her sides, as much of a display of emotion as he'd get from her. She'd always had remarkable self-control. A Cooper trait. Emotion was for the lower classes.

Emotion was what got Doe Garrison killed.

It was what got Chris Browning killed.

Mattie had heard Jason Cooper explain as much to his

kids around the kitchen table. Doe got herself worked up over a minor squabble, and she drowned. Chris got mad because of what happened to his wife, and he was shot.

"Don't worry. I won't tell the FBI you slept with the town drunk." His voice caught, annoying him. He didn't care about Grace anymore—he'd stopped caring a long, long time ago. "And I won't tell them you were in love with one of their own."

"You're odious, Mattie." She didn't raise her voice. "I want to have sympathy for you and remember what we had those few months with affection, without regret. But I look at you, and I just want to be sick."

"That's it? You want to be sick? You don't want to club me on the head with a rock or shoot me in the heart?"

"I wouldn't waste my time."

She crossed her arms tight over her chest and stalked back out to the road.

"Did you drive over here?" Mattie asked her calmly.

"I parked around the corner. I told my father and Linc that I was running an errand."

"Not worried the FBI's following you?"

"No." She paused, giving him a long, cool look. "I have nothing to hide."

"Say it enough times and maybe you'll believe it."

He watched her swallow and thought he saw a glimmer of a tear, but she turned and walked away.

The woman had everything. Brains, poise, a sense of decency. Money. A future. But she couldn't be honest with herself.

Mattie headed up his front walk. He was no judge of character, but he could recognize another liar.

Grace lied to other people—about him, for one—but

most of her lies, the worst of her lies, were to herself. Like now, he thought. She was lying to herself about just how scared she was—of him, of her own past.

Had she guessed what kind of trouble Linc was in?

Mattie told himself he didn't give a damn. Grace Cooper didn't care about him. Fine. He didn't care about her, either.

He headed into his little rented house. It could fit into the Coopers' kitchen—of their summer house. Mattie had never seen any of their other houses. Jason's place in New York, Grace's in Georgetown, Ellis's in Alexandria. But as well-off as they were, Mattie didn't envy them. He didn't want to be a Cooper.

He wanted to be a photographer.

He wanted a fresh start.

But as he pushed open his front door, he felt a prick of guilt at how he was getting it.

CHAPTER 13

"Your husband had secrets."

Abigail sat up in bed, fully awake after grabbing the phone on the second ring. "Who is this?"

"Just listen. Chris's secrets got him killed. He wouldn't talk to you. He wouldn't talk to anyone."

"Tell me more. Please." She struggled to keep her tone firm but nonthreatening. "Don't hang up."

"He didn't want to see you hurt."

"Hurt how? Physically—or emotionally?"

There was no hesitation on the other end. "Both."

"So he didn't tell me these secrets?"

"He couldn't. He loved you."

She leaned back against her pillows and headboard, the early morning sun angling into her small bedroom through gaps in the curtains. The caller's voice was disguised, as before. "How did you get my number here?" she asked. "It's not listed."

"Be careful who you trust while you're in Maine."

"Are you here? Are you watching me?"

"You have nothing to fear from me. I don't want anyone else to get hurt. That's all."

"Why would anyone else get hurt? What's going on? I need more information."

"Your husband was an FBI agent and a Mainer. Don't forget."

"I won't—I haven't. Why don't we meet? Just the two of us—"

The caller cut her off with a short, sarcastic laugh. "I don't think so, Detective."

Click.

Abigail glanced at her bedside clock. *Five-oh-nine.* She hung up, then picked up again and dialed Lou Beeler's home number. He answered on the first ring. She tried smiling into the receiver. "Don't tell me you're already on your second cup of coffee—"

"Third," he said. "What's going on?"

"I had another call," she said, and told him.

When she finished, Lou sighed. "I'll be there in an hour. I'll collect Chief Alden on my way. Want me to bring doughnuts?"

"I'm not hungry."

"Yeah. I'll bet. See you soon."

Abigail was shivering by the time she climbed out of bed. She slept in the smallest of the three bedrooms. The largest had been Chris's grandfather's room, the second largest Chris's room. She'd cleaned out all their belongings and painted the furniture, bought new rugs and lamps and picked out inexpensive artwork, but the rooms still had the feel of the Browning men. She let her renters use them.

Moving quickly, Abigail showered, the hot streams of water calling up sensations she didn't want to think about, of Owen's hands on her, his mouth—her reaction. They hadn't gone beyond their kiss last night. A bit more than a kiss, really, she thought. But afterward they'd had wine. Talked. He'd walked with her back to her house, then left with just a good-night, as if he, too, knew that was enough. Their attraction to each other was out on the table. That was plenty to get used to at least for now. She'd never brought a man here. It'd never seemed right. Too many ghosts in Maine. Too many memories. Easier, she thought, just to keep that part of herself out of reach.

Owen was different. He'd known Chris forever, and she didn't have to explain to him what had happened, how he'd died, how she'd felt in those awful days.

And in the years since, he'd never patronized her because of her situation. He'd experienced tragedy himself, and he'd seen countless others who'd had to find a way to carry on after the worst kind of loss—babies, young children, entire families, entire communities.

Abigail switched off the water and grabbed a towel, rubbed herself dry. Never mind the rest of it, she thought. She'd responded to Owen for purely physical reasons. He felt good. The taste of him, the heat of his skin.

He's bored.

He was a man of action with nothing to do. She'd be out of her mind if she got too far ahead of herself with him.

She pulled on jeans and a sweatshirt and slipped on sports sandals, leaving her hair to dry on its own as she headed downstairs. She grabbed her gun and checked outside, but she saw no sign of spies or intruders, just cormorants diving for fish and brightly colored lobster buoys bobbing in the glistening water.

Satisfied, Abigail went back inside and put on coffee. While it brewed, she sat at her kitchen table and wrote down every word of her conversation with her anonymous caller.

"Your husband had secrets."

She finished her transcript and returned to the back room, grabbing her sledgehammer and tackling another section of the wall while she waited for the local law enforcement officers to arrive.

Ellis couldn't remember the last time he'd been to Jordan Pond House, a tourist trap, if a pleasant one, famous for its postcard-perfect location and its tea and popovers. Daytrippers to Acadia National Park would take in the Visitors Center, Cadillac Mountain—the tallest peak on the Atlantic seaboard and the only one in the park they could drive up—and Jordan Pond House. Some would venture out along the twenty-mile Park Loop Road and stop at Thunder Hole, a favorite with its dramatic rock cliffs and crashing waves. Ellis hadn't done the loop road in years, either.

But everything was changing, he thought. Why not his habit of avoiding tourist hot spots?

Lunch at Jordan Pond House was his brother's idea. He and Grace already had a table out on the terrace, the sun warm and bright on a perfect Mt. Desert Island summer afternoon. Ellis noticed that his niece had put on a crisp blouse and a touch of makeup. An improvement. She'd arrived on the island exhausted—and far more tense about her appointment and the background investigation it required than she wanted to admit. She was at a crossroads in her life. Big changes were ahead.

And she preferred to have everyone think she had nothing to hide. Open nervousness would imply she did have something. Ellis, who'd been around Washington a long time, had come to believe, and accept, that everyone had something to hide. The FBI wouldn't expect perfection.

He sat next to her, across from Jason, who seemed distracted, staring across the sloping field down to the most famous of Mt. Desert's glacial fresh-water ponds. Mountains rose around its sparkling water. Ellis had climbed all of the park's peaks in his day. Now, he preferred to wander in his gardens.

For as long as I can, at least.

His throat tightened at the prospect of the house selling. He'd hoped its high price would deter buyers, perhaps delay the sale until next year. He understood Jason's reasoning. But whenever he'd convinced himself he actually liked the idea, looked forward to a smaller place, to new gardens, his stomach would twist into knots. He needed more time to adjust.

He wouldn't be getting it. Jason had arranged for lunch with potential buyers from Connecticut. Ellis didn't even know their names.

"Our guests will be a few minutes late," Jason said. "I've ordered tea while we wait."

"Where's Linc?" Ellis asked.

"There's no need for him to be here."

Grace winced almost imperceptibly at her father's callous tone. "He's out there." She nodded toward the pond. "He and Owen are hiking around the pond. Owen seems to be taking him under his wing."

"Does he understand Linc's limitations?" Ellis asked. "He won't push him too hard, I hope."

"It'll do him good to be pushed," Jason said. "Linc's spent too much time in front of a video screen. I'm glad he's finally doing something physical. And Owen's the best."

Jason glanced at his daughter, who pretended not to notice as she picked up a dark green teapot and filled a matching cup. Her father had long nursed the hope that she and Owen would fall for each other, but there'd never been a hint of that kind of attraction between them. And Grace was in her late thirties now. Marriage seemed more and more a remote possibility. If she minded, she never said. Ellis, who'd long ago given up the idea of marriage for himself, understood a single life could be rewarding and fulfilling. His brother, who hated being alone, would never understand—he was between marriages now, but dating. There'd be a fourth Cooper wedding before too long.

"The FBI has arrived on the island," Ellis said, changing the subject.

Grace nodded. "Yes, I know. I'm afraid—" She faltered, quickly setting the teapot down. "Father, why don't you tell him?"

"We don't know much," Jason said. "The two agents stopped by the house before we headed over here. They didn't say what's going on but it's clear something's up."

"Abigail." Grace picked up her earthenware teacup. "I got the impression it has to do with Abigail. The agents had no real reason to stop by. I think they were just checking on us—I don't know. Something's going on. That's for sure."

Ellis frowned. "With Abigail? Nothing's happened to her, I hope, but I can't see why her presence on the island would have any bearing on your background check."

Grace sipped her tea, avoiding his eye. They'd never openly discussed her relationship with Chris Browning, but she and Ellis had arrived nonetheless at the unspoken understanding that he was aware of the feelings she'd had for their murdered friend.

"Her father is these two agents' boss," Jason said, apparently oblivious to the look exchanged between his daughter and half brother. "Abigail has never come up here this close to the anniversary of her wedding and Chris's death. I'm sure that alone is enough to put Agents Capozza and Steele on alert. We just have to be patient. It'll all sort itself out in due course."

Ellis nodded. "I agree." He reached for the teapot, wondering if his brother even gave a damn what he thought. But Grace would. They'd always had a good relationship, in part because of her father's womanizing. Ellis provided a steady, relatively dull presence in her life. He smiled across the table at her. "No popovers?"

"When our guests arrive," she said with a smile. "You know I can't resist."

But Jason stiffened. "Damn it," he said under his breath, nudging Ellis with his elbow. "Look. Just what we need."

Abigail Browning ducked past a waiter with a massive tray and arrived at their table. "Well, hello," she said breezily. "Fancy meeting you all here. It's a perfect day for tea and popovers, isn't it?"

"Actually," Jason said, "we're meeting guests for lunch."

"I can't think of a better spot."

A muscle worked in Jason's tight jaw. He'd lost patience with Abigail a long time ago and made no secret of it. Ellis got to his feet. "Do you have a table yet? Perhaps—"

"I'm sitting out on the lawn. The flowers are gorgeous,

aren't they? Not as spectacular as yours, of course, but still, very beautiful."

Grace sat back in her chair and eyed the younger woman. "Abigail—are you all right? Is something wrong?"

"What could be wrong?"

"I'm hoping you'll tell us, because obviously—" Grace stopped, shifting her gaze from Abigail to her tea. "Oh, dear. It's the second Thursday in July. Chris was found—" She looked up, her face pale. "I'd forgotten."

Ellis could smell the strong tea and see his niece's distress, but she hadn't forgotten what today was.

Jason pushed back his chair. "Abigail, please—"

"I'm fine," she said.

Putting a hand on his brother's arm, Ellis nodded toward Owen and Linc as they made their way across the sprawling lawn, dotted with stray hikers, onto the terrace. People at the sturdy wooden outdoor tables glanced at the pair—or, Ellis thought, more specifically, Owen. Without trying, he commanded attention just by the way he moved.

Linc, on the other hand, favored his right side, all but staggering toward his father's table.

His son's presence only added to Jason's frustration. Ellis understood. His brother was losing control of his carefully planned lunch. "Owen, Linc," Jason said tightly, rising. "Did you have a good hike?"

Linc grinned, nodding proudly. "Yeah, it was great. It's more of a haul around the pond than I expected. It gets rocky on the back half. I'd never gone that far."

"Well, good for you," Jason said, quietly handing his son a napkin. "You've worked up quite a sweat."

"Yeah." Linc wiped his brow with the napkin. "I didn't expect to find you guys here. What's up?"

Grace started to answer, but Abigail said, "They're meeting guests for lunch."

"Oh. All right, then."

Owen, who wasn't sweating at all, seemed to read the situation. "I'll see Linc home—"

"No, it's okay," Linc said, "I'll manage. I don't mind walking, actually. It'll help loosen me up after clambering over all those rocks. Abigail—good to see you." He spun off before anyone could stop him.

"Father," Grace whispered. "It's too far for him to walk. Can't he stay? He could get cleaned up in the men's room—"

"He'd be bored." Obviously expecting no further argument from her, Jason turned his attention to Owen. "You don't look as if you went on that hike at all. I'd invite you to join us—"

"You didn't invite me," Abigail said.

Jason took a half step back. "What?"

She smiled at him. "Just getting under your skin, Jason. Who're you meeting for lunch? Washington power brokers? Advisers? Private investigators? Sometimes people hire their own investigators to conduct a background check at the same time as the FBI."

Ellis appealed to Owen. "Perhaps you and Abigail—"

"Relax," she said. "I'm off to tea before the waiter gives away my table."

She headed over to the sunny lawn, and Owen watched her a moment, then said to Jason, "Linc did well today. He's got guts. If you'll excuse me…"

"Of course. Thank you for showing an interest in Linc." Jason made a face. "Abigail isn't herself. I think something happened."

Owen nodded. "On my way."

Jason returned to his chair, watching Owen sit across from Abigail at one of the sturdy wooden lawn tables. Ellis could feel his brother's relief. He'd managed to get rid of both his sweaty son and Abigail before his guests arrived.

Ellis noticed a well-dressed couple in their fifties walk out onto the terrace.

The potential buyers, he thought. Did they have the look of garden lovers?

It doesn't matter.

He'd dig up the plants that were most special to him and plant them at his new place, or in his gardens at his main house in Washington.

The rest of the plants—what did he care?

"Here they are," Jason said, then turned to his younger brother. "Ellis? You'll be okay, won't you?"

He nodded. "Yes, of course. I'm with you on this deal, Jason. All the way."

He could see his brother's relief. "I knew you would be."

Grace, Ellis noticed, seemed hardly to notice what her father and uncle were saying, her attention fixed instead on Owen and Abigail at their table, as if they might be talking about her, as if they held the keys to her future. Ellis reached across the table and took her hand. "It'll all work out, Grace."

"Yes." She pulled her gaze from the table out on the lawn and managed a quick, fake smile. "Of course it will. I'm letting this background check get to me, and I know it shouldn't. I just feel so exposed."

"And you're worried about Abigail."

"Yes." She nodded, as if to convince herself. "Aren't we all?"

"Maybe Owen can find out if anything's happened. In the meantime, just try to relax and enjoy lunch."

By the time their lunch guests got to their table, Grace was on her feet, smiling, and Ellis knew he'd succeeded. His niece would sail through the background check—no matter what Abigail Browning was up to, and the constant reminder her presence was of a man Grace had wanted for herself.

CHAPTER 14

Abigail broke open a browned, steaming popover, aware of Owen's probing gaze on her. "Do you have my number here in Maine?" she asked him.

"Your phone number? Of course. It's the same number it's always been. Why?"

"Because I had a strange call this morning. It was on the heels of another strange call Saturday night."

Owen lifted a popover out of the basket her waiter had brought and set it on his plate. But he had no visible reaction to what she'd just told him. "First things first," he said. "I didn't call you on Saturday or this morning."

"Could someone have used your phone?"

"I doubt it, but if you'd told me Sean and Ian Alden would manage to sneak out a window without my knowing, I'd have said that was impossible. Do you have any reason to believe the calls were made from my house?"

"None."

She dipped her knife into the softened butter, which she spread liberally on one half of her popover. Owen's steady calm did not have a soothing effect on her. She had an urge to reach across the table and slather butter on his popover, just to penetrate his self-control. She could dump a tub of strawberry jam in his lap. Grab him by the shoulders and kiss him. Why the hell not?

"Can you tell me about these calls?"

She nodded. "Lieutenant Beeler gave the okay to tell you. He's not giving a press conference or anything, but you deserve to know, in case this guy's a threat. If you value your quiet spot on the water, you'll want to keep the information to yourself." She reached for the strawberry jam. "FBI Director's widowed cop daughter gets anonymous tips—well, you can imagine the media reaction."

"I can, indeed. And unleashing reporters out here would only muddy the waters of finding this caller."

"Correct," she said, then gave him a rundown of the two calls. When she finished, she ate a piece of her popover and gazed out at Jordan Pond, a lone bird of some kind soaring overhead. A hawk? She didn't know her birds that well. Finally, she looked back at Owen. "I know you're not the caller. I don't think you could disguise that mix of Boston and Texas in your voice."

But he didn't smile, his gray eyes narrowed, intense. "Do you think it's Mattie?"

"Lou and Doyle are talking to him. So far, there's no reason to believe it's him—or anyone on the island."

"What are you doing out here?" Owen asked.

"I followed Jason and Grace. Ellis came in a separate car. I was out on the road, and there they were—and I figured, why not? Sometimes if you stick your fingers in enough eyes, things happen."

"That's one way to look at it." He ate part of his popover, without butter or jam. "The Coopers looked as if they wanted to choke you. All three of them."

"They did, didn't they? They're too repressed to admit as much."

"Or too polite."

She shrugged. "That, too. Do you see them during the off-season, when you're not in Maine?"

"No."

"I thought you and Grace were betrothed in the cradle."

"Her father might like to think so, but, no, we weren't betrothed in the cradle. We knew each other growing up. We see each other here from time to time. That's about it." His mouth twitched with unexpected amusement. "Satisfied?"

"What about Linc?"

"I put him through his paces today. We did the pond hike at a fast clip. It's not a difficult trail, although it's rough in spots, but I made him hoof it. He kept up. He's walking back to his place now. It's a trek—it'll do him good."

"Think he's seriously interested in search-and-rescue?"

"We're offering different levels of courses at the field academy, from basic instruction for the novice through advanced coursework for specialists who could end up on a Fast Rescue team."

"Like yourself," Abigail said. "Except you're probably past coursework at this point."

"Not in this field. There's always something new to learn." He finished off his popover. "I hope Linc will apply at least for a weekend course."

"How did you get into search-and-rescue?"

"I took a first-aid class in high school. I was hooked after that. Abigail—"

"I've told you what I can about the calls. The first one was easy to dismiss. I get crank calls from time to time. Lou Beeler does, too. Doyle, less so. We all took this one seriously, but the odds are it was nothing."

"This second call this morning changes things."

She nodded. "Whoever's calling wants to manipulate me. I was married on the second Saturday in July. Chris was found—" She didn't finish, simply added, "The timing of the call is deliberate."

"Why would someone who claims to want to help you try to get under your skin?" Owen asked.

"To be in the middle of the drama. To feel important." She shrugged. "Or maybe to mislead me. Obviously it's not someone who wants to come forward."

"Why not?"

"Your guess is as good as mine."

Owen pushed his plate aside and leaned over the wooden table. "You'll be careful, won't you, Abigail? This isn't an investigation in Boston. It's not part of your job. You're personally involved."

She smiled. "Now you sound like Doyle and Lou. They told me to leave the heavy lifting to them."

"Will you?"

"Of course."

He gave her a skeptical look, grabbing the tab when the waiter dropped it off. "My treat. I haven't had tea and popovers in ages. I'd forgotten how good they are."

"Owen?" She tried to keep her gaze on him but found she couldn't. "About last night…"

"About Mattie, you mean?"

She heard the humor in his tone and scowled at him. "Very funny. I meant about—you know."

"The fire in my woodstove. It was too damn hot."

"You're making fun of me, Owen Garrison, and if you think I'm going to sit here and take it, you can think again." She finished the last of her popover, doused in butter and jam, and brushed off her fingers with her napkin, but he didn't take the hint. "You're going to make me say it, aren't you? Okay. The kiss. I have no regrets."

"I would hope not." He smiled. "It was a damn good kiss."

"We did get a bit carried away. As I said, I have no regrets, but it can't happen again."

"Why not?"

"You're looking for distractions, I'm looking for distractions. I'm getting strange calls. Mattie Young's acting weird. Doyle Alden's in a sour mood. The Coopers are in the middle of an FBI background check that might not be as routine as they want us all to believe. Jason's selling his brother's house." Abigail paused, catching her breath, wondering what her litany of goings-on was all about, why she'd rattled them off. "I can't be sneaking kisses in the dark."

"Hands off, then?"

She didn't answer right away, which surprised her.

Owen seized on the delay. "Not as easy as you thought, is it? Abigail, we've been thinking about kissing each other for a long time. I know I thought about it that time I caught you in Austin pestering my grandmother. Last night was meant to happen." He laid a few bills on the table and placed the check over them. "It's going to happen again."

"Not today," she whispered, her chest clamping down on itself, until she thought she wouldn't be able to breathe.

His eyes darkened, and he nodded. "No, not today."

He had the grace to let her get out of there first. She picked up her pace, moving in a half run by the time she reached her car. She drove out to the entrance to the Park Loop Road and paid for a pass, joining a car from Colorado and an SUV from West Virginia on the quiet, scenic drive.

"Chris...don't go. We can run errands another time."

He touched her cheek. "I won't be long."

She smiled, falling back onto the couch in the front room. "Good. I'll read for a little while and take a nap."

"Yes." He laughed, kissing her softly. "Rest up for later."

After he left, she read a few pages and fell asleep, wishing he'd stayed with her.

The breathtaking, classic Maine coast beauty steadied her even as it conjured up memories, the whisper of long-ago kisses, the shudder of long-ago orgasms. She could see Chris's eyes, as dark a green as the fir trees around her, as he'd watched her in the night.

To ease the pain, she would tell herself she was a different person now, but she wasn't. Sure she'd changed—she didn't know if Chris would recognize her anymore. She wasn't a twenty-five-year-old law student who'd never endured serious loss, who'd never been called to a scene of a triple homicide or looked into the eyes of someone who'd killed in a fit of rage and now couldn't go back and undo what he'd done. Yet with all she'd done in the past seven years, she wasn't a different person. Deep down she was the same woman who'd fallen in love with her guy from Maine, her FBI agent.

He'd been her first proper lover, and he'd relished that role in their eighteen months together.

That their life together was over didn't mean it had never happened.

Or that she needed to pretend that she didn't want to fall in love again. It wouldn't be the same—it couldn't be the same. And it didn't have to be.

She wanted it, she realized. She wanted to love a man, to be in love with a man—not out of desperation, not just to have someone in her life, but to let it happen if it was meant to, to be open to the possibility of it.

She made no stops on the winding drive.

When she arrived back at her house, the air was still, only the distant cries of seagulls to disturb the silence. Inside, she smelled plaster dust and the faint odor of fresh paint.

She dialed Lou Beeler's pager. When he returned her call, she was in the back room, shaking open a black trash bag, standing up to her mid-calves in debris from her gutted walls. Any more frustrations, and she'd have all the walls in the house ripped out.

"I don't have anything for you," Lou said.

"Did you talk to Mattie Young?"

"I did. He wants to get a restraining order against you."

Abigail snorted. "Let him try."

"Doyle doesn't have anything, either. Abigail—you know these calls could be B.S. You must have made your share of enemies over the past few years. One of them could have dug around on the Internet and figured out just enough to push your buttons."

"Is that what you believe happened?"

"I don't believe anything. I just follow the facts." He paused. "So should you."

She sat on a chair covered in white plaster dust. She'd meant to throw sheets over the furniture, but hadn't gotten around to it. Now, she had a bigger mess to clean up—and Lou Beeler doubting her objectivity.

She didn't blame him. In his place, she'd do no different.

She smiled to herself as she continued over the phone, "Does that mean I still have a green light to look into the calls myself?"

"As if you need a green light from me. You know what I'm saying, Abigail."

"You'd like for me to go back to Boston."

"Your caller could be there."

"Or not," she said.

Lou sighed. "Or not."

"What about the FBI guys doing the background check on Grace Cooper?"

"What about them?"

"Come on, Lou. You know what I'm asking. Did you talk to them about the calls?"

"Yes."

She waited, but he didn't go on. "All right. I can take a hint."

The Maine CID detective broke into laughter. "No, you can't," he said, still chuckling as he hung up.

Abigail scowled at the dead phone and debated driving out to the local police station and finding Doyle Alden, but what good would that do?

Instead, using an ancient dustpan and brush—and her hands—she swept up the chunks of plaster, bent nails, mice skeletons and yellowed drywall tape, shoving the debris into her heavy-duty trash bag.

She needed answers. But how could she get them with such an elusive caller? Without the law enforcement resources she usually had at her disposal?

"You're the only person the killer fears."

Was it true? If so, what leverage did it give her?

She could hardly breathe in the thick dust she'd stirred up. She tied up the overstuffed bag and dragged it out to the back porch, down the steps and around to the side of the house, coughing as she shoved it into the garbage bin.

She knew what she had to do.

Before she could change her mind, she ran back into the house and grabbed the phone, dialing her father's private number.

"Abigail," he said when he picked up. "I thought you might call. Where are you?"

She was sure he knew where she was. "Maine," she said.

He took an audible breath. She pictured him in his office or in his car, taking her call because he was between meetings. He was a busy man with an important, high-pressure job, but he was like any father with a daughter whose life had taken a hairpin turn from what he'd wanted for her.

John March had started out as a Boston cop. Bob O'Reilly remembered him and said they'd all known— even the rookies like him—that her father wouldn't stay in uniform. He had drive, ambition and a willingness to sacrifice. He'd gone to law school, joined the FBI, moved his family from one city to another as he worked his way to the top. He was fifty-nine, handsome and unstoppable. He was also absolutely convinced that no one would ever crack the only unsolved murder of one of his own—FBI Special Agent Christopher Browning.

Abigail never doubted her father's love or his desire to see her happy, only what they might lead him to do.

"You know about the calls, don't you?" she asked him bluntly.

"I was briefed earlier today. You're my daughter, Abigail. You can pretend I'm a plumber all you want, but I'm not—"

"Do you have any reason to believe the calls are related to your position?"

"No." He spoke without hesitation, and he wasn't a liar. If he didn't want to tell her something, he simply wouldn't. "Do you?"

"I don't know anything. It's frustrating. I'd hoped coming up here would get the caller to come out of hiding, but so far, no luck. And I have zip for leads." She smiled into the phone. "But I did have tea and popovers at the Jordan Pond House today."

"Alone?"

"With Owen Garrison, actually."

"And the Coopers. They were there, weren't they?"

Abigail sat at the kitchen table and frowned. "Dad, are you having me watched?"

He gave a small laugh. "That'd send Washington aflutter. Just imagine. To answer your question, no, I'm not having you watched. The two agents doing the background check on Grace Cooper saw her there with her father and uncle." His humor vanished as quickly as it had appeared. "Abigail, you *are* my daughter. If you're getting anonymous calls, for any reason, I need to know about it."

In other words, she should have called him on Saturday after the first call—or, at the latest, this morning, not left it for the news to work its way to him. But she hadn't, and she didn't know why.

"Next time, I'll let you know sooner," she said.

"Right now, it doesn't sound as if this caller has shed any new light on the investigation into Chris's death."

"So far, no."

"Do you want protection? An agent—"

"Good heavens, no. Tell Mom I said hi. Don't worry

about me, okay? I've been painting and knocking out walls and having tea and popovers." *And kissing Owen Garrison.* "I rousted Mattie Young from the old Garrison foundation. He was drinking beer and smoking cigarettes out there in the dark. The Alden boys thought he was Chris's ghost."

"You don't fool me," her father said quietly. "You're all over this case. You'll do what it takes to wring out of it whatever you can."

"Maybe we'll finally know—"

"Maybe, but if I had my way, it wouldn't be now, not this way, with you all alone up there."

She smiled. "I can take care of myself."

"See that you do."

After she hung up, she returned to the back room, saw that fog and gray clouds were moving in from the south and west. She could feel the dampness in the air and pictured herself by Owen's woodstove, cozy under a warm blanket.

She grabbed a hammer and attacked nails and bits of plaster stuck on the beams of the gutted walls. Two more walls to go, and she'd be done.

Tonight, she decided, was for her and her memories.

CHAPTER 15

She's harder.

There's an edge to her that wasn't there before. She tries to keep others from seeing it, but I see it. I know. She's small and mean and doesn't care about anything but her own pain.

She won't stop.

She won't ever stop.

Calling her isn't easy. Hearing her voice. Hoping I didn't slip up. She would pounce if I did.

Abigail.

She would treat me like a common criminal if she knew what I have done.

I hate the thought of trying to defend myself. Trying to explain what she will never let herself understand.

I don't kill out of passion. I don't get caught up in the moment and regret later what I've done.

I act quickly. Decisively. I capitalize on what's going on around me.

I see things.

Everything.

I know how to be patient when I have to be. To act when I must.

Abigail can be my freedom if I don't allow the thought of failure to undermine my courage.

I cannot write that script for myself.

"Abigail!"

I remember how Chris called his wife's name.

"Tell her to be happy. Please. Tell her not to grieve too long for me."

He'd always known he would have a short life. He lived each day to its fullest and never looked back, never indulged in self-pity.

I remember.

And I've never told her what her husband's dying words were.

How could I?

Then she would know I killed him.

"Abigail…Abigail…"

I remember.

And now I must be patient. Calculating. Willing to capitalize on events.

Just as I was seven years ago.

As I had to be.

I remember.

CHAPTER 16

Linc Cooper bounded over the wet rocks below Owen's house, slipping but not falling, his hair soaked. He was wearing just a sweatshirt, not appropriate, Owen knew, for long periods in the cold rain.

"Hey, Owen." Linc grinned at him, rain dripping off his nose, his shoulders hunched against the damp chill. "I can't hike today. I have something else I need to do."

"Suit yourself."

"It's not the rain—I don't care about that."

"You're not dressed for the conditions. When you're cold and wet, you stay cold and wet."

Linc gave him an awkward, self-conscious grin. "That can't be good, right?"

"Not if you want to avoid hypothermia."

"Yeah, well, I do. Look—I just wanted to let you know."

"No problem."

"I mean, everything's okay. I'm still interested in training with you."

"You don't owe me anything, Linc. I said I'd hike with you for a few days. If you want to get serious, you can sign up for training."

His eyes, which seemed bluer in the gloom, sparked. "Think I could do it?"

"Yes, I do."

"Thanks. Okay—I'll see you later." But he paused, looking down at the rocks, at the spot where Chris had died. "This place. It's where…" He didn't finish his thought. "How can you stand being out here?"

"I don't think about it just as the place where Chris died. He loved it out here."

"Yeah. I guess you're right." Linc pulled his gaze away from the rocks, but the spark had gone out of his eyes. "I'll see you later."

"Anytime, Linc."

The rain picked up. Linc pulled his hood over his head and shoved his hands into his sweatshirt pockets, jumping from rock to rock, slipping once but correcting himself quickly. He was obviously wobbly from pushing himself on the previous hikes with Owen, but he was gutsy and strong—and he had something to prove.

Owen glanced up the coastline toward Abigail's house, out of view behind trees and in the fog and rain. She'd needed to be alone last night. The two calls—the timing of them—had gotten to her. She tried to take them in cop mode, but they had to remind her of the twenty-five-year-old bride who'd stood out here and watched her husband's blood mingle with the tide.

Rain pelted on Owen's hat, dripping off the brim, turning into a downpour.

He walked back to his house and filled the woodbox, wondering what Abigail would do if he knocked on her door and said he was at a loose end on a rainy day.

Shoot him, probably, he thought, and smiled to himself.

Abigail almost didn't answer her cell phone when she saw Bob O'Reilly's number on the readout. She could pretend she was back at her house, where there was no cell service, instead of standing in front of the Abbe Museum in downtown Bar Harbor, crowded with scores of rained-out tourists.

"Hey, Bob," she said.

"Where are you?"

"I'm in Bar Harbor watching a seagull devour the remains of an ice-cream cone some kid threw on the sidewalk. Too cold for ice cream if you ask me. Is it raining there?"

"Pouring. What're you doing in Bar Harbor?"

"I just toured the Abbe Museum. Have you ever gone through it? It's dedicated to the Native Americans of Maine. Fascinating." She brushed raindrops off her hair. She didn't have a hat or umbrella, but the rain had tapered off to an intermittent drizzle. "And I just bought a moose sweatshirt."

"You're not playing tourist," Bob said. "What's in Bar Harbor that you think might lead you to your anonymous caller?"

"Nothing specific. I'm casting a wide net."

"Owen Garrison's new field academy is setting up in Bar Harbor."

"So it is." She'd stopped by on her way into town, and

no one was there. "Katie Alden's going to be its director. The chief of police's wife."

"Good for her. What about the FBI? They poking around in Bar Harbor?"

"Not that I've noticed."

Bob sighed. "I wish I had something to report on my end. Now that you've had a second call, we're taking another look at the one you got on Newbury Street. Nothing but dead ends so far."

"I gave Lucas a list of people who know I frequent that particular restaurant."

"We've already gone through the list. The truth is, anyone could know. Wasn't it in the papers one year? Some reporter said how you spend your wedding anniversary having dinner alone there—"

"That was at least five years ago. Who'd think I still went there? And why wait until now to act?"

"Because 'things are happening' now," Bob said, a bite of frustration in his voice. "Craziness. We'll figure this out, Abigail. You just keep your eyes open and stay safe."

"I will, Bob. Don't worry about me."

"Oh, no, why should I worry? You're up on an island in the rain, all alone, with some maniac calling you at five o'clock in the morning, and you're going to museums and buying moose sweatshirts. Who the hell would worry?"

By the time he finished, he had her laughing. "Goodbye—"

"And Owen Garrison. Let's not forget the studly rich guy. I've seen him, you know. I'm doing my homework— guy's in Maine resting up after a year of nonstop rescue and recovery work. Guys like that, they don't rest."

Fair warning, that, Abigail thought, suddenly feeling warm. "Are you done now?"

"Yeah. No—" He bit off a sigh. "If you need anything—*anything*—you know I'll be there. Scoop, too. Just say the word."

"Thank you. I do know that. And I appreciate it."

But Bob couldn't resist. "Anything you need, kiddo. Bail money, a spare set of handcuff keys—"

She laughed and disconnected, slipping her cell phone into her jacket pocket. She hadn't lied to him. She *had* visited the museum and bought a moose sweatshirt. But she'd also asked around about Mattie Young, making up a story about having heard that his old photographs were in demand. A woman in the sweatshirt store had pointed to a small gallery that, she believed, had some of Mattie's work in stock.

Abigail walked down the street and ducked into the gallery, its display window offering the obligatory water-color of the rockbound coast and a red-and-white striped Maine lighthouse—and she could understand why. If she could have afforded the painting, she'd have bought it herself. On a bad day in Boston, she would close her eyes and conjure up just such an image, of bright sky, rocks and glistening ocean. Why not add a picturesque lighthouse?

She eased off her wet jacket, careful not to let it drip on any of the wares, and wandered among shelves of carved waterfowl and pottery painted with wild blueberries and cranberries, and walls crammed with original paintings and photography.

A wiry older man—he had to be at least eighty—greeted her. "May I help you?"

"I'm looking for the work of a local photographer, Mattie Young."

He seemed surprised. "Mattie? Heavens. I haven't had anyone ask about him in ages. Yes, we do carry his work. A few pieces. We don't have anything on display right now— we haven't in a long, long time."

"May I see what you do have?"

"Of course."

But as he led her through an open doorway to a small room lined with cabinets, Abigail saw Owen entering the gallery. He waved to her as he crossed the gallery toward her.

"Fancy meeting you here, Abigail."

She noticed the older man straighten his spine as he inclined his head in greeting.

"Mr. Garrison. We haven't seen you in some time. I'd heard you were on the island."

"It has been a long time, Walt. Too long."

Abigail didn't know why she was surprised at the exchange between the two men. The Garrisons had been fixtures on Mt. Desert Island for more than a hundred years. She wondered if Walt had known Owen's grandfather, too.

Not that their reunion stopped her from speaking her mind. "Did you follow me?" she asked Owen.

He smiled. "Tough to miss you in that red jacket."

It was *very* red. "You're not wet. What, were you driving past the gallery, saw me and decided to pop in?"

"I was on my way to the field academy."

"You must have had good parking karma," she said, then turned back to Walt, who had stopped in front of a cabinet of thin, deep drawers.

"We might have one or two other pieces," he said. "But most of what we have is in here. Do you know Mattie?"

Abigail didn't look at Owen as she answered. "He and my husband grew up together."

"Your husband?"

"He died seven years ago. Chris Browning."

The man's aged eyes settled on her a moment, any awkwardness fleeting. He nodded. "I knew your husband's grandfather. I didn't know Chris well. He's the one who persuaded Mattie to display his work."

"Mattie's had his ups and downs over the years."

"Yes. They started long before your husband was killed."

And before she turned up on the scene. Although he didn't say as much, Abigail knew Walt must have thought it. She, the FBI—they'd taken Chris away from the island and his friends. At least in their minds. But Abigail knew that Chris had always considered Mt. Desert Island home. Since she'd moved a lot growing up, that was fine with her.

Owen stood behind her, not crowding her, but not going on his way, either. "Has Mattie brought any new work in lately?" he asked Walt.

"Not recently, no. It could help us sell his older work." The older man unlocked the drawer and opened it, gesturing at the contents. "Mattie has an incredible, unusual talent. You'll see. These photographs are some of his best work. The earliest were taken when he was a teenager. They're not as refined as his later work, of course, but his eye is there. Well, I'll leave you to them."

Walt withdrew to the outer room, and Abigail lifted a black-and-white print from the drawer. She took a breath, immediately recognizing the cliffs just down the waterfront from her house. Mattie had captured the dramatic beauty of the sheer granite face and the white-capped waves crashing onto massive rectangles of rock.

But the danger was there, too, palpable, unrelenting. The cliffs and the sea would be unforgiving of a carelessly placed foot, a reckless paddler, a poorly dressed hiker—a fourteen-year-old girl, Abigail thought, upset after a meaningless fight with a friend.

"Mattie took that picture the day Doe drowned," Owen said.

"*This* picture? You're sure?"

"He had his camera with him on the boat with Chris and his grandfather. This was later, after they'd gotten Doe to the harbor. He went back to the cliffs."

"But there are no police—"

"They'd gone. Everyone had gone by then."

"Were you with him?"

Owen shook his head, staring at the stark photograph. "No."

"Then how do you know—"

"Chris told me years later. He didn't want Mattie to put this particular photograph out into the public."

"Mattie?"

"He didn't agree."

"But no one's ever bought it," Abigail said, setting the photograph on top of the cabinet and digging back into the drawer for more of Mattie's work.

Owen touched a corner of the old photograph. "Would you buy it, if you knew the circumstances of when it was taken?"

"No. I wouldn't. But you never know what some people will do. Besides, most tourists wouldn't have a clue."

"I suppose so." He kept staring at the scene of the cliffs. "I convinced myself I wasn't alone out there that day. I thought someone followed Doe and me to the cliffs, or was there already, hiding in the trees."

"Someone who could have helped her," Abigail said.

He shrugged. "At least someone who could have screamed for help. I couldn't—I tried, and no sound came out."

"What an awful memory to live with."

"I know now it wouldn't have made a difference. Doe hit her head on a rock, and had early-stage hypothermia. She fell in a tough place to get to by land or by boat. Help wouldn't have arrived in time." He pulled his gaze from the picture, his gray eyes taking on the color of the gloomy afternoon. "Doe was a gentle soul. She never liked difficult, scary hikes. The cliffs terrified her. She never meant to fall."

"But she was upset that day, wasn't she?"

"Grace Cooper had teased her about backing out of a hike up the Precipice Trail."

"It's not my favorite trail, either," Abigail said. "If I have to use rungs, it's too vertical for me."

"Not going to turn you into a rock-climber, are we?"

"No way." She saw that her humor had broken through his darkening mood. "Did your sister go down to the cliffs to prove herself somehow? Or just because she was upset and wanted to get away from everyone?"

"I don't know why she went down there. She was used to Grace teasing her. Doe would tease her back." He shook his head. "It's been twenty-five years. Hard to believe. The truth is, what happened wasn't anyone's fault."

"Grace must feel guilty, even if she knows your sister's death was an accident."

"She's never said one way or the other, at least not to me. The Coopers aren't ones for big emotional displays."

"I suppose not." Abigail remembered how she'd clawed at Owen, trying to get to Chris's body. She'd never been repressed, but she'd learned self-control. "Mattie was just a teenager himself."

"Seventeen."

She glanced at the picture once more, imagining Chris and Mattie and Owen as boys, all of them trying to make sense of what had happened to pretty, gentle Doe Garrison.

"These other pictures are amazing, too," she said, pulling out a stack of prints.

Although she wasn't an expert in photography, Abigail could see that Mattie's later pictures were better, technically and artistically. Presumably, he'd kept all the negatives. She flipped through the prints, seeing Mattie Young in a different light, understanding better why Chris had been so reluctant to give up on his friend.

"Look," someone in the outer gallery said. "Sunlight!"

Abigail turned away from the photographs. Owen said, "We should dry off an outdoor table somewhere and have a drink."

"That sounds wonderful. Then you'll show me your new field academy?"

"It's just a big empty building right now." He angled a look at her, as if trying to figure out if she had an ulterior motive for wanting to see the training facility. "But I'd be happy to give you the grand tour."

On their way out, Abigail bought a small, carved black duck, noticing Walt carefully returning Mattie's photographs to the cabinet drawer, on top of the one he'd taken the day Doe Garrison drowned.

Linc watched Mattie lift a fat, squirming worm out of the wet dirt of a hole he'd dug in a small garden near the back gate of Ellis's house. "Your uncle doesn't like working in the rain." He tossed the worm aside. He had on a half-shredded denim jacket, not warm enough for the chilly temperatures. "But he doesn't mind me working in the rain."

"It's not raining now. What are you doing?"

"I'm dividing perennials. How's that for a day's work?"

"At least it's an honest day's work," Linc said, sarcastic. He didn't care.

Mattie rolled back onto his heels. "You're an arrogant little fuck, Lincoln Cooper. I'm enjoying making you sweat. It's about damn time someone did."

"I don't care what you think of me. I know what I've done and what I haven't done."

"You care what your family thinks of you. Those FBI agents sneaking around town, checking into your family's business so they can give your sister the stamp of approval she needs. The local cops. Who's that skinny guy from the state police? Lou Beeler. He'd like to know what I know about you. Get your nuts into the wringer. Find out what you were up to the day Chris Browning was murdered."

Linc felt himself flush but refused to let Mattie see he was getting to him. "Having fun, aren't you?"

"Oh, sure. I like cutting worms in half in the mud."

Linc felt his stomach roll over at the thought of cut-up worms. "You're lucky I'm not a killer. If I were, I wouldn't be paying you to keep your mouth shut. I'd have you buried in a deep, dark hole where no one would ever find you."

Mattie wasn't the least bit rattled. "Doesn't matter if you're a killer or not. You're a snot-nosed kid who stole from your family's friends. Even if you didn't break into Chris's house and hit his wife over the head, steal her necklace, you gave whoever did the idea."

"A copycat," Linc said. "Except that doesn't make sense.

With all the rich people on this island in the summer, why target the Brownings?"

"Wedding money, maybe."

"There was none."

"Doesn't mean the thief knew that or—" Mattie rolled onto his knees, digging with his bare hands into a tangle of greenery and roots. Linc wasn't good with his flora and fauna. He had no idea what kind of plant it was. Without looking up, Mattie said, "Do you have my money?"

"It's under a flowerpot next to your bicycle."

"All of it?"

Linc hesitated. He'd done a cash advance on his credit card, cleaned out his bank accounts, hauled a bunch of stuff no one would miss to Ellsworth, the closest real town, and pawned it. He'd debated swiping a watch from his father, getting into his or Grace's cash. But he hadn't gone that far.

"Damn it, Linc—"

"No. I don't have all of it. Two thousand. It's all I could manage without drawing attention to myself. I can get more in a few days."

Mattie sat on his butt in the wet grass and leaned back, spots of blood where he'd nicked his mud-encrusted hands. He'd worked in the rain. He wouldn't care. "I don't have a lot of patience left."

"It won't do either of us any good if I'm caught. My father's not stupid. He'll ask questions—he'll see through me—"

"All right, all right. We don't want Daddy getting all suspicious and pissy. Just get it done. I want my money. I deserve it."

Linc could feel his blood roaring into his face, pounding in his ears. He noticed a scratcher lying in the grass and pictured it embedded in Mattie's head, silencing him forever. But he couldn't picture himself doing the embedding.

It had to be easier just to shoot someone, he thought. The coward's way out. Just close your eyes and pull the trigger. If the target wasn't moving, it wasn't that hard to do.

He couldn't picture himself shooting someone, either.

"I'll do what I can to get you the rest as soon as possible." Linc straightened, aware of Mattie's amusement, and realized how frightened and sickened he must look. "Then it's over. You can threaten me until you choke. There'll be no more money, not from me."

"I just want the ten grand. I'll keep my word. Your secrets will be safe with me."

His secrets. What did a creep like Mattie Young know about his secrets?

Linc saw the sun breaking through the clouds, felt a cold breeze against his back. Why did he want to hear Mattie say he didn't believe he'd killed Chris? Why did it matter?

He gave the scratcher a little push with his toe. "Like I said, I know what I've done and what I haven't done."

"Yeah?" Linc grinned at him, reaching for a pack of cigarettes. "I know what you've done and haven't done, too. Best to keep that in mind."

CHAPTER 17

Sean and Ian Alden scrambled out of Owen's truck and onto his rain-soaked deck. He appreciated their energy after a full day of camp. Doyle had called him on his cell phone, while Owen was having iced tea and chowder with Abigail, watching the skies clear under a yellow umbrella at a table overlooking Bar Harbor's famous waterfront. They'd never made it to the academy building. Doyle was bogged down and needed Owen to pick up the boys and keep an eye on them until evening.

By the time Katie got back, Owen figured Doyle would have worked out how to manage without her.

Sean bent down and picked up papers—something—propped up against the French door. He made a face. "Gross. Owen, is she one of the people you couldn't rescue in time?"

Ian leaned into his brother and took a peek. "Oh, yuck. She's *dead*."

Owen leaped onto the deck. The sun sparkled on the

small puddles left by the rain, and he could hear the tide washing onto the rocks, seagulls, the engine of a far-off lobster boat. Not wanting to panic the boys, he said carefully, "What do you have there?"

"Pictures," Sean said. "Aren't they yours?"

"No. Let me see, okay?"

Sean handed him a clear plastic sleeve, dotted with raindrops. Inside were at least two, maybe more, eight-by-ten prints. Owen held the plastic by the edges, but it had been sitting out on his deck in the rain, Sean had handled it—any trace evidence would likely be long gone by now.

The top picture came into focus. His mind resisted taking in what he was seeing.

Doe...

"Owen?" Ian's voice was low, panicked. "Owen, what's wrong?"

She was lying on a blanket on the dock where the Brownings had taken her and rescue workers had tried to revive her. Only his sister—her lifeless body—was in the shot, as if she were out there all alone.

Strands of her wet hair covered her face.

Owen pictured the rest of the scene. His parents, holding each other in shock and grief. His grandmother, the indomitable Polly, her hands clasped in prayer. Chris and his grandfather, talking to the rescue workers and police, explaining what had happened. The Coopers, horrified, trying not to get in the way.

He didn't remember seeing Mattie Young.

Sean froze, staring up at Owen. "Do you want me to call my dad?"

"It's okay." He forced himself to make eye contact

with the two boys. "I need to look at the other picture in here. Hang on."

The plastic sleeve had no clasp or other kind of seal, and he was able to slip his fingers inside and lift out the print that was under the one of Doe. But he didn't need to take it all the way out. He recognized the rocks, the tall pines on the waterfront below the remains of his family's original Mt. Desert house.

And he recognized the woman in the picture.

And himself.

"Abigail," he whispered. "Hell."

He had his arms around her, holding her back as the police arrived and she tried again to go to her husband.

She'd fought him with all the strength she had.

She was so young, in the grips of such terrible grief.

Ian gulped in a breath. "Owen." The boy sobbed. "Owen, what—"

"Easy." He slipped the pictures back into the plastic sleeve. "Let's go inside."

Whoever had left the pictures hadn't broken into his house. He unlocked the door, but kept the boys close as they went inside. He put them on the high stools at the breakfast bar, then dialed Abigail's number, letting it ring.

No answer.

He hung up. He had no idea what she'd done after he'd left her in Bar Harbor.

He dialed the local police station and spoke quickly to one of Doyle's officers, who promised he'd send someone out there and get hold of the chief.

"Be sure to tell him his sons are fine," Owen said.

Sean looked at him thoughtfully after Owen had hung up. "Why don't you just leave us here and go check on Abigail?"

"I'm not leaving you here by yourselves."

"We'll be *fine*."

Owen gave the boy a quick smile. "But *I* won't be if I can't get back here before your dad arrives."

Neither boy laughed, and Ian, sucking in a succession of shallow breaths, said, "What about Abigail? Is she all right?"

"She's probably out for a hike or running errands."

Ian clutched Owen's hand. "Go find her!"

"We can go with you," Sean said.

Owen shook his head. "That's not going to happen. Abigail will be all right. She's a police officer like your dad."

Footsteps sounded out on the deck, and the two boys jumped, even as Owen moved between them and the door.

"Owen?" Abigail's voice. "It's me—everything okay here?"

Ian clutched his heart in a display of drama and slumped in relief. "She's okay."

Owen smiled at him. "Told you."

Sean eased down off the stool and ran to the door. "Abigail! My dad's on the way. Someone left Owen pictures of dead people."

When she pushed open the door and entered the cool house, Owen noticed the gun on her waist, her focused, cop-mode look as she frowned at him. "Dead people? Owen, what's going on?"

He nodded to the plastic sleeve of pictures on his kitchen counter and tried to explain, without further alarming Sean and Ian, what had happened. Abigail listened without interruption. When he finished, Owen noticed that her cheeks had drained of any color. "Abigail? Did you come back to the same pictures?"

"Different ones," she said. "They were inside my front

door. Three shots taken at Ellis Cooper's house the day Chris was killed."

"Did you see anyone?"

"No. No one. I checked around outside and walked over here. No sign of anyone."

Mattie, in other words.

"Lou Beeler's on his way." She made an effort to smile at the two boys. "Your dad, too."

Owen sensed her restlessness. "Where are the pictures that were left for you?"

"On my kitchen counter." Her eyes, dark and intense, leveled on him. "There's something I need to do. Tell Lou and Doyle I'll be right back."

"You're going to confront Mattie."

"Just because the pictures are disturbing doesn't make it against the law to leave them on our doorsteps."

"You know damn well the police will investigate."

But she ignored him, saying goodbye to the boys before she slipped back out to the deck, barely making a sound as she headed back across the rocks.

Owen swore under his breath. There was nothing he could do. He couldn't leave Sean and Ian, and he sure as hell couldn't take them with him and go after Abigail.

"Owen?" Ian slipped a cool hand into his. "I'm scared."

He wanted to tell the boys there was nothing to be scared of, but someone had just left him a picture of his drowned sister and a picture of a terrified, grief-stricken widow. How could he say, with any degree of confidence, there was no reason to be afraid?

"Hey, guys," he said. "Come on. Let's get a fire going."

Abigail parked in front of Mattie's house, walked up to his front door and rang the doorbell, just the way she was supposed to. It was after four. He would have knocked off work by now. She noticed bent vertical blinds hanging in a picture window of the small, one-story bungalow. He hadn't planted flowers in his own yard.

When the door didn't open, she pounded on it, its white paint chipped and yellowed. "Mattie, it's Abigail. Abigail Browning. I'd like to talk to you."

She waited two beats. Still no answer. She tried the knob. The door was unlocked.

"Mattie."

She called him again as she pushed open the door. Before entering, she heard the clatter of a bicycle behind her on the walk and turned, sighing at Mattie. "There you are. Don't you lock your doors?"

"What for? I don't have anything worth stealing." He waved a hand at her, showing no indication of surprise or irritation at her visit. "Go ahead. Go inside if you want."

"Thank you, I will."

She stepped into a simply furnished living room, surprisingly neat and clean given Mattie's general appearance. He followed her in and flopped down onto the couch. "Okay. What do you want?"

"I'd like to talk to you about your photography."

"My photography? Why?"

"I was at a gallery in Bar Harbor today. The owner, a man named Walt—"

"Oh, yeah." Mattie grinned, putting his feet up on a coffee table. "Good old Walt. He's full of shit, isn't he? Pompous ass."

"He thinks you're very talented."

"See what I mean?"

"Where do you keep the negatives of the pictures you've taken?"

"I burned them."

Abigail wasn't sure whether or not to believe him. "When?"

"One night when I was drunk and feeling sorry for myself. Well." He gave a fake laugh, no hint of self-deprecation. "I guess that describes a lot of nights. It was sometime after Chris was killed. I was living in Bar Harbor—it feels like civilization compared to living out here."

"Did you destroy all your negatives?"

He hesitated. "I don't remember."

"You remember, Mattie. You're a photographer. Those negatives are your life's work."

"I don't know why I let you in here."

"You didn't burn the negatives of the pictures you took the day Dorothy Garrison died," Abigail said.

He shot to his feet, bolting for the front door, but she intercepted him, grabbing his arm and twisting it behind his back.

He squealed. "Hey!"

"Just calm down." She eased off. "Running isn't going to solve anything."

"You have no right—"

She released him and stepped back. "I want to know about the pictures, Mattie."

"What're you talking about?"

Abigail didn't answer him. She walked into the adjoining dining room, where a dusty faux-crystal chandelier hung above a scratched and nicked dark-stained pine table. "You have a decent setup here." She ran her fingers over the table. "Keep your day job and work on your photography on your off-hours. That's your plan, isn't it?"

He rubbed his arm where she'd tackled him. "Yeah. Yeah, that's the plan."

"Why sneak off to the old Garrison foundation to drink in the dark with the mosquitoes?"

He shrugged. "Why drink?"

"Good point."

"You used to be nicer. When you and Chris were together."

"Maybe so."

She started toward the kitchen, off the dining room, but noticed a fat envelope tucked under a clear glass vase on the sideboard, which matched the table. She walked over to it and lifted the vase with one hand and picked up the envelope with the other hand.

"Hey—that's mine. You need a warrant to search my place—"

"I'm not here as a police officer. I'm here as a friend." She could see the stack of green bills inside the envelope and fanned them with her thumb. Most were fifty- and hundred-dollar bills. "How much is in here? A thousand?"

"It's not against the law to have cash in my own house."

"I thought you said there was nothing here worth stealing. Do the Coopers pay you in cash?"

He snapped his mouth shut. "Get out." He pointed toward the front door. "Now go, before I call Doyle."

Abigail made a show of checking her watch. "By my calculations, he should be here soon."

"What?"

"Doyle and Lieutenant Beeler. I wouldn't be surprised if they come together." She replaced the envelope under the vase. "Feel free to tell them we've talked."

Mattie swore at her. He got himself onto a roll and kept swearing, calling her a long, not particularly inventive string of names, but Abigail ignored him as she walked past him to the front door. She held it open with one hand and looked back at him. Something about her expression worked, because he shut up.

She said, "Tell Chief Alden and Lieutenant Beeler everything you know, Mattie. Whatever you're hiding, whatever angle you're playing, isn't worth the risks you're taking."

He held up both his hands, splaying his fingers. "Look at these. Look at the dirt and the dried blood. The calluses. You think I'm playing an angle? You're fucking crazy. I get up in the morning and I ride my bike to rich people's houses, and I work my ass off. I'm doing the best I can to pull my life together."

"Lie to yourself all you want. And to me, if you have to. Just don't lie to the police."

"Go fuck yourself."

On that lofty note, Abigail left, getting to her car and back onto the main road without running into any of her colleagues in law enforcement.

But they were waiting for her at her little house on the Maine coast. Lou Beeler, Doyle Alden *and* Special Agents Capozza and Steele.

"Lucky me," she said aloud.

She pulled over into the grass and parked.

No way did she want to block the driveway and prevent any of the cop cars from leaving.

CHAPTER 18

There were three color photographs in Abigail's clear plastic sleeve.

The top one—the one she saw through the plastic—was of a thirteen-year-old Linc Cooper standing by the iron gate in his uncle's garden with his shirt half untucked and a martini glass in his hand.

Abigail knew it was taken at Ellis's party seven years ago because of Linc's age, the little umbrella in his drink and the decorative lights on the fence. She'd seen many other pictures of the party.

The second photograph was of Grace Cooper in the shade at the top of the steep zigzag of steps that led up to Ellis's house from the private drive.

On the step just below her, almost out of view, was Chris, his hands balled into fists, a tight look of anger on his face.

There was no fear, Abigail had decided after studying his expression.

No premonition that he was about to be murdered.

He'd gone up to Ellis's after finding her unconscious, obviously intent on finding whoever had attacked his wife. Just the Coopers and the caterers and a few stragglers were still at the party. Grace had told the police that she had seen Chris at her uncle's house, but never indicated they had spoken.

But how could they not have, with him coming up the steps and her right there?

The third photograph was of Owen, on Ellis's stone terrace, clearly later—after Linc had snuck his martini, after Grace and Chris had said whatever they'd said to each other.

Hours before Owen had gone down to the rocks and found Chris's body.

Abigail had jotted down detailed descriptions of each photograph before Lou Beeler could send them off to the lab. The prints were fresh, probably run off an inkjet printer. She'd suggested to Lou that he check to see if Mattie had put his negatives onto a computer disk before burning them, or put the ones he hadn't burned—if he'd burned any—onto a disk, but the Maine CID detective had already covered all the bases.

Her fellow law enforcement officers were gone now, off to find Mattie, having taken her and Owen, separately, through their paces, all of them trying to make sense of the pictures and why they'd been left, what they meant.

Abigail was restless. There wasn't much she could do for the moment, other than take out her frustration on her walls.

She tied a purple bandanna over her hair and lifted her sledgehammer, the wind gusting off the water, blowing through her porch door and stirring up more plaster dust. There seemed to be no end to it, no matter how much she swept.

One more to go, and she'd have the room gutted. Then she could put up new wallboard and tape, slap on primer, pick out a paint color—something bright, but that didn't clash with the lupine-blue in the entry.

Thinking about wallboard and paint colors gave everything else a chance to simmer. The calls, the pictures, Mattie's parties in the old Garrison foundation, the stash of money under his vase.

The Maine cops, the frightened Alden boys.

Owen.

Abigail jumped.

The man who'd just been in her thoughts stood in the doorway to her front room, watching her angle her sledgehammer at the final section of wall. It was dusk, but night was coming fast. "You should wear goggles and a mask," Owen said.

"I've got some in my trunk."

He didn't offer to go fetch them. "You rent this place to cops most of the time. I bet you could get a half dozen of them together to help you tear down walls and put up new ones. Throw a few lobsters in a pot, buy a couple of six-packs—they'd be thrilled."

She grinned at him. "Are you implying we cops come cheap?" But she didn't wait for an answer. "Stand back. I don't want to nail you in the head with this thing."

"Abigail—"

Her first whack penetrated the wallboard. "Hey, I'm getting good at this." Before she lost her steam, she heaved the sledgehammer twice more, then gave up and set it against an exposed support beam. "That's enough. Best to pace myself before I tear my rotator cuff or something."

"You've got a dead body there."

"Mouse skeleton." Using her toe, she dragged it out of a corner. "It's the one I missed earlier."

"Where there's one dead mouse, there's another."

"It's live mice I don't want to run into."

Owen stepped into the room and walked over to her, running his thumb under her eye. "Don't want to get plaster in your eyes."

"That wouldn't be good." She took a breath. "Owen…I'm sorry you and Sean and Ian had to see those pictures."

"It's not your fault—"

"I could have stayed in Boston. I didn't have to come up here."

Doyle Alden appeared on her back porch. "That's right," he said, opening the screen door. "You didn't."

Abigail ignored his sour tone. "Did you find Mattie?"

"Yeah. We found him. Beeler's talking to him." Doyle glanced at her array of tools, as if he wanted to take a crowbar to her himself. "Maybe you should talk to the Coopers about including this place in with the sale of Ellis's. Jason's a smart guy. Shrewd. He'd probably get you a better price than you could get on your own."

"Probably would. How are Sean and Ian?"

"They're fine. My next-door neighbor's watching them while I deal with this mess."

"Listen, Doyle, if I'd known about the pictures—"

"No way for you to know," he interrupted. "The bastard who left them could have stuck a piece of paper in front of them. Instead…" He trailed off. "Doesn't matter. What's done is done."

"Have they talked to their mother?" Abigail asked. "That might help."

Doyle stiffened. "I don't need you to tell me how to raise my sons."

"I'm sorry. I didn't mean—"

"Doyle," Owen said, "nobody wanted the boys to see those pictures. I've had the image of my sister burned into my brain for twenty-five years—of Chris for seven years. I'd have done anything to keep Sean and Ian from having to see that. We all would have."

All the air seemed to go out of the chief of police. He swore under his breath, but quickly pulled himself together, pointing a finger at Abigail. "You need to remember what your role here is and what it isn't. Understood?" He didn't wait for an answer. "Knock out all the walls in this whole damn house, Abigail. Paint. Decorate. If we learn anything about the phone calls and the pictures, we'll let you know."

Abigail gave him a cheeky smile. "Lou told me the same thing."

Doyle managed a grudging smile back at her. "Smart guy, that Lou."

Doyle climbed into his car, the window down, mosquitoes thick in the cool, salt-tinged air. Owen had followed his friend outside and could feel Doyle's frustration and resentment—his powerlessness. "Let me know if you want me to talk to the boys about what happened."

"Some days, I swear—" Doyle shoved the key into the ignition with more force than was necessary. "I swear Katie and I should just pack up the boys and get off this damn rock. I should find another line of work."

"Your work didn't cause what happened today."

"I'm not talking about today."

Owen knew he wasn't. "You're a small-town cop,

Doyle. You're good at what you do. You enjoy it. You just never thought you'd have to investigate the murder of your best friend."

"You'd think after seven years…"

"What, that we'd all have forgotten? I'd think after seven years we'd be itchy and irritated that Chris's murder was still unsolved, and worried that other people might be at risk."

Doyle gripped the wheel, shaking his head. "We're never going to find the killer. That's the truth, Owen. Abigail knows it. She's trying to create leads where there are none. For all we know, she planted those pictures herself. She's been collecting her own stash of evidence for years. She's—" He eased off the wheel and turned the key in the ignition, starting the engine. "I've said too much."

"Forget it."

But Doyle looked at him through the open window. "She's not going to tell you anything she doesn't want to tell you. She's got a tight lid on herself. Never mind those dark eyes, Owen, my friend."

He smiled with feigned innocence. "What dark eyes?"

When he returned to Abigail's kitchen, she had dumped lobster bisque into an ancient saucepan and had it simmering on the stove. "Big confession," she said. "I've never cooked my own lobster. Then again, I've never claimed to be a real Mainer. I just have a house here." She peered into the saucepan. "I think there's enough butter in there to give us six heart attacks apiece."

Owen stood behind her and peered over her shoulder as she stirred the bisque with a wooden spoon. "I can't remember the first time I was in this house. I must have been a toddler. Not much has changed. Chris's grandfather used to heat up chowder in this same pan."

"I wish I'd had a chance to know him better. He died nine months after Chris and I met."

"He was a great guy. Salt of the earth. I used to come over here all the time before my sister drowned. After that—" He eased his arms around her waist, wanting to feel her warmth as much as to provide some kind of reassurance for her. "It wasn't easy for my family to be here."

"But you came back."

"After I was on my own, yes. Chris was off to school by then. I'd come over here and sit on the back porch with his grandfather, and he'd tell me stories about lobstering and living out here. He was laconic—it took some doing to get him going. Once he did, he was mesmerizing."

"That's what I remember about him. Chris was like that, too. He didn't tell me everything." She stared at the pinkish bisque, the smell of lobster, butter and sherry filling the air as the pot heated. "I think he believed there'd be time for all that. Time to fill in the gaps. Tell me his secrets."

Her matter-of-fact tone only added to the intensity of her words. Owen kept his arms around her. She sank her weight into him. He tried to picture all the horrific images that were seared into her brain, not only of her husband's bloodied body on the rocks, but of other murder scenes, other grieving loved ones.

"The police will talk to Ellis Cooper and anyone up at his house," Abigail said. "Anyone who might have been out here today and seen something."

"If the pictures were Mattie's doing, people wouldn't necessarily notice him. He's a fixture around here. Part of the landscape."

She nodded. "Fair point. They'll interview Jason and Grace, too. Not great timing for her, but right now, as far as we know, no crime's been committed."

She continued to speak in that same deliberate, calm tone. Owen could feel the heat of her skin under his hands and suspected that, underneath that cool exterior, Abigail Browning was churning.

"Mattie took those pictures, Owen," she said.

"I know."

"I'm just not convinced he's the one who left them here."

Owen tightened his arms around her. "You don't trust any of us, do you?"

She slid out of his embrace without answering and got bowls down from a cupboard. He noticed the pull of her shirt against her skin. She'd taken off her purple bandanna and cleaned up, but she'd still managed to get plaster dust in her dark curls.

She let the bisque simmer until it was heated through but not boiling.

"Abigail, I want you to trust me."

She turned the heat off under the saucepan, keeping her back to him. "I've been fighting for answers on my own for a long time."

"We should have done more to help you. All of us."

She ripped open a drawer and pulled out a dented soup ladle. "I tell myself that everyone wanted to give me the space to get on with my life. And you had your own grief. You all knew Chris longer than I did."

"We weren't married to him," Owen said, making a face. "Hell."

She gave him a small smile. "Fair enough. I have got on with my life, but—I want to find his killer. I want answers. I know I probably should have sold this place that first year after Chris's death, but—" She shrugged. "I didn't."

"The pictures." He sighed. "They're tough to look at."

"If we'd gone to Ellis's party that day…" She shook her head, making it almost a shudder. "We were invited, but we didn't go."

"You were on your honeymoon."

"When I saw those pictures, I felt the breeze off the water and smelled the salt and the roses in the air as I went into the back room and got my head bashed in. It all came back." She switched the heat off under the pan. "Was that what it was like for you, seeing the photo of your sister?"

He nodded.

"At least I was an adult when Chris was killed. Twenty-five." She kept her tone even as she dipped the ladle into the bisque. "You were a little kid when your sister drowned. I can't imagine. Or maybe I can, somewhat. When you've lost someone close to you that young, that tragically—people treat you differently. It's like all of a sudden there's a circle around you that people have to step into before they get close to you. Where before there was no circle."

"Abigail, don't—"

She swore, dropping the ladle, and spun around at him, into him. His mouth found hers, and if he was tentative, she wasn't. She took his hand and placed it on her breast, and he found her nipple with his thumb, even as their kiss deepened. Her urgency fired his own. She lifted his shirt, and he felt her fingers cool on his back, inside his belt.

But he felt her tears, dripping onto his cheek, hot, and pulled back, his heart breaking for her. "Abigail—I'm sorry."

"It's not you."

He knew it wasn't. But he was sorry, anyway, and didn't know how to explain it even to himself.

Without a word, she fled from the kitchen.

Owen stared at the simmering bisque. What the hell was wrong with him? Why not carry her upstairs and make love to her? He wouldn't be taking advantage of her. It was what she wanted as much as he did.

He walked into the front room and stood in the doorway of the torn-apart back room where she'd been attacked so long ago. "Bisque's going to get cold."

She kicked at the debris on her floor. "I don't know what the hell I was thinking, making this mess. I should get Bob and Scoop up here." She smiled over her shoulder at Owen. Self-deprecating. Tears dried. "Have you met Bob and Scoop?"

"Cops?"

She nodded. "My upstairs neighbors." She gestured to her pile of debris. "They'd be like Doyle and want me to stay out of trouble, to keep knocking out walls. Well, maybe I will. I'll head to the hardware store in the morning and order some wallboard. Buy a new hammer."

As if she wasn't going to think about the call, the articles, the pictures. Mattie Young. As if she would just switch off her cop mind, her sense of obligation to her murdered husband.

Owen kept his expression neutral. "Sounds like a plan."

She blew out a breath and angled a look at him. "I was this close—" she held up two fingers, a quarter inch apart "—to throwing you over my shoulder and carrying you upstairs. You know that?"

He laughed. "It would have been a fight, then, for who carried whom."

"Nah. I'd have let you win."

But when she hooked her arm into his and walked him back into the kitchen, Owen realized what had just happened.

Abigail wanted to make love to him.

But not here, he thought. Not in the same house where she'd spent her short-lived honeymoon.

"Owen…"

"It was a very nice kiss, Abigail. We're not just distractions for each other. We both know that much now, don't we? But let's leave it at that."

He could see the relief wash over her.

After their lobster bisque, he walked back to his house and started a fire in the woodstove to take the chill out of the air, to hear the crackle of a fire and feel its warmth and coziness. Did Abigail worry about staying in her house alone tonight? He reasoned she was a police officer, and a widow, and she'd spent more nights alone than not.

Once he got the fire going, he walked outside, the stars and the moon guiding him out to the far end of the point, waves crashing on three sides of him.

He looked back toward the old foundation of his family's original house and saw a solitary silhouette.

Abigail.

No way was she out there contemplating life. She was checking to make sure Mattie Young hadn't returned to his party spot.

Owen gave a loud whistle and waved to her.

She waved back.

But he thought he heard her call him a jackass, presumably for startling her but who knew—who cared? It made him laugh, which, he decided, was a good way to end such a day.

CHAPTER 19

Abigail woke before dawn and drove out to Cadillac Mountain and up the twisting access road to its pink granite summit. She jumped out of her car, the wind brisk at almost sixteen hundred feet, the sky awash in the lavenders, pinks and oranges of the Maine sunrise.

Below her, ocean, bay and islands came into view, and she could hear murmurs of pleasure from other early risers. She emptied her mind as she walked along the well-traveled granite trails, enjoying her surroundings and the feel of the crisp mountain air. But thoughts of last night crept in. Lou Beeler had stopped by her house before heading home. Mattie had declined to tell the state police anything, either, and denied all knowledge of the pictures or how they'd ended up on Owen's and Abigail's doorsteps.

On Lou's way out, Mattie asked him to demand Abigail stay away from him.

She had sensed the senior detective's frustration—and

his misgivings. The calls could have come from a faraway crank with nothing better to do. The pictures were another story. They'd come from someone on the island. Lou admitted he'd never seen any of the shots taken at Ellis's party, nor the one of her and Owen at the murder scene.

He definitely had never seen the shot of Dorothy Garrison's body.

That picture, even more than the others, clearly troubled the older detective.

Abigail had dreamed about the drowned teenager. She'd awakened with a start, unable to breathe. She'd been a little kid getting ready to move to Boston twenty-five years ago, but the scene she'd created in her nightmare of the Brownings, the Coopers and the Garrisons on the dock that awful day was so vivid, so real, that she might have been there herself.

Why leave such a photograph for Owen? To get under his skin?

Why?

On her way back from Cadillac, Abigail stopped at a popular roadside restaurant on impulse and took herself out to breakfast. Wild blueberry pancakes, pure maple syrup, bacon, far too much coffee. She was wired on caffeine and sugar by the time she turned onto her shared driveway.

She parked at her house, debating how she'd tackle Mattie Young today. Unless ordered to do so, she had no intention of staying away from him—and Lou had all but given her the green light to get under his skin a little more. Get out of him whatever it was he knew and wasn't telling.

She thought of the cash in the envelope. Did it mean anything? Had to. Mattie wasn't one for saving his money.

As she climbed out of her car, she noticed a robin

perched on a high branch of the spruce tree at the corner of her driveway. Why couldn't she sit on her porch and watch the birds?

"You could," she said aloud. "You absolutely could."

No one would blame her if she did.

The spruce branches rustled in a strong breeze off the water. The robin fluttered off.

Abigail unlocked her front door, immediately feeling the fresh breeze off the water blowing through the house. She'd left the windows open all night. It'd gotten chilly, but she didn't care. She wanted to get rid of the last of the paint fumes, any mustiness, anything that would slow her down and clog her mind.

In the entry, she remembered that she'd left the porch door open, too.

Not much point locking the front door and leaving the back door unlocked, but she hadn't given it a second's thought before heading up to Cadillac.

With no pockets in her lightweight hiking pants, she dropped her keys on the stepladder, still set up in the entry, and headed to the back room. She could see specks of plaster dust suspended in the sunlit air.

The smell of the room was off. Different.

Sweat.

She heard a sound behind her, in the short hall leading from the back room to the cellar door and kitchen. But even as she reacted, the blow came to the outside of her right thigh. She went with it, didn't fight it, putting out her arms as she dropped forward, allowing them to absorb the force of her fall. She hit hard, the rough floorboards scraping her left forearm, then rolled instantly to her feet.

But no one was there.

She heard her front door bang open and shut.

Damn it.

Her thigh ached, stinging, slowing her pace as she grabbed a crowbar and charged through the front room. She realized whatever she'd been struck with had managed to rip through her pants and bloody her. It wasn't her sledgehammer. A knife? Hell, had she been stabbed?

She reached the front door, tore it open.

No one. Nothing.

She turned to get her car keys off the stepladder, but they were gone. She shot outside, hobbling as fast as possible down the steps and out to her car.

No one was there, either.

She shuddered at the pain in her thigh and felt warm blood oozing down her leg. She'd never catch up with her intruder, even if he was on foot.

Mattie.

That was his sweat she'd smelled.

"Damn." Abigail gulped in a breath and cupped a hand over her injured leg. "Damn, damn, damn."

What killed her wasn't that she'd been caught off guard or that she'd been cut. She'd had no reason to suspect anyone was in the house until it was too late. And if her assailant had sliced at her again, she'd have tackled him.

No, she thought. What killed her was having to explain her stolen car keys to Owen Garrison, Doyle Alden, Lou Beeler, the FBI agents in town, Bob, Scoop, her father and whoever the hell else would find out about them.

Owen had worked with enough victims of accidents, violence and disaster to recognize those who found their sudden vulnerability more difficult to deal with than the pain of their injuries.

Abigail was one who hated her vulnerability. Hated having to ask for help.

She leaned over his stainless-steel sink with her sweater on the floor in a heap as she stuck her scraped arm under cold running water. Despite her bloodied leg, she'd staggered across the rocks from her house, burst in from his deck and gone for his phone, not explaining, just calling Lou Beeler, then Doyle Alden. She hadn't bothered with 911.

She told Beeler she was at Owen's house because the phone line at hers had been cut, presumably before she'd arrived back from her trip up Cadillac Mountain.

Owen sat on a tall stool at the counter. He'd gotten out his first-aid kit. He tapped its plastic box. "You're welcome to help yourself to whatever you need."

"I don't need anything. Thanks." She glanced back at him, her color slightly improved since she'd called in the law and got the cold water running on her arm. "I didn't even know anyone was in the house until I had a drywall saw slicing through my pants leg."

"How do you know it was a drywall saw?"

"Because he dropped it in the entry on his mad dash out. I'm never going to live that one down."

"You're positive it was Mattie?"

"I am. Enough to question him, if not convict him. Assuming we can find him. He must have taken off on his bike. If my damn leg…" She scowled and turned back to the sink. "And my car keys. I could have followed him in my car."

"I can take a look at your leg—"

"My leg's fine." Using her elbow, she shut off the faucet.

"It's a superficial wound. I don't think he wanted to hurt me. I surprised him, and he wasn't planning to stick around and explain himself."

"Any idea what he was doing there?"

"It wasn't to help me hang wallboard." She raised up the dripping forearm and inspected her scratches. "Looks clean enough, don't you think? Just a couple good scrapes. Kind of like a road rash. Stings a little."

"I can wrap it for you. It's hard to wrap your own arm."

"It doesn't need wrapping."

"There are ice packs in the freezer," Owen said.

"I don't need ice."

He flipped open the first-aid kit and lifted out a nonstick bandage, a roll of gauze, tape, scissors and antibiotic ointment, laying them on the counter. "You're bleeding on my floor."

"Oh. Yeah, I guess I am. Not much, though."

"We're wrapping your arm."

She grinned at him. "I'm being difficult?"

"Not unless you try to shoot me. Otherwise you're just someone who's injured and doesn't want to be." He walked over to her and took her hand, turning her arm and taking a look at the injury. "You've got a couple of fairly deep scratches here."

"They're about a quarter-inch long. Big deal. I think I hit a nail from my gutting project."

"Tetanus shots up to date?"

She nodded. "Doyle and Lou are going to land here any second. I don't want them to see you patching me up."

"Of course not." He used a dish towel and dabbed at her arm, drying it as best he could. "Why are you so convinced it was Mattie?"

"He left an odor."

"Do you think he'd been drinking?"

"I have no idea. If he was, it didn't slow him down any. He had to move like a jackrabbit to get out of the house and out of sight."

"Well, if I had you coming after me with a gun—"

"I had to get my gun. That created a small delay." She winced as Owen applied the antibiotic ointment, then placed the bandage over it. "I didn't take it up Cadillac with me."

He wrapped gauze around her arm, covering the bandage, and secured it with tape, then glanced down at her right thigh. The bleeding there looked to have stopped. "You should go to the E.R. about your leg, at least."

"I get worse cuts picking blackberries. If it starts looking infected, I'll see a doctor."

"You might need stitches."

"I don't need stitches." She had a perceptible limp as she walked toward the deck door, then leaned against it and sighed at him. "This isn't going to be my finest hour. You ever do anything stupid?"

"Me? Never."

She laughed. "Oh, sure. Let's see all your scars." But color returned to her pale cheeks, and she made a face. "Umm. Forget I said that."

"Sorry, Detective. I'm not letting that one go." Owen walked over to her and slipped an arm around her waist. "I'll drive you back to your place. Don't argue."

"I won't—I don't know how I made it across those rocks to get here as it is. Must be the pancakes I had for breakfast."

"And for the record," he said, half lifting her out to the deck, "you can see my scars anytime."

* * *

He'd gone and done it now, Mattie thought, feeling terrible as he slipped through the iron gate on the border between Ellis's gardens and the woods. Ellis was at the family estate on Somes Sound. Mattie had seized upon his absence to sneak down to Abigail's house, hoping she wouldn't be there—hoping he'd have the window of time he needed.

He'd taken what precautions he'd thought of. Cutting the phone line, hanging on to the drywall saw. He just couldn't get out of there fast enough.

He crept along the fence, behind a swing that had been there since the Garrisons had owned the property. When he reached the shed he checked his trail for any footprints.

He'd just sliced open a cop. They'd all be looking for him now.

But he had his story ready. Doyle would believe him. Didn't Doyle always believe him?

You don't have your license because Doyle didn't believe you when you said you hadn't been drinking.

Mattie silenced the voices of doubt in his head and unlatched the shed door, stepping inside its crowded but ultraneat single room of tools and garden supplies. Thankfully, he could relatch the door from the inside and wouldn't have to leave it swinging open.

Sunlight angled through the small, paned windows, somehow making him feel more claustrophobic, more trapped.

He worked his way past bags of fertilizer, peat moss and dried cow manure to the back of the shed, where he pushed aside a stack of old wooden lobster pots and got down on his hands and knees.

Using his fists, he banged on the piece of plywood he

himself had tacked onto the opening the chickens had used. It was bigger than necessary, really, for chickens, but that could help him in a pinch. The wood came free easily, but he left it leaned up against the hole. It was unlikely anyone would notice it, one way or the other, but he'd taken enough chances already.

If he had to, he could crawl out the tiny door and get into the woods, disappear.

He'd expected to have to disappear at some point, just not until he had his money. The whole ten grand. More. Damn it, Linc could spare it. He deserved to pay up for what he'd done. For the secrets he'd kept. The blackmail would help cleanse his soul.

Excuses. You should have told Doyle everything last night.

Mattie shook his head. He couldn't afford to let any doubts creep in, undermine him. Not now. Not when he'd gone past the point of no return.

He sat on the floor, his back against a lobster pot. Was it one of Will Browning's old pots? Pa, Mattie used to call him. Ol' Pa Browning. He was the Browning who'd lived a long life.

"Two wrongs don't make a right. Remember that, Mattie."

Ah, Pa.

"I'm trying," Mattie whispered. "I'm trying hard."

At least Pa Browning hadn't lived to see his grandson murdered. A small blessing, at least.

Mattie didn't know if he fell asleep, or if he'd simply gone into some kind of trance, but he became aware of the shed door creaking open. He went very still, silently reassured himself that he couldn't be seen from the door. If it was Ellis, returned from paying homage to his brother, he'd never come this far into the shed.

The door shut—Mattie could hear it, feel more than see the change in light.

"It's me," Linc Cooper said. "I'm alone."

Mattie got to his feet, but stayed close to the little chicken door. "Ellis isn't back yet, is he?"

Linc shook his head, making his way to the rear of the shed. "The cops have gone out to talk to him and my father. They're looking for you. They think you attacked Abigail Browning."

"I didn't attack her—that's not what happened."

"Then tell that to Chief Alden. He knows you. He won't want to believe you'd deliberately hurt anyone. Running just makes you look guilty. What about your bike? Mattie, they'll find you—"

"I haven't done anything wrong."

He'd hid his bike in the woods, where no one would find it, but he had no intention of giving Linc that information—that much power over him.

Linc sneered at him. "Always innocent, aren't you?"

"I don't have to explain myself to you." Mattie felt a surge of impatience. "You'd better hope our Detective Browning doesn't think *you* attacked her."

"Me? Why would I?" The kid squared his shoulders and gave Mattie an icy, superior look. "I'm not playing your game."

"This isn't a fucking game."

"Whatever." Linc stepped closer to him, holding out an envelope to him. "Here's another two thousand. That's four thousand, total. Take it, Mattie, and get out of here. Before you go too far. What if you'd killed Abigail today? She's the daughter of the director of the FBI. She's a cop—"

"You're a bastard, Linc, you know that?" Mattie kept his

voice calm, never mind the lousy situation he was in. He hadn't meant for things to go this way. "You're just like your father. Don't think you're different, because you're not. You're a cutthroat son of a bitch just like he is. A chip off the old block."

Linc's cheeks flamed red. "Better than being a foul-smelling drunk who betrays his own friends."

Mattie snatched the envelope from him and inspected the contents, the mix of green bills. A new beginning. But his eyes welled up with tears. He coughed, covering for himself. "I want the rest."

"I can't—"

"I have Abigail's necklace."

He relished watching the shock seize Linc, turn him ashen, force him to take a step back, stumble on a bag of cow manure. "Mattie…*Christ*…"

"You remember her necklace. It was her grandmother's. Abigail wore it on her wedding day. The 'something borrowed.' Pearls, with a cameo pendant. You grabbed it."

"I didn't."

"You thought no one was at the house. I'll give you that. But she was there, and you hit her on the head—"

"Show it to me." Linc had recovered slightly, his cockiness, his natural arrogance, rising to the challenge. "If you've got the necklace, show it to me."

Mattie shook his head. "I don't trust you not to hit *me* over the head."

"If I stole it, how did you end up with it?"

"I know where you stashed it."

Linc looked as if he'd throw up any second. "I don't know how you can sleep at night. A six-pack of cheap beer makes all the difference, though, doesn't it?"

"You're not helping yourself."

"I don't care. I'm not paying you another dime. If you've got evidence that ties me to Chris's murder, take it to the police. I don't care anymore."

He cared. Mattie could see the fear—the self-loathing—in the kid's eyes. "I'm not greedy."

Linc snorted. "You're such a creep, Mattie."

"You should have thrown the necklace in the ocean. That's what you're thinking now, isn't it? But you panicked."

"I'm leaving." Linc straightened, looking less green. "I'm not going to turn you in. Sink in your own slime. But I'm through, Mattie. Do what you want to do with the necklace. I didn't steal it. I didn't kill Chris. I don't know who did."

He spun on his heels and marched out of the shed, latching the door behind him.

Mattie sank back onto the cold concrete floor. He had four thousand dollars on him, in his possession. When had he ever had this much cash? Why not take it and go?

Let it be enough. *Make* it be enough.

He'd just attacked Abigail Browning. Chris's wife. His friend's true love.

"You should have been at our wedding, Mattie. It was something."

But Mattie hadn't been able to see beyond his outrage at his friend the FBI agent cutting him off.

"You're drinking again. I'm through."

Mattie got out his cigarettes, tapped one out and stuck it on his lip. He didn't dare light it. He sank his head against the stack of lobster pots.

"Hell, Chris. I've done it now, haven't I?"

And there was no going back.

CHAPTER 20

Owen stood on the rock cliffs where his sister had fallen to her death. A family of black ducks bobbed in the outgoing tide below him. Tall firs and spruces grew along the edge of the vertical rock face, their roots bulging out of the thin soil, some of them hanging over the water.

Linc stayed two paces behind him. "You're not worried about falling?"

"No. It's not slippery." Owen grinned at him. "And I've got one hand on this tree."

"I don't like hanging my toes over the edges of cliffs." Leaning forward, very tentatively, Linc peered down at the water, then pulled back, his cockiness—a cover for everything—returning. "I've never spent much time out here. What's the point? There's nothing to do. Maybe if I were into rock climbing."

"Or bird-watching."

"Bird-watching?"

Owen stepped back from the cliffs. "Never mind."

"Oh." Linc seemed slightly embarrassed. "Your sister. I remember Grace saying she was into birds. I wasn't thinking about…" He grimaced. "I wasn't thinking this is where she, you know, fell."

"It was a long time ago."

The five wooded acres of waterfront were included in the property Jason Cooper was selling, and presumably would go to the new owners. Linc, obviously, wouldn't care. But he'd looked anxious and preoccupied since he'd arrived on Owen's deck an hour ago. Owen had suggested walking out to the cliffs as much to burn up some of Linc's nervous energy as to see if they could pick up the trail of Abigail's attacker.

After dropping her off at her house, Owen had left the law enforcement officers and returned to his deck, dragging a chair close enough to the rail that he could put his feet up and stare out at the water and think. He'd gotten about two minutes of thinking done when Linc had turned up.

He shoved his hands into his pockets. "Mattie's worked for my family for years. I can't believe he'd hurt anyone. Abigail pushes his buttons, but she pushes everyone's buttons."

"Let's see what Mattie says when the police catch up with him."

"It's not good that they can't find him, is it?" Linc asked.

"Depends." Owen noticed dark smudges under Linc's eyes. "Are you sleeping okay? Did I push you too hard on our hikes?"

"No, no. I'm fine. I'm sleeping okay. It's just—" He shrugged, looking out at the horizon, sky and water the same clear blue. "I guess with my sister and everything she's got going on, and then Abigail showing up—I'm just on edge."

"Where's Grace today?"

"I don't know. She doesn't tell me what she's doing. She's probably at the house." He paused, clearing his throat, then asked abruptly, "Does Abigail think that Mattie killed Chris?"

"That hasn't come up between us."

"In a way, it'd be easier if he did and we knew it, could prove it. Then it'd be over. The not knowing."

"You were just thirteen when Chris died," Owen said. "That's a tough age to be a part of something like that."

"He was my friend." Link blinked rapidly, keeping any tears at bay. "I remember the morning he was found. No one wanted to tell me. My father—he just said Chris was hurt. I didn't find out for hours what'd really happened."

"Who told you?"

"My dad, finally. Chris…" His voice cracked. "He believed in me. After he was killed, I learned I don't need anyone to believe in me in order to believe in myself."

"We all want someone to believe in us—"

"Wanting's different from needing."

"Maybe so."

Linc brushed the back of his hand across his cheeks. "I should get back."

Owen eyed the younger man. "Linc, you want to tell me what's going on?"

"Nothing. Everything's getting to me is all."

They headed back along the path through the woods and out to the private drive. When they reached Owen's house, Grace Cooper was on the deck, arms crossed on her chest as she paced, preoccupied, oblivious to her surroundings.

She saw her brother and gave a small gasp of relief. "There you are. Your car's at Ellis's—"

"I know. I left it up there and walked down here. What difference does it make?"

"We were worried."

Linc rolled his eyes. "We?"

"Yes, we. Father, Ellis." She dropped her arms to her sides. She had on expensive-looking sailing clothes—white slacks, a navy-and-white top—that somehow made her look older than she was. "With this attack on Abigail, who knows what's next."

"I'm not afraid." Linc sounded more belligerent than convincingly unafraid. "It wasn't a random attack. Whoever went after her isn't going to beat me over the head."

Her brother's confrontational tone didn't seem to get to Grace. "That's a good point. You don't believe it was Mattie? The police are looking for him."

"Doesn't matter what I believe."

She turned to Owen, her poise faltering slightly, but she managed a polite smile. "I don't imagine you're getting the rest you thought you would this week."

"Not a problem."

"No, I suppose it wouldn't be for you. " Her smile faded, offering a glimpse of the emotions she kept so tightly under wrap. "Everything's a mess right now."

"Her appointment," Linc said, as if Owen couldn't guess that was what she meant. "It's all-important, you know."

His sister swung around at him. "That's not fair!"

He flushed. "I guess not. I'm sorry." He shrugged, self-deprecating all of a sudden. "Being a jerk helps me not think about everything else."

Grace nodded, instantly accepting her brother's explanation. "It's okay. Forget it. Owen—we'll run along. Please let us know if there's anything we can do. I hope Abigail's all right."

As she and Linc headed off the deck and back to her car, Doyle Alden pulled into the driveway, Abigail in the front seat next to him. When they got out, they greeted the Coopers, who mumbled quick hellos before continuing on their way.

"Two of Lou's guys are up at Ellis's house," Doyle said as he stepped up onto the deck. "They'll be talking to Grace and Linc next. It's Mattie's day off. No reason for them to know where he is, I suppose."

Abigail walked up to the deck, her limp less noticeable. She'd put on fresh clothes, but blood had seeped through her khaki pants where she'd been cut with the drywall saw. Not a lot, Owen noted, but enough. She paid no attention, taking in a deep breath. "We could hit eighty degrees today. Imagine that."

Doyle frowned at her. "You look like shit, Abigail."

"One of those days, Chief."

"Yeah." He sighed heavily. "I guess it is."

"At least we found my car keys. Mattie threw them in the grass by the driveway. He must have thought better of stealing my car."

"We don't know it was Mattie."

"*You* don't. If I were in an official capacity, I wouldn't, either. But I'm not." With a slight wince of pain, she moved to the glass door. "I'm the one who forgot to lock her damn door."

"Might not have made a difference," Doyle said. "Easy enough to put a chair or a rock through a door or window, if someone's determined to get in."

They'd evidently been over that ground already. Doyle

obviously relished being able to reassure Abigail about a mistake she'd made.

"Anything new on Mattie?" Owen asked.

Doyle shook his head. "He knows every inch of this island. He's got friends who'd give him a ride, pick him up in their boat—loan him a boat. If he doesn't want to talk to us, he can make himself very hard to find."

"Cutting my phone line was a smart preemptive strike," Abigail said, not going inside just yet. "It delayed getting you all out here. He knew he only had a bike."

"That's what doesn't make sense to me," Doyle said. "How did he know you weren't home? Did he happen up your driveway, see your car gone and seize the moment? I don't know. None of it makes any damn sense. Maybe he just walked in to wait for you and decided he couldn't explain himself—"

"So he grabbed a saw and knocked me on my ass?"

Doyle rubbed the back of his neck, the sunlight and heat—the frustration—turning his face red. "I'm just saying we don't know until we talk to him."

Abigail looked at Owen and gave a small smile. "The state guys confiscated my drywall saw as evidence."

"Take a trip to the hardware store," Doyle said. "Buy a new one. It'll give you something to do."

"Don't want my help searching Mattie's house? You've got enough for a search warrant—"

"Thank you for your advice, Detective Browning," Doyle said with open sarcasm.

She was unaffected. "I should have found a stick or something to use as a cane before you all got here. Garnered some sympathy."

"We're all just glad you weren't hurt worse."

"Yeah, tough one, that'd be," Abigail said. "Chris's widow, John March's daughter—"

"Just stop." Doyle stuck a finger up at her. "Stop right now before you go too far. I try to be decent, and you—" He abandoned that thought and dropped his hand. "You try my patience, Abigail. You always have."

She grinned at him, unrepentant. "Sorry."

"I need to go pick up the boys. You want me to have a cruiser posted at your house?"

"Doyle—"

"Payback," he said, with almost a chuckle. "I'll let you know if we find Mattie."

"I know you two go way back," Abigail said. "I meant what I said to Lou and his guys earlier. I don't believe Mattie attacked me with the intention of hurting me. He just wanted to get out of there without getting caught."

"But he did attack you," Doyle said. "Someone did, anyway. Hell, your leg's still bleeding. You should have it looked at."

"It's nothing. I just overdid it. I'll borrow Owen's first-aid kit and put on a Band-Aid. Owen? Is that okay?"

He smiled at her. "Of course. I'll be right here if you need me."

"I'll be in your downstairs bathroom." She smiled back at him. "And, thanks, but I won't need you."

Owen kept his mouth shut as she went inside, but Doyle called to her, "Damn thing could get infected." He didn't wait for an answer and growled at Owen. "You understand the position I'm in? And Katie's not here. I've got all this on my plate…" He bit off a sigh and shut up. "Bring the boys by here anytime."

"And what, let someone hack at them with a saw?"

"That's not going to happen."

"Maybe not." Doyle didn't meet his eye. "I wish I knew what Mattie was up to. And Abigail. Hell. I can't get my head around what all's going on here. I'm hoping nothing. That when it's all done and said, it's just a bunch of nothing."

Something banged inside in the bathroom. *"Damn!"*

Doyle glanced at Owen and smiled. "Sounds as if our detective needs some help, after all. I'll leave you to it."

"Chicken," Owen said, and headed inside.

Abigail picked herself up off the bathroom floor and got out of there, leaning against the pineboard wall in the hall just as Owen arrived, steady, not at all panicked.

"All set," she said. "I lost my balance and had a little spill."

"Going through my bathroom cupboards?"

"Your shelves, actually. There must be five million of them in there. I checked them all for ibuprofen. I got up on the edge of the tub to see into the high ones." She could feel her heart thumping rapidly from the near-disaster. "But no ibuprofen. And there's none in the first-aid kit."

"It's in the kitchen."

She noticed him glance down at her leg and was grateful that she'd had the good sense to put her pants back on before pawing through his shelves. She'd stood there, in the middle of his bathroom, pants in hand, and considered the matter—pictured herself falling, and him charging to her rescue, only to find her in her skivvies, writhing on the floor. Unfortunately, her premonition hadn't compelled her to skip climbing onto the edge of the tub altogether.

"My leg's fine," she said. "Honestly."

"All patched up?"

"I found a proper bandage that I could manage on my own. All I need now are a couple of ibuprofen, a glass of wine and a hot bath."

Owen moved closer to her. "All can be arranged."

He was close enough that Abigail could see the black flecks in his fog-gray eyes. She pressed the small of her back against the wall. If she could do magic, she'd make herself melt into the pine boards. The man was messing up her head.

He studied her with that mix of steadiness and intensity that, in him, weren't at all contradictory. "Doyle's gone."

"Arresting Mattie won't be easy for him, if it comes to it."

"Would it be easy for you?"

"No. It wouldn't have been for Chris, either. The three of them—" She pulled herself slightly away from the wall, her heart rate adjusting to the jolt of her fall. "They grew up like brothers. I could see that when I first came to Mt. Desert. I didn't understand the push-pull Chris felt about his life here until I met Doyle and Mattie."

"If Mattie has an explanation for why he was in your house, why he attacked you—"

"He'll have an explanation. He always does, doesn't he?"

"Will you press charges?"

"It's not that simple." She thought of the two pictures the Alden boys had found on Owen's deck. "Doyle wasn't on the lobster boat the day you lost your sister, was he?"

"No. I don't know where he was. Abigail—"

"He'd have been fifteen. It must have been an awful time for him, too."

"I'm sure it was. He, Mattie and Chris were all friends. Abigail, what do you want to do? Do you want to go look for Mattie? Because I can go with you. We can take my truck."

She banged her head back against the wall. "Sure. Yeah,

we can go look. It beats climbing around in your bathroom and driving myself nuts trying to put all these disparate pieces together. But we won't find him, not if he's squirreled himself away somewhere and doesn't want to be found."

Owen traced a crooked finger along her jaw. "You're worried about him, aren't you?"

She nodded. "Crazy, I know. The bastard jumps me, cuts my best pair of hiking pants—okay, so my only pair of hiking pants—and humiliates me in front of a bunch of Maine cops, not to mention two very serious FBI agents—" She blinked back totally unexpected tears. "And I'm worried about him. *Damn.*"

"Your father…"

"No cell service out here on the rocks and Mattie cut my phone line." She smiled through her tears. "There you go—maybe he cut the line just to keep me from having to talk to my father. He was doing me a favor."

"Is the line fixed now?"

She nodded. "One of Lou's guys knew what to do. I'm not good with wires."

Owen let his finger trail up her cheek and catch a tear, then kissed the spot where it had been. "I hate to see you cry."

"I'm not crying."

"And your leg's fine, and your arm's fine, and you can take anything."

"I'll take anything I have to take if it means finding Chris's killer." Her voice was little more than a whisper. "Anything. I don't care."

"How far will you go to find his killer? As far as you have to, regardless of the consequences?"

"There are lines I won't cross."

"What lines?"

"Ethical lines. Legal lines. But I won't cover up for anyone. I won't look the other way just to avoid hurting people. Hurting myself."

He slipped his hand behind her neck. "You've thought it all through, haven't you?"

"I've had seven years."

"As much as I want to kiss you now," he said, "and as much as I've wanted to kiss you for a lot of those seven years, if I could go back in time and stop Chris from leaving you that day, I'd do it."

"Owen—" Her head spun. "Chris always said you were one of the best people he knew. He wished he'd known you better. I can see why Linc Cooper and Sean and Ian Alden idolize you. You're one of the most highly-regarded search-and-rescue specialists in the world. But to me—" she touched the scar under his eye "—you're also a tumbleweed and just a little reckless."

"I've never fallen off the edge of a tub while sneaking through someone's bathroom shelves."

When they kissed, Abigail closed her eyes, hearing the ocean, smelling the salt and pine in the air. She wrapped her arms around his hard middle and drew herself tight against him, ignoring any sting of pain in her scraped arm and cut leg. Instead of putting her on her guard, scaring her, the hunger and desire—the soul-deep yearning—that surged through her energized her.

Owen caught her by the waist and lifted her, kissing her throat. She hooked her legs around his hips and gave herself up to the exquisite pleasure of his mouth and tongue on her flesh.

When she threw herself back in his arms, the strain on her thigh was too much, and she gave a small cry at the tug of pain. She immediately tried to cover it with a moan of pure desire, but the man who had her aloft was an expert in pain.

He unhooked her legs and set her back down on the floor. "Okay?"

"A little more wild abandon than my body's ready for."

"Part of your body, anyway."

"Well—there's that." She suddenly felt self-conscious. "Is the offer of driving me around in your truck still open?"

He kissed her on the forehead. "Let's go, Detective."

CHAPTER 21

Ellis Cooper guessed that Abigail was trying to picture the party at his house the day her husband was killed. She stood near the gate that opened into the woods. Although she had to be tired and in pain from that morning's confrontation, she looked focused and alert.

Owen was another matter. Ellis had no idea what he was thinking.

He pointed his walking stick at an arborvitae. "This wasn't here seven years ago. An old maple was here. It was struck by lightning, and I had to have it removed."

"I remember that maple," Owen said. "Doe and I used to climb it as kids."

Ellis tried not to show his awkwardness at Owen's mention of his early childhood there. Throughout the gardens, there were still Garrison touches, reminders of pretty Doe's presence. Ellis had preserved what pleased him, what meant something to him and his own memories.

He decided to ignore his neighbor's remark and went on. "I've added more plants and trees and changed things around since the party. A garden's always a work in progress. It's never finished."

Abigail seized on his comment. "But you're looking forward to starting fresh somewhere else?"

"Yes, absolutely." He refused to admit a contradiction. "I'm just tinkering here at this point."

"I think I'd like tinkering." She ran her fingers over the gate latch, giving no sign that her bandaged forearm hurt. "Did many of your guests that day use the gate to come and go?"

"None that I remember. I wasn't paying that close attention."

"Maybe some were tempted to take a walk on one of the hiking trails," she said.

Ellis shrugged. "Perhaps." He shifted his attention to Owen. "What's this all about?"

But Abigail moved on toward the garden shed, and Owen didn't answer, instead motioning to Ellis that they might as well follow her. Their take-charge manner irritated him. They were on *his* property.

Well, his brother's property.

They came to an old cedar-wood swing, a true treasure that hung from a massive red oak tree. Abigail gave the swing a little push. "Must be a nice spot to sit and read a book."

"I have very little time to read," Ellis said stiffly.

"I love to read. Helps keep me sane."

"My sister used to read here." Owen touched the chain holding the swing to a thick branch. "She must have read *Anne of Green Gables* a dozen times."

Abigail's tight control faltered. "I'm sorry to remind you—"

"Don't be. It's a good memory."

When Owen smiled at her, Ellis was taken aback by the affection he saw. The *physical* attraction. He'd never anticipated a bond forming between Owen Garrison and Abigail Browning. What would Jason say? And Grace. Despite her protestations, she'd always believed Owen was there for the taking. He'd had fleeting relationships but there'd never been anyone with any threat of permanence. It was obvious to Ellis that so long as Owen was available, Grace would assume she could have him if she wanted him.

Ellis quickly returned to the subject at hand. "Most of my guests at the party stayed over by the patio. Some used the steps to go down to the water and check out the cliffs—"

Abigail moved away from the swing, past a mass planting of pink and white astilbes. "Did you turn over all the pictures you took that day to the police?"

"Of course. I didn't take many myself, but I had disposable cameras available for guests. Some snapped pictures and left the cameras. I turned them all over to the police—voluntarily. They didn't have to ask. I'm quite sure they were of no help whatsoever in their investigation. I wish they had been."

"Was Mattie here taking pictures?"

"I didn't hire him to, if that's what you're asking."

"What about on his own?"

"He could have been. Abigail, please—what's this all about?"

She gave him a quick smile. "I know I'm asking a lot of questions. Something's going on around here, and it obviously involves me." She came to the shed. "Mind if I take a look inside?"

"Of course not, but—"

"Don't let us keep you from your dinner."

Ellis sighed, resigned to the intrusion. "I don't mind. You're welcome to join us."

Jason, Grace and Linc were in his kitchen. They were to have dinner together and discuss what was going on with their yardman and Chris Browning's widow—John March's daughter. If word of the attack on Abigail that morning reached the media—and Jason was convinced it would—then all bets were off concerning Grace's appointment. A cold murder case of a friend was a difficult enough public-relations hurdle. But a hot, immediate investigation would be impossible. Ellis had counseled enough Washington types to know her appointment would get pulled at that kind of whiff of scandal. They'd find a graceful way out, but they'd be done with it. She'd worked hard and developed a solid reputation for her expertise in international affairs but none of that would matter.

Owen stepped in front of Abigail and unlatched the shed door, but she went in first. As she moved, Ellis noticed the weapon under her lightweight jacket. He didn't blame her. After that morning, he wouldn't take any chances, either. He followed them inside, more bored than irritated.

"I keep my garden supplies in here," he said. "Mattie's in and out all day when he's working, but—"

Abigail put up a hand. "Hang on."

She drew her weapon. Owen, right behind her, said nothing, as he followed her through the garden materials back to a stack of lobster pots.

Ellis saw now. The pots had been moved. Someone had been back there.

Mattie.

"Is everything okay?" Ellis asked, hearing the note of panic in his voice.

Using one foot, Abigail shoved one of the old wooden pots aside. A wave of fresh air blew into the stuffy, enclosed space, and he realized that the plywood covering the chicken door had been removed.

Owen said quietly, "My grandmother kept chickens."

Abigail bent down and peered through the two-foot opening. "Hell, an ostrich could get through here."

"She wanted to have pigs. My grandfather balked."

"Do you have any eccentric hobbies, other than fast-roping out of helicopters?" But she didn't look around at him, her attention focused on her task as she squatted down and peered through the opening. "Looks as if he crawled through here and made good his escape."

Ellis felt his heartbeat increase. "I haven't seen him. I can't recall hearing anything out of the ordinary."

She stuck her head out the small door and looked around, then pulled it back in, standing up. "I'm not going out there. I don't want to disturb any tracks. Ellis—I need to use your phone and get the police up here."

"Of course." His throat was constricted now; he hoped he wasn't having a heart attack. "But Mattie's in and out of here all the time…"

"Through the chicken door?"

"No. I imagine not."

Owen pushed past him to the front door, but Ellis couldn't move. He leaned on his walking stick, feeling deflated—embarrassed. Had Mattie been hiding in the shed all day? His brother and his niece and nephew would witness Abigail Browning calling the authorities from his phone.

She touched his arm. "Ellis?"

He gave himself a mental shake. "The potential consequences for Grace—"

"Because Mattie Young hid in your garden shed? People aren't that shallow, Ellis, and we still don't have Mattie's side of the story."

Despite her conciliatory words, Abigail's expression told him she didn't need Mattie's side of the story. "Go ahead," he said, motioning for her to move past him.

She shook her head. "You first."

"What? Oh." He inhaled through his nose, irritated now. "You want to be the last one out. You don't want to risk that I might tamper with evidence."

She didn't answer.

Ellis walked out into the beautiful evening air and stood next to Owen. "Abigail won't care who she catches in the cross fire," he said, more to himself than to the man next to him. "She never has."

"She cares. She just can't let it stop her."

"How can you be so calm?"

Never one to overreact, Owen gave him a wry smile. "I don't know about you, Ellis, but I'm having a hard time thinking anyone who'd crawl out of a chicken door is all that dangerous."

Ellis tried to return the smile and match his neighbor's sense of humor, but he couldn't. He didn't have Owen's knack for distancing himself from a difficult situation in order to maintain his composure. Owen had learned to thrive in a crisis. Ellis was different. He did what he had to do, but he didn't look for adrenaline highs. He preferred a quiet life. He didn't need to get out there like Grace and subject himself to the scrutiny of a background check, political gamesmanship, having his every decision examined and politicized. Nor did he need to put his life on the line the way Owen did.

And Abigail.

She was complicated, and yet, right now, her mission was simple and straightforward. Find Mattie. Figure out if he was Chris's killer.

But as he used his walking stick to make his way back across the yard, all Ellis could think was that his own life was spinning out of control. It had been for a long time. He'd taken too long to see what was happening. Now he was beginning to realize that the only way to stop it—to bring his life back into balance—was to be bold.

He wasn't like Abigail and Owen, he thought. Boldness and courage weren't in his nature.

"You're a behind the scenes type, Ellis," Jason had told him a thousand times. *"You get other people to do what needs to be done."*

He'd meant it as a compliment.

Ellis glanced back at the shed, the door swung wide open. *Where are you, Mattie? What have you done?*

Spinning, spinning.

Calming himself, Ellis placed a palm on his rapidly beating heart and took a deep breath. He hated being thrust in the limelight, but now he had no choice. The police would arrive in droves. They'd have search teams, dogs— who knew what.

Out of control.

It wasn't his brother or his niece who needed his counsel this time.

This time, it was his turn to listen to his own good advice.

Evening fog rolled in over the island, unexpected, impenetrable, as if Mattie Young had conjured it up himself, willed it to cover his tracks and slow the search for him.

As he took his plate to the sink in his uncle's perfect kitchen, Linc realized he was rooting for Mattie, and not just because of the blackmail and how terrified he was to have anyone find out about it.

He was rooting for Mattie because the guy was such a loser, and everyone was against him. Everyone was after him. Linc had seen cops go off through the gate, into the woods, with a German shepherd the size of a tiger.

The stupid bastard didn't stand a chance.

Maybe he'd take the four grand and start fresh. Maybe he'd hit bottom this time, finally, and blackmailing Linc over something he'd done at thirteen would turn him around.

Attacking Abigail. Hiding in a garden shed. Crawling out of a chicken door.

He'd see what a creep he was and decide he wanted a different life for himself.

And, Linc realized, he was rooting for Mattie because of his father's attitude.

The great Jason Cooper, who'd been born to privilege, who'd never had to fight alcoholism—who'd never lost a friend to murder.

Linc knew his father had never cared about Chris Browning. That his murder remained unsolved and Chris's widow stayed on the case, relentless, not giving a damn who she pissed off, was just an annoyance to him.

"Linc?" A note of concern had crept into his father's voice, but Linc had no illusions that it was about *him*. His father would only worry that his afterthought of a son would do something to attract police attention. "Son, why don't you have a cup of tea with us. Then we'll go home. Mattie will have an explanation for why he was in the shed."

To pressure me with Abigail's missing necklace. Linc

rinsed off his plate. It was handmade pottery, as carefully chosen as everything else in his uncle's kitchen—the cool tile floors, the muted colors, the custom cabinets. Dinner had been clay-pot chicken with rosemary from the garden, locally grown early peas, crusty bread from a Bar Harbor bakery. Linc had shoved his food around his plate, pretending to eat.

"I don't want tea," he said, turning from the sink.

Grace sighed, her reserves worn thin. "Oh, Linc. This day's been difficult enough without you getting sullen."

"I'm going to look for Mattie."

"No!"

His sister jumped up, but their father shook his head, saying calmly, "Let him go. The mosquitoes will chase him inside soon enough."

"But Mattie *attacked* someone today."

"Abigail," Jason said, as if that explained everything.

Grace spun around at him. "You make it sound as if she deserved what she got."

"Not deserved." He didn't raise his voice. "She's capable, Grace. She's an experienced homicide detective. She can handle herself."

"Mattie could have slit her throat today."

"I don't think so. He had a rusted saw that probably hadn't been sharpened in fifteen years, and he had only a split second to act—not enough of an opening for someone of his abilities and limitations to have succeeded in doing more than what he did."

"You can be so calculating sometimes," Grace said.

"I'm just trying to be objective and understand the situation."

Linc had heard enough. He let the screen door bang shut

on his way out. Abigail and Owen had headed out to look for Mattie even before the police had arrived, but as well as they knew their way around the surrounding woods, Mattie knew them better. He'd grown up there, he'd photographed them. With the fog and the oncoming darkness, no one would find him unless he wanted to be found.

The police hadn't asked Linc outright if he'd seen Mattie. He hadn't volunteered what he knew, but he hadn't lied.

One of the FBI agents—Special Agent Capozza—stood in front of the shed door, brushing at a cloud of mosquitoes hovering over him.

Linc gave him a sympathetic smile. "They're bad tonight, aren't they? Early morning and early evening are the worst times. You want to be careful of West Nile." He peered past him into the shed. "Was Mattie in there for sure?"

"You'll have to talk to Lieutenant Beeler or Chief Alden."

"Right. Sorry."

Capozza whacked a mosquito on his arm, grimacing when it spurted blood. "Looks like I got that one too late. Your father and sister still here?"

"They're having tea in the kitchen. I want to go look for Mattie."

"Why?"

Linc felt a surge of emotion. "Because he's my friend. Because I don't think he'd ever hurt anyone. I don't want some trigger-happy cop to shoot him just because—"

"Whoa, whoa. Watch what you say, Mr. Cooper."

"He didn't kill Chris Browning."

The FBI agent tilted his head back and eyed Linc. "Why do you say that?"

"Chris was my friend, too. And he was Mattie's friend."

"Sounds like everyone's friends up here." Capozza

wasn't paying attention to the mosquitoes now. "But we've got a string of unsolved burglaries, an unsolved attack and robbery, an unsolved murder, and now—"

"I need to go." Linc sniffled, pushing back an urge to cry. "Ellis has bug repellent inside if you want some."

"Suppose you and I go in together and find it?"

"What?"

"I'd like to talk to you."

An hour later, Linc sat stiffly in his sister's car as they headed back to Somes Sound. She was driving too fast for the conditions. Thick fog, high emotion. He was too scared to say anything in case he threw off her concentration and she wrapped them around a tree.

"What did you and Special Agent Capozza talk about?"

"Nothing much. How well I knew Chris. How well I know Mattie. I didn't tell him anything people around here don't already know." *I didn't tell him about the blackmail and the four grand.*

"Did he ask about me?" She gripped the wheel with both hands. "Because I deserve to know if he did."

"He was trying to get all our relationships straight in his head. That's all."

She took in his words with a nod. "I don't want anything to happen to Mattie, but if it does, it's not my doing. Or yours. Or Father's, no matter how frustrating he can be. And Ellis—did you see him, Linc? He's a wreck."

"He just doesn't want Mattie to slit his wrists under one of his rhododendrons."

"Linc!" She pounded on the brake, the car screeching to a halt in the middle of the fog-enshrouded road. "Damn you. You inconsiderate little bastard. I've stood by you as you've flunked out and gotten yourself thrown out of school after school."

"Two."

"Two colleges. How many prep schools? Father and I both pulled strings to get you into good schools. He's not an easy man, but he's only ever wanted the best for you."

"What's good for me is good for him."

"Just *stop*."

Linc sank back into his seat and sighed, as if he didn't care how upset she was. "I wish you'd start driving before someone rear-ends us."

"I was proud of you for going to Owen and asking him to train you." Grace was half crying. "I hope he does. I hope it works out. You can make a difference, Linc, if you'd stop feeling sorry for yourself and being mad at the world."

"Who says I want to make a difference? Maybe I just want to train with Owen so I can look good."

"He'd see through you in a heartbeat."

Linc paused for a beat. "If you admire him so much, why don't you marry him?"

"We've never had that kind of interest in each other."

"Because you're in love with a dead man."

His sister reacted instantly, slapping him across the face.

In the darkness, his face stinging, Linc could see tears shining in her eyes as she turned back to the wheel and pressed her foot on the gas.

"Oh, shit." He choked back a sob. "Shit, Grace. I'm sorry."

"I'm not staying here. I'll leave tomorrow. I have plenty to do back in Washington." She was crying openly now. "Linc—my God, Linc. I love you. I don't want anything bad to happen to you."

"Nothing will, Grace. I promise."

"I'm here for you. Always. Do you understand?"

Tell her. But he couldn't. "I do understand. And you—I'm here for you, too."

She smiled at him, tears still streaming down her face. "I don't think anyone's ever said that to me before."

"I mean it. Grace—I really am sorry about what I said. About Chris."

"Chris. My God, Linc. I did love him." She sucked in a breath, slowing in the thickening fog. "We were just never meant to be."

"Did he ever love you?"

"He loved Abigail."

CHAPTER 22

I don't want to think about death tonight.

I want to think about love.

I don't want to think about violence.

Again. Love.

I don't want to hear Abigail's voice.

Love.

My heart bursts with a love so deep and pure and fulfilling that it alone is all I need to sustain me.

So few ever have this kind of love in their lives.

I don't pity them so much as I stand apart from them.

Separate.

Alone.

Isolated.

All those words come to mind and yet don't describe how I feel, because they imply loneliness and desperation. Incompleteness. But I am not lonely or desperate or incomplete.

Because of my love.

I love.

It's not just a state of being but of action.

Love as a verb.

I've lied. I've misled. I've cried. I've killed.

Ways of loving. All of them.

I feel so free, writing in this stream of consciousness manner. Allowing myself to put aside all my inhibitions.

I don't want to kill again but to say I won't is to say my ability to love has weakened.

And it hasn't.

It won't.

Not ever.

CHAPTER 23

Wherever Mattie was, he'd be there through the night. Abigail didn't like the idea, but who did? The warm day had turned cool with nightfall and the fog. If he didn't have proper attire, a good blanket, water, food—if he panicked and got lost, or kept running in the woods—then anything could happen.

She watched Owen, crouched down on one knee, build a fire in his woodstove. She'd pulled a fleece throw over her as she sat in one of his fireside chairs, but he showed no sign of cold or fatigue. "If you'd climbed Cadillac and got whacked today, you'd be as wiped out as I am," she said.

"You didn't climb up Cadillac. You drove up."

"I walked all over the summit. And it was freaking dawn. That counts."

He looked back over his shoulder at her. "The only reason you're shivering is because of what you have on."

"Not enough?"

He turned back to his fire-building. "Depends on how you look at that one."

She gave him a shove in the back with her foot. She'd left her wet shoes at the door. "You know what I mean."

"You're in the wrong clothes for charging through the woods in these conditions."

"And you?"

He struck a match. "I'm fine."

"Uh-uh. You're in jeans. Jeans aren't the best choice for cool, wet conditions. They're not good insulators, especially when wet. See? Not bad for a city cop."

The kindling and rolled-up newspapers caught fire, bright flames crackling as Owen shut the screen and leaned back on his outstretched arms, stretching out his legs. His toes were almost in the fire. He'd taken off his shoes, too. His feet struck her as casual, intimate.

They'd joined the search for Mattie, but the trail was cold, visibility marginal. Any sign of him—footsteps, trampled plants—ended after a few feet. He could be anywhere.

"Who knows about Mattie," Abigail said. "I've never seen him in anything approaching clothing appropriate for a night out in the elements."

"He could have supplies with him."

"Or he could be shacked up with a friend, or hiding on some derelict pal's clunker of a boat. He could have caught a ride off the island with someone…"

"Abigail—"

"I'm just saying." She breathed out a sigh. "I don't want to find him dead, Owen. No one does."

"Do you have any clue what he's up to?"

She shook her head. "I wish I did."

"Think he's your caller?"

"I don't know. The caller supposedly wants to help—" She broke off. "Whatever Mattie's doing, it's not helping."

"Your caller—whether it's Mattie or someone else— isn't helping, either. Just stirring the pot."

"Good point."

The local and state police and the two FBI agents had all departed from Ellis Cooper's house. Ellis had pointedly refused to have any cruisers posted in his driveway, insisting to Lou Beeler that he wasn't afraid of Mattie—that it wasn't as if Mattie had done anything horrible—if he'd done anything at all.

"Ellis might as well have said I was bad luck," Abigail went on.

"He's upset."

"Jason and Grace weren't much better. But I only came up here after I got the first call. Maybe whatever Mattie's up to has more to do with what the Coopers have going on than with me. The appointment, the sale of the house—they could be the catalyst."

"Could be," Owen said.

She slipped her arms over his shoulders and down his chest, leaning forward and touching her cheek to his. "You don't care, do you?"

He grabbed her hand. "At the moment, no." And in one move, he'd lifted her off her chair and over his shoulders, onto his lap, his arms circled around her. He grinned. "I had a feeling you wouldn't put up a fight."

"Fight? I'm injured."

"I thought it was just a few scratches."

She draped her arms around his neck. "It is. Traipsing over hill and dale after Mattie didn't hurt my leg. It's a little stiff, but that's it." She smiled, feeling the heat of the fire on her back. "I just didn't want you to think I'm easy."

"Easy isn't the first word that comes to my mind when I think of you. More like determined, single-minded, dedicated..."

She rolled her eyes. "Gee, I'm feeling better already."

He tightened his hold on her. "Attractive. Sexy. Brown-eyed."

"Shapely?"

He laughed. "Definitely."

"Liar. I'm not shapely. I'm–" she thought a moment "—fit."

"That's it," he said, his mouth lowering to hers. "I could watch you trek up and down mountains all day with that fit butt of yours."

"Bastard," she said with a laugh, their lips coming together before she could add anything else.

She opened her mouth to the kiss, giving a small gasp at the urgency with which he responded—all eagerness and heat. There was nothing tentative about him. He wasn't tip-toeing around what he wanted.

He lifted her shirt and placed his palm, warm from the fire, on her stomach. "Stay with me tonight."

"You can trust me not to go out a window on a bedsheet."

"I'm not talking about staying in a guest room."

"Owen..."

He eased his palm higher up her abdomen and smiled. "Yes, Abigail?"

"You're direct, aren't you?"

Without answering, he smoothed his palm over one breast, outlining the shape of it, curving his fingers around the nipple. "Lace," he said. "Somehow I expected a lace bra, Detective."

"Ah-ha. So you've been imagining what kind of bra I wear."

"And you? Want to admit what you've been imagining about me?"

She smiled. "No."

He slid her off his lap and got to his feet, tossing another log on the fire, then caught her by her hand and helped her up. The fresh chunk of wood caught fire with a crackle and a spark of heat. Owen didn't let go of her hand. They walked together down a short hall to his bedroom, all dark woods and deep, earthy colors. The air was cooler there, away from the woodstove.

"It's a beautiful spot," Abigail said.

He lifted her into his arms and laid her on his bed, smoothing back her short curls. "Don't think for a change. But if anything doesn't feel right—"

"I won't shoot you. I promise."

He ignored her attempt at humor and kissed her forehead, her nose. "Just tell me."

She touched her fingertips to his mouth. "I will. Thank you."

They helped each other get undressed, her shirt going first, her lacy bra and underpants going last. Owen was very careful of her bandaged scratches, but she hardly noticed them at all, her entire body screaming out not with pain but desire, an ache that had nothing to do with getting attacked with a drywall saw.

"Owen," Abigail said, letting her mind spin away from all that had brought her to Mt. Desert. "I like saying your name."

She ran her hands up his back, skimming the ripple of scars, of hard muscle. She had nothing on him when it came to being fit. Every inch of him betrayed the work he did. He was tough, sexy, focused and absolutely relentless.

"Stop thinking," he whispered, as if he'd been reading her mind.

"I'm not thinking. Not really. I'm feeling your scars." Her fingertips caught the tip of his erection. "I guess that's not a scar."

"I hope to hell not."

He took her nipple into his mouth, scraped his teeth erotically over it, then down her stomach, and lower. There were no more words after that. And, she thought, no going back. She moved under him, guiding him to her. He eased into her just a little, as if to give her a chance to change her mind, but she responded by taking him deep inside her.

That was all he required. She could feel his shudder of total abandon as he thrust into her. She threw her arms over her head and shut her eyes, sensations washing over her, emotion and physical need melting together, indistinguishable.

He didn't slacken his pace, didn't relent. She grabbed hold of his hips and drove him even deeper into her. She knew she was on the edge. She tried to hold back, but he urged her on, thrusting faster, harder, until she was spiraling into an orgasm that took over her entire body. She cried out, but still he didn't stop, taking her higher, deeper, holding her there.

"Owen!"

She shattered and melted into the warm bed under her. She didn't move. Couldn't.

But he could, and did, still hard inside her, but moving more slowly now, as if to test her, tempt her, make her prove to him that she was spent.

Amazingly, her body responded. Desire coursed through

her like a hot, oozing trickle that turned quickly to a flood, overwhelming everything in its path. She clutched his arms, digging her fingers into his muscles as he quickened his pace, his energy and stamina without limit.

For an instant, their eyes locked.

Then he smiled, shuddering with his own release, even as she pulled herself up against his chest and felt the heat there, tasted his sweat as her body convulsed yet again, this time with him.

They collapsed together, then fell onto their backs, breathing hard.

Bit by bit, the room came back into focus. The wood walls. The rich colors. Abigail could smell the fire in the other room and hear the sigh of the ocean, the rhythmic hoot of a nearby owl.

She'd just made love to Owen Garrison.

She hadn't held back even a little. She sat up, aware of her nakedness. In the dim light, she could see spots reddened by his teeth and tongue, still sensitized. A touch—just a glance, probably—and she'd be fired up again, eager for more wild sex.

His eyes drifted from her breasts downward and back again with a frankness she found both comforting and unbelievably erotic. He made no effort to cover himself. She could see it wouldn't be long before he was ready to take her again.

"You're one good-looking bastard," she told him.

He sat up. "Am I?"

"You know damn well you are. A good-looking daredevil. And bloody rich, too."

"And?"

"Oh, there should be more, should there? Glutton. Well, you're also good at what you do, and committed to it, and—" All the fun went out of her tone, and she finished. "Rootless."

"All true. Everything you say." He sat up halfway and flicked his tongue over her nipple. "Every word."

She gulped in a breath. "Owen…"

He flicked his tongue over her nipple again. "I think you're the sexiest woman I've ever met." He cupped his lips around the nipple, holding it in his mouth as his tongue did its work and she started to melt. He released it, saying, "I love your dark eyes," then captured it again.

Barely able to sit up any longer, Abigail ran one hand up his back. "Never mind my eyes. I'm—"

"And your heart." He let go of her nipple and sat up higher, so that his eyes were level with hers. "I love your heart. You're not cynical. You've seen the worst that human nature can offer, and you still believe in the rest of us."

She sank back onto the bed, taking him with her. "Don't be too sure," she whispered. "Just make love to me again. Now. If you can…."

"Oh, I can," he whispered back, taking her hand and guiding it to him.

As she stroked him, she pressed him against her most sensitive flesh, slowly, the hard tip inflaming her. When he entered her this time, he didn't move. He filled her up with him and held her close.

"I'm falling in love with you, Abigail," he said. "I have been for a long time."

This time, their lovemaking was slow and tender as they explored each other, giving as well as taking, a meeting of souls and not just of bodies. She could feel his release starting and moved in such a way to heighten it. He moaned, shuddering with each thrust.

She didn't think she'd have another orgasm—didn't care—but before she realized what was happening, it was upon her, rocking her to her core.

"Owen," she said. "Owen, I…"

But she couldn't get another word out. She was done, exhausted. Satiated. She rolled into him, aware only of his arms around her as she fell asleep.

Doyle kissed his sons good-night and lumbered downstairs as if he were a million years old. Will Browning in his last days at ninety-five had walked with more of a spring in his step.

No one thought this thing with Mattie would end well.

He'd gone on self-destructive binges before, but luck and friends would walk him back from the brink. This time, luck meant not that he'd passed out before getting behind the wheel of a car but that Abigail Browning hadn't caught him cutting her phone wires or pawing through her house. Armed or not, she'd have nailed his skinny ass.

Luck meant he hadn't nicked her deeper with the drywall saw.

And friends.

Mattie might have other friends he could count on, but Doyle was through. The DUI over the winter had just about done him in. If Mattie had been bugging Abigail with the anonymous calls—if he'd *attacked* her—there was just no going back to any kind of tolerance between them. Any kind of friendship, no matter how ragged.

The stupid bastard was working an angle.

It was one thing to hurt himself. It was another thing altogether to hurt other people.

And yet when he sat down at his computer and opened up an e-mail to Katie, Doyle's first words betrayed his anguish. "I'm worried about Mattie."

CHAPTER 24

Bob O'Reilly took one look at Abigail on her front doorstep and scowled. "Damn it, Browning."

"What? Do I have dirt on my nose or something?"

But she knew what he meant. With the fog burning off, she'd put on shorts and a T-shirt, and he could see her scraped arm—she'd pulled off the gauze wrap—and the lower edge of her bandaged thigh.

"Looks like you need a refresher on how to fight off a man with a saw."

"I did fight him off."

It was eight o'clock in the morning, but she'd awakened early in Owen's bed and beat a path back to her place for a hot shower, coffee and a get-a-grip session with herself. A good thing, because she wouldn't have wanted O'Reilly showing up unannounced and not finding her there. Having him privy to her love life or lack thereof in Boston was bad enough—one of the unintended consequences of him living two floors above her.

Explaining Owen Garrison would have been impossible. Abigail wasn't sure she understood what had happened last night herself. Whatever was going on between them wasn't just a fling. She knew that much.

"What are you doing here?" she asked Bob. "Taking a break from city life? Is it too hot in Boston, or is there nothing for an experienced detective like yourself to do?"

"You know why I'm here."

She did, indeed. She'd have headed north if he'd been the one attacked.

"Scoop would be here, but he's working a case right now. He said I have his permission to smack you up the side of the head for him, too."

"And you boys wonder why you have trouble with women."

"I don't have trouble with women. It's relationships that kill me."

"This is what I'm saying."

He stood at the bottom of the steps. He wore jeans and a navy polo shirt, yet no one would mistake him for anything but a cop. "And you're not a woman. You're a detective."

"Ha-ha."

He walked up the steps, and she moved aside, letting him go in first. He made a face at the brightly-colored entry. "The blue's a change."

"Doesn't it remind you of lupine?"

"Right. Yeah. First thing I thought of."

She smiled. Bob was even worse with plants than she was. "Lupines aren't native to Maine, actually. They're a Japanese import. They've naturalized."

"Been reading about lupines?"

"Ellis Cooper told me."

"Ellis, the amateur landscape designer whose brother is about to sell his summer house out from under him."

"He has a pink lupine in his garden that's incredible."

Bob moved into her front room; he'd obviously heard enough about lupines. "Your assailant was hiding in here?" He didn't tone down his skepticism. "How the hell did you miss him?"

"Because he wasn't in here." She walked past him into the back room and pointed to the short hall that led past the cellar door and into the kitchen. "He must have heard me coming and ducked in there."

"Why not just run through the kitchen and out the front door?"

"Because I'd have heard him and followed him."

"And he knew that," Bob said with just a hint of a challenge.

"It's a logical conclusion—"

"For someone who knows you're a police officer." He nodded in agreement. "Otherwise, you'd just get out of here and try not to be seen."

"Another indicator it was Mattie Young."

"No word on his whereabouts?"

Abigail shook her head. "You heard he was holed up in Ellis's garden shed?"

"Yeah. Lou Beeler gave me a call late last night."

"Lou? Why?"

Bob's expression told her that he wasn't buying any pretense of confusion on her part. He said, "No one wants to see you get hurt or spin out of control."

"Thank you for your concern, but—"

"But nothing." He pulled open her porch door, the cool morning breeze gusting into the small room. "Turning out to be a nice day. I left Boston at two o'clock this morning."

"If you want to take a nap, you're welcome to crash upstairs."

"I don't want to take a nap, Abigail."

At least he was using her first name again. "Coffee?"

"I drank a gallon on the way up here." Standing in the doorway, he looked back, scanning her half-gutted room. "You do all this work yourself?"

She nodded. "Wielding a sledgehammer is a great tension reliever. Helps focus the mind."

"I'd have helped. Scoop, too."

"I know."

"Leave the rest for us. We can all come up one weekend—"

"Bob, I'm not going back to Boston until I figure out what's going on up here."

"Yeah." He gave her a grudging smile. "It was worth a try."

"At least let me make you breakfast," she said.

But he was staring out at the water, tufts of fog yet to burn off, lobster boats making their way to the buoys that marked their dozens of pots. "It's gorgeous here. I remember when I first stood right in this spot. The scenery literally takes your breath away." Without turning, he went on, "I couldn't help thinking what a damn shame it was for this beauty to be marred by the memories you have."

"I have good memories, too. They're not all bad." She sat on the edge of a chair. "You're not here just because a Maine state detective called you."

Bob kept his gaze on the water. "You've got a few spots of fog that haven't burned off yet. Kind of neat looking."

"Bob."

"The FBI stopped by to talk to Scoop and me about you."

Abigail didn't react. "Because of Grace Cooper's background check?"

He turned to her with a half grin. "We didn't get that far."

"Scoop was in a bad mood?"

"That and your father called right while these G-men were sitting in my living room."

Abigail sprang up. "My father called *you?*"

"We knew each other in the old days."

"So?"

"Better he should call me about his daughter than about five thousand other people he could have called, don't you think?"

She was only slightly mollified. "What did he want?"

"For me to come up here."

"And here you are. Great, Bob. Just great."

"He talked to me as a father, not—"

"Not as the FBI director? And you didn't think of his position for one second, did you?"

O'Reilly shrugged off her irritation. "He asked me to put eyes on you and reassure him you were all right. If he came up here himself, it'd be a show. You know that."

And if he'd called—which he probably had tried to—she wouldn't have been there to answer the phone, but that was a point Abigail preferred to keep to herself.

"Some asshole comes after my kid with a saw," Bob said, "I'd want to know she was all right, too. It's natural. It's got nothing to do with what's going on up here or what you're doing or not doing."

"It's got everything to do with what's going on up here. He wants to make sure it's not about him—that someone's not using Chris's death to play games with my head and get at his somehow."

"That'd be a stretch."

She shrugged. "Anything's possible. Isn't that what my father told you?"

"You and your dad aren't as different as you think." Bob paused, nodding at her waterfront. "Isn't that your neighbor? Batman Garrison. Guy can move on those rocks, can't he? He's like a billy goat."

"Owen's here?"

O'Reilly must have heard something in her voice, because he turned to her. "Browning, are you blushing?"

"I never blush." She walked to the door, but he didn't move aside. "I should go down there and meet him. Maybe he has news."

Bob didn't budge. "He patch up your injuries for you?"

"What difference does that make? He's trained in first aid."

"So he did patch you up. I'll be damned. Should I report this to your father?"

"You should mind your own damn business."

Her half-faked irritation only further confirmed whatever he was thinking—and she had a fair idea of what it was. His grin broadened. "So it's not just the weird shit happening that's keeping you up here."

"If you don't mind, I'd like to go out to see what he wants."

"Am I in your way, Detective?"

"Bob."

"Don't you want me to meet your neighbor? I've seen him a couple times when I've been up here, but he's usually off to a disaster. We've never officially met."

"You don't need to meet now."

"Abigail? Hell—are you *sleeping* with this guy?"

"Bob."

"You get involved with Batman, and everything changes. You know that, right?"

He wasn't letting her go to Owen without him. "You're a pain in the neck, Bob. You know that, right?"

He ignored her. "You get involved with a guy like Scoop, nothing changes. You're both a couple of working stiffs, never mind who your father is. You rent out one of your apartments, put his TV set and stereo system in with your IKEA stuff, and that's it. You're done. With Owen Garrison—" Bob squinted out at the rocks. "Do you know who the Garrisons are? Who he is?"

"Yes, Bob, I know who the Garrisons are, and I know who Owen is. And why come up with Scoop for your hypothetical? Why not that cute guy in narcotics?"

"Abigail, the Garrisons used to *own* this island."

"Not all of it."

"The half the Rockefellers didn't own."

"His grandmother grew up dirt-poor in Texas. She kept chickens up here. She wanted to keep pigs, but her husband—"

"The guy throws himself into the mouth of danger every chance he gets."

Maybe that described why he made love to her, she thought. He'd gotten turned on by the risk of having a relationship with her. *The forbidden woman.* But she found herself smiling at the thought.

As Owen crossed her narrow strip of yard, Bob elbowed her, still not letting her get past him in the doorway. "He's even better-looking than that guy in narcotics."

Owen trotted up the porch steps. Abigail could have

smacked Bob for successfully stalling her long enough to make sure she didn't get a word with Owen alone first.

Bob opened up the door as if he owned the place, and Abigail, with no other real option, stepped back out of the way and made polite introductions. She didn't explain why Bob was there. She didn't ask why Owen was there.

Owen, casually dressed, as good-looking as ever, handed her a small paper bag. "You left these at my house."

She gave him a questioning look.

"Your socks."

Avoiding Bob, Abigail snatched the paper bag and dumped it on a chair. "Thanks."

"Doyle stopped by," Owen said. "They found Mattie's bike in the woods. It was hidden off a hiking trail behind Ellis's place. No sign of him. Lou Beeler asked Doyle to let you know, and Doyle asked me—"

Bob snorted. "Sounds like no one wants to talk to you, Abigail."

"Everyone's busy." She sighed, then addressed Owen. "Bob's humor takes some getting used to. I should get rolling. I want to help search for Mattie." She turned, motioning at her mostly gutted room. "Never mind that everyone would rather I stay here and work on my walls." She frowned, but her mind had gone elsewhere. "What's that?"

Before either man could respond, Abigail was across the room, kneeling on the floor, picking up a tiny white ball. She held it up in the light. "It's a pearl."

Bob was there instantly, and she placed the pearl into his big hands.

"How did the crime scene guys miss this yesterday?" Bob asked.

"We all missed it. We weren't looking for pearls."

"The wall," Owen said.

He didn't need to explain further. They all recognized it as the same wall that she and Chris had worked on the morning before she was attacked and robbed.

Abigail, still on her knees, leaned into the gutted portion and reached down inside the wall, lowering her arm as far as she could, wiggling her fingers for any more pearls. "That pearl didn't jump out onto the floor by itself," she said, touching something soft and dry with her fingers. "Gross. I think I hit mouse pooh."

Neither man smiled at her attempt at humor. She dug through a ball of fuzzy gunk of some kind, scraping her already bloodied arm on a two-by-six.

"Let me do that," Bob said.

"Your arm's too big. Owen's, too."

She scooped up a brown-and-gray heap and dumped it onto the floor.

Another pearl, covered in dust, rolled out.

And, in the middle of the fuzz, Abigail saw her grandmother's cameo pendant.

She dropped back onto her heels, her arm stinging, her cut leg aching. "My necklace was in the wall all this time. And Mattie—" She took in a breath, calming herself. "That bastard knew."

Owen lowered a hand to her and helped her to her feet. "That's what he was after yesterday."

"He must have used the drywall saw to dig into the wall and hook the necklace." She pushed a hand through her hair. "*Damn* him."

Bob frowned at the heap of dust, mouse droppings, mouse fur, pearl and cameo. "Why go after it now? Why not seven years ago?"

"Because I was gutting walls. He knew I'd find it. I'll call Doyle and Lou." She caught her breath and faked a smile. "Heck. Now maybe they'll want to talk to me."

If Lou Beeler wanted to smack his detectives or himself for having missed the pearl, he never let on. But he obviously wasn't happy about it. He looked as if he could kick out the rest of the half-gutted wall, a feeling Abigail well understood. She leaned against the doorway to the front room, her house filling up with local and state cops. Doyle Alden was still en route—she had no desire to see him. Mattie Young was a lifelong friend, and discovery of the necklace would just be another implication for Mattie, another blow for Doyle to absorb.

And somehow Abigail felt responsible. If she hadn't come along, would Chris still be alive? Would Mattie have straightened out and become the kind of photographer everyone believed he was meant to be?

She hadn't sat down since Lou had arrived, tight and preoccupied but also, she thought, energized. Discovery of the pearls and the cameo pendant were breaks. Although she hadn't been a detective for as long as he had and didn't have a seven-year cold case, Abigail thought she understood how he felt.

If anyone could identify with Detective Lieutenant Beeler, it was Bob O'Reilly, but he was staying out of the way—if not, Abigail noticed, out of earshot.

Owen had excused himself as soon as Lou had told him he could go or stay. She'd known he would leave. He would consider his presence an unnecessary distraction.

Lou shoved his hands into his pants pockets. "It never occurred to me the thief dropped your necklace into the wall," he said. "Doyle Alden was the responding officer when it was stolen, but I did a walk-through here after your husband was killed. And I did the final walk-through yesterday."

Abigail pictured the back room and the descriptions she'd written so many times in her journals of how she'd heard the clatter of tools, felt the breeze, smelled the salt and roses in the air. Every detail of what had happened.

"I've looked at that wall for seven years," she said. "Some of the best detectives in Boston have looked at that wall for seven years. It never occurred to us, either."

That didn't mollify Lou. "Why toss the damn thing into the wall?"

"I don't know. It doesn't make sense."

"I figure the thief—"

"Mattie," she said.

Lou wasn't going that far. "It looks that way, I know, but it's possible the real thief confessed to Mattie, or he saw what happened and just has never said."

"I suppose."

He pulled his hands out of his pockets and eyed her, not without sympathy. "Must be tough for you right now."

"I'm just trying to wrap my head around what happened." She had no intention of getting into her emotions right now. "I interrupted you. You figure the thief what?"

Lou sighed, then went on. "I figure he didn't expect you. He already had the necklace when you woke up from your nap, and once he hit you, he knew he didn't want to get caught with it. He panicked and did the first thing that came to his mind."

"Dropped it in the wall and ran."

"It's logical, not that I think he was using logic."

"There's a perfectly good ocean right out my door. If he wanted to get rid of it, why not toss it in the ocean? Much less likely to be found there."

"You could have come to and seen him. If he'd tried to run with it, he could have been caught. Ellis Cooper's guests were down this way during the party to check out the cliffs. A wonder he wasn't spotted as it was."

But Lou and his detectives had questioned every one of Ellis's guests that day, and no one had seen anyone.

Then again, would anyone have noticed Mattie Young?

"We'll go through every piece of dust in that wall, Abigail," Lou said, moving past her into the front room. "And we'll keep an open mind."

She gave him a grudging smile. "If you're reminding me of the dangers of jumping to conclusions, your point is well taken. I shouldn't have dug into the wall. I should have waited for the crime scene guys." She glanced back at her fellow BPD detective in the entry. "O'Reilly, why didn't you stop me?"

He shrugged. "Didn't seem like a good idea at the time."

"I just…"

She couldn't go on. She saw herself on her wedding day, putting on the pearl-and-cameo necklace with her grandmother and mother watching her, happy for her, none of them ever imagining the horror and tragedy that would come their way in a matter of days.

And not because of the necklace.

The thief—the person who'd attacked her seven years ago—had never been after the necklace.

It was nothing she needed to tell either detective with her.

"Lou, what else do you know?" She spoke quietly, saw

him stiffen as he stopped, his back to her. She went on. "What haven't you told me all these years?"

He turned back to her. "Lab guys will be here any sec—"

She swallowed. "I should talk to my father, shouldn't I?"

"You should always talk to your father." He cleared his throat and nodded to Bob. "Good to meet you, finally."

"You, too, Lieutenant," Bob said, stepping aside for Lou to pass him.

After Lou headed outside to meet more arriving officers, Abigail frowned at O'Reilly. "'Finally?' What does that mean? Have you two talked behind my back more than I think you have?"

"Probably."

"I don't like being thought of as a complication."

"Well, you are. Tough. You're also a damn good detective. If not for you, Boston would have a few more cretins on the street."

She hadn't expected any kind of compliment, not today. "Thanks for that, Bob."

"I'm just stating the facts. I'm not trying to be nice." His big frame took up most of the doorway. "Abigail. Detective Browning. You get burned up here—you cross the line—I can't help you."

"Understood."

"Having a father who's the director of the FBI isn't a point in your favor. It's not why you're a detective today. Neither is having the unsolved murder of a loved one in your background. These are liabilities."

"I like to think I'm a detective today because of my own hard work."

"You are. You didn't let your liabilities sink you." He made a face, as if he'd been planning what to say to her but, now that he was saying it, didn't like it. "I'm being blunt here, but I have to be. Your liabilities set you apart. They make people look at you and wonder, and that's not good. I've stood up for you because you should have a chance to prove yourself on your own merits. And you have."

"Your faith in me means a lot."

"Yeah. That's great. I'll tell Scoop that we need to keep that in mind when reporters are camped out on our front stoop." But O'Reilly wasn't finished. "Tell me, kid. What are you going to do if you come face-to-face with Chris's killer? Have you thought about that?"

"Every day for the past seven years."

He wasn't satisfied. "Do you see yourself calling 911?"

"Bob, I know what you're getting at."

"Or do you see yourself taking out your Glock and pulling the trigger and blowing this guy's head off?"

"I see Chris." Abigail crossed her arms on her chest and refused to look at her friend and mentor, a man with almost thirty years of law enforcement experience. "I see him nodding and saying, 'That's the one, babe. That's the one who killed me.'"

Bob had no response. He walked into the front room and stood next to her. Lou had posted troopers at the porch and hall doors. No one was touching his seven-year-old crime scene wall.

"Beautiful spot," O'Reilly said, looking out at the ocean. "I'm starving, though. Anyone up here serve lobster this early?"

CHAPTER 25

Grace picked at a wild raspberry scone on the screen porch overlooking Somes Sound, possibly her favorite spot on earth. Mattie had wanted to make love to her out there when she'd slipped away from Washington for a long off-season weekend with him, months before Chris's death, but she'd refused. She'd known, even then, at the height of their affair, that she and Mattie Young weren't meant to last.

But Chris had met Abigail by then, and when Grace had seen them together, she'd known he was lost to her.

It was late morning now, the sunlight and shade shifting with the wind on the lush grass that Mattie so carefully, so grudgingly, tended, and as beautiful as the scene was, she would have preferred to be anywhere else.

Her father and uncle watched her from their seats at the round table, set with the breakfast dishes her mother had picked out long ago and decorated with a crystal vase of delphinium Ellis had brought down with him.

How, Grace asked herself, could she explain to them that she didn't give a damn anymore what they thought?

Let them try to read her mind. Let them try to manipulate her. She just didn't care. Her father knew he'd asked her the impossible. He knew he'd asked her to cross a line she wouldn't cross.

Maybe it would have been easier if he'd been oblivious, but he wasn't. Jason Cooper never spoke without knowing exactly what he was going to say and the impact it would have.

"I'm not telling Linc to leave the island." Grace wrapped her long, baggy sweater more tightly around her, although she wasn't cold. "I can't do that. I won't do it."

Her father inhaled audibly, one of his tricks to show his displeasure. It was a cue. They were all supposed to understand what he was thinking and feeling without him actually having to say so. "Your brother listens to you."

"That's why I'm not telling him. I can't ask him to leave because of me."

Ellis, in one of his country-squire outfits, broke off a piece of his scone but didn't eat it. None of them had eaten much. He'd picked up the scones in Northeast Harbor and arrived while they were still warm. He said, "Whatever Linc's hiding could cost you this appointment."

His tone was patient, not at all condescending. Grace abandoned her scone. "He's not going to cost me anything. If the appointment gets pulled, it will be because of me and who I am—not because of my brother."

"But you don't deny he's hiding something," Ellis asked quietly. "Do you know what it is?"

Her father, an elegant man, always composed, studied her as he and her uncle awaited her answer. At that moment, she hated them both. Her most trusted confidants, her biggest supporters. She could turn to them with anything—but not, she thought, this. Not Linc. They would sacrifice him to save her appointment. They wouldn't believe they were hurting him because they were convinced he'd never amount to anything, anyway.

What would they do if they knew she'd slept with Mattie Young?

What would they do if they knew she'd lied to the local police, the Maine State Police, the FBI—herself?

"I have no idea what Linc's hiding," she said, finally. "He's gone to see Owen."

"Owen." Her father grimaced, pushing aside his plate. "He's part of the problem. I admit that I liked the idea of him taking Linc under his wing at first. Now, I don't know. Linc needs baby steps. Owen's not a man for baby steps. As much as I respect him, he must see that Linc isn't seriously interested in search-and-rescue."

Grace could feel herself growing warm at her father's almost clinical way of discussing her brother. "He's getting some positive attention from Owen. That can't be a bad thing."

"Linc gets plenty of attention from everyone. Including me."

Grace had to stop herself from snorting in disbelief. Did he actually believe he gave Linc any attention at all? She lifted her napkin off her lap and placed it next to her plate. "I'm going for a walk," she said, getting up from the table.

She ripped open the screen door and pounded down the stone steps, picking up her pace as she ran across the lawn to the water's edge. Sprawling beach roses formed a thick border between the yard and the shoreline, the morning dew glistening on their pink blossoms.

As she calmed herself, she watched a lone kayaker out on the water. How long had it been since she'd kayaked? She'd been so wrapped up in her work for so long. She'd hoped some time in Maine with her family would be a good break, that she'd have a chance, finally, to do things just for fun—never mind the damn background check.

She became aware of her uncle behind her. "I know what you and my father are doing," she said. "You're not worried about Linc. I'm not even sure you're worried about me. You're worried about Abigail Browning. Bad enough for the FBI to be right here on the island, digging into our lives. But Abigail—having her know our dirty little secrets…"

"Grace, Grace." Ellis stood next to her, leaning on his walking stick. He didn't look at his niece but out at the sound, the kayaker, the seagulls, the mountains, as if he were trying to absorb their beauty through his skin. Finally, he sighed. "I don't care about Abigail or the FBI. Neither does your father. We're worried about you. About what's best for you."

She blinked back tears. "I know. I'm sorry."

"Listen to me." He touched her elbow through her heavy cable sweater, too warm for the conditions. "Please, Grace. Listen carefully."

He waited for her reaction. She nodded. "All right. I'm listening."

"Abigail only cares about finding her husband's killer. Her only interest in any of us is related to that desire—that commitment. She wants closure."

"And justice. Don't you think she also wants justice?"

Ellis seemed untroubled by her sharp tone. "Right now, I would say justice isn't on the top of her list of concerns. I've no doubt she tells herself it is. Do you believe it's any coincidence this drama with Mattie is going on this week? It's the seventh anniversary—"

"I know what week it is."

"Yes," he said, without inflection. "I know you do. Grace, Abigail is stirring up people, and she's doing it on purpose. You saw her last night at the house, when she realized Mattie had been in my garden shed. She has no boundaries."

"She's a detective, for heaven's sake."

"And that makes what difference?" This time, he didn't wait for an answer. "I like Abigail. We all do. That doesn't mean I can't see the dangers her obsession poses."

"What if she finds Chris's killer?" Grace turned into a sudden gust of wind that burst up the sound and hoped Ellis would blame it if he saw any tears. "As far as I'm concerned, then all her pushing will have been worth the aggravation."

"Even if you suffer needlessly?"

"I don't think any suffering of mine matters—or is needless."

"Grace," her uncle said, and now she could feel his eyes on her, probing, knowing. His style was different than his much older half brother's, but he could be as ruthless when he wanted to be. "It's time to get over Chris."

She gulped in a breath. "Don't."

"Someone has to say to you what you already know in your heart. Chris was never real to you. He was always a fantasy. It's time to break free of him."

"He's dead. Don't you think I know that?"

"Intellectually, yes. Emotionally...I don't know,

Grace." He didn't relent. "Do you? In a way, his death makes it easier for you to hold on to him."

She dropped her arms to her sides and spun around at him, the wind blowing at the back of her head, sending her hair every which way. "Ellis. Stop. I'm not some weak-kneed, lovesick nitwit. I refuse—"

"You refuse what, Grace? To face the reality that you're thirty-eight years old—seven years older than Chris was when he died—and unmarried? To face the reality that with him gone, you don't have to deal with the fact that he was in love with another woman?"

"He *married* that other woman."

"You can pretend he didn't, or that it wouldn't have worked. You don't have to see him and Abigail have children. You don't have to watch their children grow up, learn to drop lobster buoys, climb on the rocks, hike—"

"I was over Chris before he was married." She tried to sound convincing, mature, not as if she was churning inside. "I was well over him before he was killed."

"No, Grace, you weren't. You aren't over him now."

She couldn't stand Ellis's scrutiny any longer and took off down a narrow path between the roses, their prickly branches slapping at her hips and thighs, soaking them with dew. A thorn scratched the top of one hand. The bank was short, fairly steep, but that didn't deter her; she'd walked this path since she was a child. She and Doe Garrison would play dolls on the shore and wave to Chris and his grandfather as they puttered by in their lobster boat.

She'd loved Chris then, even as a girl.

To her relief, her uncle didn't follow her down to the water. She looked up the hill and saw him heading back to the house, and she wondered if he regretted his bluntness. He was wise and understanding, in part, she thought, because he'd never married and had children of his own. She'd come to rely on his advice, his keen observations of other people. His patience. Who else could watch his own brother sell his beloved Maine house out from under him and not complain?

Yet Ellis had always lived in his brother's shadow—just as Linc was living in her shadow. And as much as she adored her uncle, Grace didn't want her brother to end up like him.

Owen walked up a sandy path through the junipers and low-lying blueberry bushes below the remains of his family's original Mt. Desert house, pine and spruce saplings popping up here and there in the thin soil. He'd caught a movement up at the foundation and was off to check it out. He wasn't practicing any measure of stealth. He was just tramping up the path.

Linc Cooper stood up from the spot where Mattie Young had drunk beer and smoked cigarettes, unwittingly terrorizing two young boys.

When he saw Owen, Linc gasped audibly and bolted, climbing over the chunk of foundation and scrambling for the woods behind it.

Owen shot out after him. He knew the kid's capabilities—he wasn't worried about catching up with him.

A few yards into the woods, on a rough path, Linc tripped on an exposed tree root and fell onto one knee, crying out in pain as he picked himself up and continued running.

Owen thought he heard the twenty-year-old sob.

"Linc—hold up," he called.

But he ran faster, unimpeded by his bruised knee, grunting as he gasped for air.

Since he had to know who was after him and still didn't slow down, Owen decided he was through with niceties. He barreled in behind Linc and knocked his feet out from under him, buckling him with one well-placed kick.

Owen pounced, pinning his wannabe protégé facedown on the ground, so that he couldn't kick, thrash, bite or otherwise move. "Be still. I'm not going to hurt you. I just need you to calm down. Understood?"

"Let me go. I'll press charges."

"Fine. The police are at Abigail's house right now. I'll take you to them."

Linc's body went slack, and he squeezed his eyes shut, tears leaking out the corners. "Just leave me alone," he said.

Owen eased up on his hold. "Don't bolt. I didn't get a lot of sleep last night." He didn't explain why. "I don't want to chase you."

"You ran like a maniac." Linc sniffled, sitting up, pine needles in his fair hair. "I thought you were going to kill me. I forgot you were in the military."

"Why did you take off?"

"You scared the hell out of me."

"I'm walking out here on my land. How did that scare you?"

He picked a bit of bark off his lip, his natural arrogance returning fast. "I don't know. I'm jumpy."

"You were looking for Mattie, weren't you?"

"I don't have to tell you anything."

"You saw him out here Sunday night, didn't you? Did you meet him, or did you just follow him here?"

It was like all the air went out of him. His shoulders slumped. Snot and tears ran into his mouth. "Shit. Owen."

"You're in over your head, Linc. The only way out is to tell the truth."

"You don't know what my life is like. My father. My sister. Even my uncle. I'm the low man on the totem pole around here. If I screw things up for them, *I'm* screwed."

"You have to do what you believe is right and let the rest of it fall into place."

"Or not."

For the past couple of hours, since Abigail had spotted that dusty, lint-looking pearl on her back room floor, Owen had been trying to let the new pieces of what had happened seven years ago fall into place.

And one of them was right here, torturing himself.

"Linc, you were the burglar seven years ago, weren't you?"

He sobbed, crying openly now.

"Chris knew," Owen said, making it a statement.

He snorted in a lungful of air and coughed, pulling himself together. "He found me the night before he was killed—before Abigail was attacked." As he spoke, Linc stared at the trees, as if he were seeing himself at thirteen, Chris Browning at thirty-one, confronting him. "He read me the riot act. And I quit. I didn't want to disappoint him."

"He believed in you."

"Yeah." Linc shut his eyes. "I'm so ashamed. But I didn't steal Abigail's necklace. I didn't hit her. I swear. But who'll believe me?"

"That's why you never told anyone?"

He nodded. "I thought no one else knew. I thought whoever did it was long gone. That's what I told myself, I guess." Linc tucked his knees under his chin. "I never lied outright to the police."

"Mattie knew you were the burglar?"

He hesitated, then nodded. "He's blackmailing me. He wants ten grand."

"How much have you given him?"

"Four."

"Who knows?"

Linc took a breath. "No one."

"You're twenty years old, and you're carrying this thing by yourself." Owen put out a hand, and Linc took it, getting up onto his feet. "That's not necessary."

"I know. I'm stupid—"

"I didn't say that."

"Owen, I'm sorry. I opened my mouth a dozen times on our hikes to tell you, but I didn't. My sister's appointment—the house going on the market—" He swallowed, his panic rising again. "I was scared."

"Linc," Owen said quietly, "if I could figure this out, the cops can, too."

Abigail ducked under a low branch that hung over the path. Owen knew she'd been there a while. "Did Mattie threaten you?" she asked.

Linc kept his cool at her presence. "Not with bodily harm, if that's what you mean. He didn't have to—just knowing what a screwup I am, knowing I could never let my family find out was enough. I never—" He raised his chin, but his lower lip quivered. "Chris died because of me."

"Did you pull the trigger?"

"No!"

"Then he didn't die because of you," Abigail said. "He died because someone shot him."

Linc obviously wasn't used to that kind of clarity in the life he lived. "What happens now?"

"You tell Detective Lieutenant Beeler everything."

"And the FBI?"

"They'll be there, too."

"Chris—"

Abigail nodded, as if she understood what Linc was trying to say. "He'll be there in spirit. Think of that, okay? You can't change what other people did. You can't change what you did. All you can do is tell the truth and rely on it."

"That's what Chris said seven years ago."

"I imagine it was." She stood back, smiling unexpectedly, if a little weakly, at Owen, taking some of the tension out of the moment. "It was kind of fun seeing you in action. I got here just in time. I'm glad I didn't miss that one."

Owen pictured himself chasing her through the woods and smiled back at her. "I suppose you'll want me to talk to the law?"

"Well, I can tell you they'll want to talk to you."

CHAPTER 26

Out on his screen porch overlooking Somes Sound, Jason Cooper was dressed for sailing and a day spent pretending he had no problems he couldn't control. He lifted little Sis into his arms and eyed Abigail with a superciliousness she found desperate more than genuine. She wasn't annoyed. And she certainly wasn't cowed.

"Where is my son now?" he asked.

"At my house talking to Lieutenant Beeler."

"Without an attorney?"

"He's twenty. He's not a minor."

"He's my *son*." Jason inhaled sharply, not easing up on the superiority. "We've all indulged your obsession over the years—your interference in our lives—because of your situation. Because we, too, loved your husband. But to accuse my son of hiding information from the police—"

"I'm not accusing him of anything," Abigail said. "If you want to talk to him, you know where my house is."

The little dog looked as if she wanted to lick her master's chin—or bite him. He set her on the floor, and she stayed obediently at his feet. "Abigail, perhaps you should leave, before you say something you truly regret."

"Or before you do," she said.

Sis barked at her, as if the dog knew Abigail had been rude. Jason stared at her, but some of the raw anger visibly went out of him. "I love my son. I'm proud of him. I believe in him."

"I wouldn't expect otherwise."

"Of course you would. Sometimes I'm not a very good father. I know that." He stopped himself. "Well. I should go to Linc. I want you to know, however, that my son had nothing to do with Chris's death."

"Did you know he was burglarizing homes seven years ago?"

Jason snapped his fingers, and Sis scampered into the house through the open porch door. He turned back to Abigail. "If I did know or suspect anything of the sort— and I'm not saying I did—I wouldn't have confronted him. That's not how we do things in my family. I would let him sort out his own priorities."

"He was thirteen."

"Yes, I know he was thirteen. Everything stolen was returned." Jason's expression hardened, as if he was daring her to contradict him. "Whatever my son did, Abigail, he wasn't the one who attacked you and stole your necklace."

Making that his final remark, he followed his dog's path back into the house. Abigail was faintly surprised that he'd left her to her own devices, but he would also know she wanted to talk to his daughter and that there was very little he could do to stop her.

She could see Grace dragging a bright orange sit-on-top kayak through the beach roses, down to the water.

Abigail quietly shut the screen door behind her and walked down the stone steps. The landscaping was more reserved than Ellis's extensive gardens, but nonetheless tasteful and in perfect condition, thanks to the hard work of their solo yardman—presumably, given Mattie's behavior, soon to be ex-yardman. She hadn't pressed Jason Cooper on what, if anything, he knew about his son's recent cash withdrawals. She'd leave that to Lou and his teams.

Following the path through the roses, she joined Grace down at the water's edge. "I think those rosebushes have more thorns than they used to. Just what I needed, more scratches."

"I do believe you relish every one of your scratches, Abigail." Grace slapped the kayak into the water and stood up straight, her baggy sweater unbuttoned, blowing out in the stiff breeze. She squinted back at Abigail. "I'll paddle with the wind and hope it dies down before I get back."

"Where are you headed?"

"I don't know. It doesn't matter." She smiled without any pleasure. "Anywhere."

"It's a beautiful day for kayaking."

"Do you kayak?"

Abigail shrugged, walking into the soft, squishy sand. "I'm not very good at it."

"I love it. I wish I could get on the water more often, but my work keeps me very busy." She pushed back her hair, strands rising up in the wind. "I'd hoped to spend more time up here, but I have to get back to Washington."

"Must be a busy time for you."

"Yes. Very." She hugged her pilled, old sweater to her. "I'm not really dressed for kayaking. Well, I don't care. I suppose I could paddle past Owen's house. Then if something went wrong, he could rescue me. Although that wouldn't look good on my FBI background report, would it?"

"Better to be rescued than—"

"Drown?" Grace splashed into the shallow water. The tide was coming in, rising steadily, the waves choppier out on the sound, away from the shore. She had on long pants and sports sandals, the gray sand seeping under her exposed feet, between her toes, as she sank into it. "I seldom paddle that way. Never, in fact. The water's often rough, but that's not the reason. I just don't want to pass the cliffs where Doe drowned."

Abigail sat on a wood bench on a grassy strip up against the beach roses. She could smell their sweet fragrance as she watched Grace lift the paddle off her kayak, almost banging herself in the head with one end.

She stabbed it onto the bow of her kayak, stopping it before it could float off. "Have you ever seen pictures of Doe?"

Grace was being provocative, mean, even. Abigail deliberately kept her tone matter-of-fact. "The other day," she said. "Someone left a picture of her after she'd drowned for Owen to find. Unfortunately, the Alden boys found it first."

It wasn't the answer Grace had expected. *"What?"*

She dropped the paddle and lunged after it, falling onto the kayak and landing on her knees in the water. She awkwardly tried to right herself and not lose the paddle or the kayak.

Feeling the barest hint of guilt, Abigail ran to her, splashing into the chilly water with her own sports sandals, and offered her a hand.

"I'm all right." Grace stood up, the bottom half of her

sweater soaked and stretched down to her knees now. She got her balance and snatched her paddle, laid it back across the kayak cockpit, then grabbed the line tied to the bow and gave Abigail a cold look. "That was intentional. To shock me. Well. Mission accomplished."

Abigail didn't apologize. She jumped back out of the water, shook as much wet sand off her shoes as she could and watched Grace slide her kayak back into shallow water, where it scraped along the sand and rocks.

"Doe was as beautiful as Owen is handsome," she said, her back to Abigail. "Even in death. The Garrisons are a good-looking family."

"That they are."

Grace plopped down onto the grass, with her feet in the rising water, up to her ankles now. "I'm surprised you notice such things."

"Why?"

"Being a detective and all. Being a woman who doesn't seem to pay much attention to that sort of thing. Being—I don't know. Stuck in the past, maybe?" But she didn't wait for the barb to strike and went on. "Do you know where this picture came from?"

"I assume Mattie took it." Abigail could feel the rough sand rubbing at the bottom of her feet. "Where it's been all these years and how it ended up on Owen's doorstep—that I don't know."

"Well, I certainly don't. And neither does Linc—or my father—or my uncle. Any of us."

Abigail didn't argue with her. "The day Dorothy Garrison drowned…"

"I was at what was then the Garrison house. We all were. Doe and I had argued. Just some stupid teenage fight that should have passed with us remaining the best of friends. She'd been miserable company all day. Sullen, teary, argumentative. I don't know if it was hormones or what. I don't suppose I'll ever know."

"She ran down to the cliffs by herself?"

"We thought she was on the steps. At least I did. I know her parents did, too. Owen realized she was gone and walked down to the cliffs to see if he could find her." Grace's voice faltered. "He arrived in time to see her slip and fall."

"You're sure she slipped?"

Grace swung around but didn't get up. "Of course she slipped! Do you think Owen pushed her?"

Abigail said nothing.

"You think Doe jumped? That's outrageous. She was *fourteen*. She was full of life. No, she didn't jump." Grace yanked her feet out of the water and stood up, red from her toes to her ankles, her pants soaked, much of her sweater too. "I can't believe you'd suggest such a thing."

"I didn't suggest it. I just asked a question."

"Well, it was an outrageous question."

"Maybe so. Did you go down to the cliffs that day yourself?"

She shook her head, her anger not taking root with a topic so tragic. "No. Chris and his grandfather heard Owen from their boat when he finally was able to yell for help. Mattie was with them. There was such a flurry of activity."

"Did someone stay with you the whole time?"

"My mother did. She and my father were in the middle of their divorce, but she was there."

"Do you remember anyone not being there, especially before you all heard Owen calling for help?"

Grace went very still. "No, I don't. Abigail, what's this all about? It's well-known that Owen believed he heard someone in the trees. He was eleven—he couldn't take in what happened. He felt guilty. There's no reason, of course, but sometimes these things have very little to do with reason."

"I'm just trying to figure out why the picture of his sister ended up on his doorstep."

"Because some twisted son of a bitch put it there."

Abigail nodded. "There's that."

"Dear heaven." Grace shivered, and she seemed all of a sudden to notice her dripping sweater and cold feet. "I can't start out on the water wet. I'd freeze in this wind."

"Grace, you know your brother—"

"I heard the beginning of your conversation with my father." She tried to button her sweater, then abandoned the effort. "That's why I came out here. Fight or flight, you know."

"You care about Linc very much," Abigail said.

"Yes, I do."

"Enough to lie for him when Chris asked you where he was?"

Grace lifted her chin, and Abigail could see the older woman's self-control assert itself—could see glimpses, finally, of the intelligence and drive that had helped land her the State Department appointment. "What are you talking about?"

"I got pictures the other day, too. You told the police you never talked to Chris when he stopped up at your uncle's house after I was attacked. But you did, didn't you?"

"There's a picture of us?"

"Yes."

"I told the police I saw him. If the picture doesn't show

us actually talking—" But she stopped herself, then went on in a half whisper. "He asked me where Linc was."

"What did you tell him, Grace?"

She looked down at her blue-red feet. "I told him Linc was at the old Garrison house foundation. That's where I thought he was. I didn't lie. Not to Chris."

Something in her voice penetrated the wall of professionalism Abigail had tried to put up to steel herself—to give herself objectivity. She sat back on the bench, its wood warming in the midday sun. Bob O'Reilly had warned her to leave any questioning to the Maine CID detectives. And yet here she was.

"Linc wasn't down at the foundation," she said. "There was another picture in the packet on my doorstep. It shows him at the gate in your uncle's yard. It was taken around the same time as the one of you and Chris."

"Linc—" Grace seemed confused. "My brother was in the gardens?"

"Sneaking a martini."

"But I thought he was…" She didn't go on.

"Why did you think Linc was at the old Garrison foundation?"

"I don't remember."

"Did you know he was the burglar everyone was talking about that summer?"

"Suspected—I've never known it for a fact. I still don't, no matter what Linc's told anyone else."

"My husband knew," Abigail said, not making it a question—not wanting, she thought, to make it a question.

"He never said. But I assume he did know, and I assume he confronted Linc and gave him one more chance. And Linc—" Grace shrugged off her sweater and balled it up in one hand, turning back to her kayak. "I have to go."

"Grace, Linc wasn't the one who broke into my house and attacked me and stole my necklace. Chris knew that. I could see it in his face. He knew who'd done it, and he knew it wasn't a troubled thirteen-year-old boy."

"You sound so confident."

"I'm not confident about much that happened that day, but about that—" She nodded. "Yeah. I'm confident. Chris wanted to know where your brother was to make sure he was safe. All this time, Grace, have you believed your brother killed Chris?"

She shook her head. "No. Never."

Grace abandoned her thought and grabbed the line on her kayak, dragging the lightweight boat farther up onto the grass. She dropped it and tossed her sweater into the open cockpit, then threw her head back, staring into the sky as if she might see Chris's ghost.

Finally, she turned to Abigail. "I just believed I sent your husband to his death."

And Abigail knew what she was hearing in Grace's voice now. She stood up, put a hand out to her. "Grace," she said. "You were in love with him."

But she pretended not to hear. She gave her kayak a little kick. "I'll come back for you later," she said to it, then squinted at Abigail. "I'm so glad you weren't hurt any worse than you were yesterday. I know you're very good at taking care of yourself, but I'd hate to see anything happen to you. We all would."

She fled up the path through the roses.

Abigail didn't follow her. Instead, she walked back into the water, the tide higher now, deeper. She spotted a bit of bright color that didn't fit with the grays and browns of the bottom and reached one hand into the water, digging among rounded stones and rough sand until she freed it.

It was a sliver of purple seaglass, its edges rounded and softened by the salt water and sand. She rinsed it off and held it up to the sun, imagining it was from a bottle Chris had tossed into the sound as a boy. She could see him out in his grandfather's boat, exploring the island's nooks and crannies, pulling lobster traps from the depths, dreaming of becoming an FBI agent.

Had he ever dreamed of the woman he would marry?

She cupped the seaglass in her hand, then threw it as far out into the water as she could.

She would find out who killed him.

On her way back from Somes Sound, Abigail stopped at the diner where she'd had her fried shrimp roll with Lou Beeler and Doyle Alden the other day. It seemed like a hundred years ago. She ordered another one to go. She hadn't eaten with O'Reilly before he headed back to Boston, after making her promise to stay in touch and behave and not do anything stupid—a whole long list.

She took the steaming roll down to the picturesque harbor and watched the working boats and the pleasure boats come and go on what was a stunningly perfect Maine summer afternoon.

The harbor was also one of the few places with cell phone service.

"Abigail," her father said when he picked up. "Is everything all right?"

"Was Mattie Young an FBI informant?"

Silence. Her question wasn't altogether the stab in the

dark it felt like now that she could hear her father's voice. Lou Beeler had hinted at something her father knew. And Chris and Mattie—the tension between them before the wedding. The pieces were coming together.

"Maybe we don't have a good connection," she said. "Let me ask again. Was Mattie Young an FBI informant?"

"It's complicated," her father said.

"No, it's not complicated. It's a yes or no question. Yes, he was. No, he wasn't."

"You should talk to Lieutenant Beeler."

"I did." She could hear the edge in her voice. But if anyone would know, it was FBI Director John March. Her father. "Have you talked to him?"

"You're a homicide detective yourself, Abigail. You understand there are details of an investigation that you keep to yourself."

"Lou, yes. But you? You're not on this case. Or are you?"

He didn't answer right away. "Mattie was Chris's informant." There was no hint of apology in her father's tone. "I didn't find out until after Chris was killed."

"And you didn't tell me."

"Lou Beeler knew."

And that was enough as far as her father was concerned. The lead investigator had the information, even if Abigail didn't. "Chris never said a word," she said.

"He wouldn't have. In his position, you wouldn't have, either. He cut Mattie loose in the weeks before you two got married. He had other things on his mind, Abigail. He was on his honeymoon. There was no need—"

"Apparently there was a need since he ended up with a bullet in his gut, bleeding to death—since he was *murdered*." She sucked in a breath. "Damn it."

"Remember, you weren't a homicide detective seven years ago."

"Yes, I know." She set her shrimp roll on the dock rail, half-covered in seagull droppings. "It's a lot to absorb. What kind of information did Mattie provide?"

"To be honest, I think Chris was just trying to help a friend, to give him a sense of purpose, keep him busy." She could hear the emotion in her father's voice, not a common occurrence for him. "I can get on a plane now and be there in a couple of hours."

"I know, Dad. Thanks. I'm okay. I just wish you'd told me about Mattie a long time ago."

"I couldn't."

"I know that, too."

After she disconnected, she fought off a seagull interested in her shrimp roll and watched a battered lobster boat circle into the harbor with a man and a boy going through their routines after a day at sea. She wanted to call to the boy to keep fishing. Be satisfied. Don't go away and fall for the daughter of the future director of the FBI.

"Your husband had secrets."

That Linc Cooper was their burglar. That Mattie Young was his informant.

That Grace Cooper was in love with him.

In time, Abigail wondered if Chris would have told her— if they weren't secrets so much as things he just hadn't gotten around to sharing with her. They'd been focused on their wedding and honeymoon, their future together.

But they hadn't had time.

CHAPTER 27

Doyle read a chatty e-mail from Katie three times before he shut down his computer and headed to the kitchen to take some pork chops out of the freezer. His wife had told him in great detail about what she was doing in England—the kinds of things she was learning, the people she'd met, the sights she'd seen. She wrote like she talked. They hadn't called each other much since she'd left, with the time difference, their busy schedules, the cost of international calls.

As much as he missed her and would have wanted her counsel—her support—if she'd been there, Doyle didn't want to tell her about what was going on at home, not when there was nothing she could do about it but worry.

The boys liked to instant-message her right after dinner. Doyle had never figured out the whole IM thing.

He looked out the window over the sink. Sean and Ian had gone off on their bikes. He'd told them not to go near

Mattie's house, but otherwise what could he do? Keep them inside all the time? Make them afraid of their own shadows?

The search for Mattie continued. If he was still up in the woods and hadn't found food and water, he risked dying of exposure, thirst. Doyle had envisioned that scene a million times over the years—Mattie Young, dead in a pile of leaves, dead on the rocks, dead in a car crash. Better than him killing someone else while driving drunk, or so Doyle had always told himself.

He left the pork chops on the counter and walked out to the living room. He'd have the chops in the oven before they could breed bacteria. So far, he'd managed not to poison himself and the boys.

Abigail Browning stood on the other side of his screen door at the front entrance. He hadn't heard her drive up. Then he saw Owen behind her, both of them grim-faced. Doyle's heart lurched. Had something happened to Sean or Ian? Katie? He immediately told himself to calm down. It'd been the kind of day for grim faces.

"Come on in," he said.

"Hey, Doyle." Owen stepped past Abigail and pushed open the door. "We saw the boys on their bikes. They look like they're having a great time."

"They know we're looking for Mattie. The rest—I haven't told them." He held up a hand, nipping any well-intentioned protests in the bud. "I'm not planning to, either, until I have to."

"Your call."

Abigail glanced around the country-style room. "I haven't been in here in a few years. You and Katie have done a nice job with the place."

"Thanks." Doyle pointed to the couch. "Have a seat—"

"I can't stay," she said. "Mattie?"

"No sign of him since we found his bicycle. I left the station an hour ago. Lou was still there. The FBI guys wanted to talk to Linc Cooper." Sighing heavily, Doyle sank onto his easy chair. "I don't get Mattie. I guess I never will. He never could get his shit together. He had his chances, just like the rest of us, but he was always looking for an angle. It was Mattie first. Always Mattie first."

"We still have a lot of unanswered questions."

He didn't even get on her for saying "we," as if she had an official role in the investigation.

"You can't know what it's like. Either of you. I have this picture in my head of Pa Browning taking Mattie, Chris and me out on the boat on a freezing cold day long after the tourist season had ended. We had the best time. And now—hell. Pa and Chris are gone. Mattie might as well be."

Abigail had that relentless look Doyle had seen in her before, and she didn't indulge him in his moment of self-pity. "You knew Mattie was an FBI informant?"

He threw his head against the tall back of the chair and thought about throwing them both out and watching television. Just not think about his work, his life, for a half hour.

Owen said quietly, "I didn't know."

Doyle sat forward. "'FBI informant' is too strong. Mattie kept his ear to the ground and told Chris what he heard. Mostly it wasn't much of anything, but he happened onto a drug smuggling operation into Canada. The feds were on to it, but Mattie had names, a meeting place. It helped. So, Chris threw some money his way. It was all on the up-and-up."

"Then Mattie started drinking again, and Chris pulled back."

"Yeah. That's pretty much the story."

"I don't want 'pretty much' the story, Doyle. I'd like to hear the whole story."

"All right." He put both hands on the arms of his chair just to keep himself from launching to his feet and strangling her. "That's the whole story. Better?"

She didn't react to his sarcasm. "And Grace Cooper. Did you know she was in love with Chris?" But when Doyle's eyes flickered to Owen, Abigail sucked in a breath and swore. "Damn it. You all knew."

"He was never for her," Owen said. "We all knew that, too. And it was over a long time ago."

"No, it wasn't." Doyle got heavily to his feet. "It was for Chris. Yeah, he never had a romantic interest in Grace. But for her? She'll never get over him. Who knows, maybe he'd still be alive today if he'd fallen for her instead."

Owen grabbed his friend's arm. "That's enough. You're upset. Don't make matters worse."

Abigail had gone pale, which, in the mood he was in, Doyle considered something of a victory. But she didn't raise her voice when she spoke. "If you thought Chris should be marrying someone else, why did you agree to be his best man?"

"Because he asked me, and he was my best friend. He thought I'd come around one of these days and see what he saw in you."

"Another of his little secrets," she said without bitterness.

A bike clattered out in the driveway, and one of the boys yelled, *"Dad!"*

Sean, Doyle thought, surging for the door, even as Ian called out to him. "Dad, Dad, come quick! It's Mattie!"

Moving like a bolt of lightning, Owen shot out the front

door before Doyle could get there, Abigail on his heels. He took the steps in one leap, then charged across the lawn to his driveway and detached one-car garage, where his sons were tangled up in their bikes.

Ian stood up, his knees skinned. "We tripped. We were running—" He sobbed. "I thought Sean saw the ghost!"

Owen knelt down, getting at eye level with Sean as the boy pointed at the garage. "Mattie was in there! I know he was. He made this bed…"

"We'll check it out," Owen said, calmer than Doyle would have been. "Did you see him?"

Ian shook his head, Owen's presence steadying him. "He's not here."

The garage didn't have an automatic door. Doyle didn't protest when Abigail went around to the side door, still half-open from when the boys were in there. "Sean and Ian didn't have to unlock the door," he told her. "Lock's busted. It's been busted for weeks. I haven't gotten around to fixing it."

She nodded, going inside. He raised the main door, entering the garage a half second after she did. Katie's sedan filled up most of the space. On various hooks and shelves were tools, supplies, snow shovels, sleds and pieces of junk that she insisted she'd use one day for various craft projects.

"Car's locked?" Abigail asked.

"Yeah. Keys are in the house."

At least Mattie—if the boys were right and he'd been there—hadn't bashed in a window and made his bed in the car. Doyle walked around to the hood, where Abigail pointed to a blue tarp that had been spread out on the concrete floor, on top of it a rolled-up car blanket and a camp pad that he'd forgotten they even owned.

"Looks as if he helped himself to your pantry," Abigail said.

Doyle saw what she meant—a box of Wheat Thins, a pop-up can of pears, a package of Oreos. Everything looked empty. What Mattie hadn't eaten, he must have taken with him.

And it was Mattie. Doyle knew he didn't have to say anything. The smell, the strands of long hair on the makeshift pillow, the hair tie—enough proof for both him and Abigail.

"He must have slipped into the kitchen while I was out looking for him last night," Doyle said. "He doesn't have a key, but he'd know where I keep mine. I never thought…"

"Don't beat yourself up. Staying here might have saved his life."

"At least I didn't have any beer in the house." But as she walked past him, Doyle grabbed her arm. "About what I said earlier. I didn't mean half of it."

She had the grace to smile. "Which half?"

When they got back outside, Sean and Ian bolted away from Owen, and Doyle scooped them up, one in each arm. He nodded to his friend. "Thanks."

"Anytime."

But Owen had his eyes on Abigail. "It was Mattie?"

She nodded without comment. She'd pulled back inside of herself, protective, focused on the job she was there to do. "I'll go call Lou," she said, moving off toward the house.

Doyle hadn't seen what was happening before, but he damn well did now. Here was another friend falling for Abigail Browning. "She doesn't trust any of us right now," he said to Owen.

"Would you?"

"Probably not."

"Dad," Sean said, "what's going on?"

Doyle knew push had come to shove. He had to tell his sons as much as he could about Mattie, about Chris. All of it. He set them back on the driveway, could feel their tension and curiosity in their slim frames. But he addressed Owen. "If you want to check the area and see if you can pick up Mattie's tracks, that'd be a help."

"No problem," Owen said, and when he started for the garage, he had the look of the experienced search-and-rescue specialist he was.

Mattie clung to wet moss and a protruding root on the steep hillside next to the zigzag steps eccentric Edgar Garrison had carved into the Mt. Desert granite a century ago.

His head pounded behind his eyes and cheeks. His teeth ached, his sinuses reacting to the strong smells of evergreen, moldy pine needles and pinecones. Hiking back out there from Doyle's garage, sticking to the woods as much as possible, avoiding the cops, had been pure torture.

He'd had little sleep. Stretched out on his tarp, scared out of his mind, he had lain in the dark garage last night, listening to his cop friend snoring through his open bedroom window. Worse than a damn freight train.

If Katie had been there, Mattie might have gone into the house and begged her to help him figure out what to do. She was levelheaded. She could stand back from the situation and think. He didn't know what Doyle would have done. Shoot him on the spot?

And the state cops. Hell. He was a freaking marked man.

Everyone thought he'd tried to kill Abigail. They thought he *had* killed Chris.

And then there was Linc's money. The blackmail.

"Fuck the money," Mattie whispered.

He crept along the slippery, treacherous, near-vertical hill to a crevice where he and Doyle had hid as kids, spying on the Garrisons. It was just a little inset in the granite. It reminded him of Tolkien and hobbits.

As he huddled against the rock ledge, Mattie pulled a cheap green camouflage rain poncho he'd lifted from Doyle's garage around him. He had a jug of water and some chocolate. He hoped to have a plan well in hand before he starved to death or died of thirst.

He shivered against the cold rock. He didn't dare light a cigarette.

"God," he whispered, "what I wouldn't give for a hot shower."

He debated going up the steps and knocking on Ellis's door. *Hey, I'll do some yard work for you if you'll let me use your shower and keep your mouth shut.*

But who knew with Ellis? He was discreet. Otherwise, no one would trust him, and in his work off-island, trust was everything. He was also a control freak who'd fuss about two Japanese beetles on his rosebushes instead of being happy there weren't hundreds. Mattie had no idea how Ellis had reacted to his yardman's predicament. Was he sympathetic to the police and determined to be helpful? Or was he more worried about having to handle his gardens by himself?

Didn't matter, Mattie thought. If he tried to move now, he'd never make it. He'd fall and crack his head open. He was exhausted and so damn confused, and there were just a few inches between him and a straight drop down to one of the crazy stone landings. He half expected to hear police sirens and helicopters, or see some big, nasty police dog drooling over him.

A drink would calm his nerves. He didn't care about "working the program" or "one day at a time"—any of it. He'd reform when his life wasn't so complicated.

He was facing too many unknowns, and was up against too many different agendas of smart, powerful people.

You're the damn yardman.

And he was a slimeball. Mattie had betrayed his friends' trust in him. He'd let alcohol and entitlement and resentment fuel his anger and screw up his judgment.

His eyes drooped and shut, and he felt his body go slack.

Would he fall off the ledge in his sleep?

Would the search dogs find him?

I don't care.

Ah, Chris.

Did you lie there bleeding in the tide thinking I'd killed you?

Did you, my friend?

CHAPTER 28

An uneasy silence had settled in Abigail's back room, which had finally been swept and wiped clean of any police presence. She'd ripped out the last of the old wallboard.

So many questions, she thought, tugging a red bandanna off her hair and shaking off the plaster dust.

Owen tied up a trash bag of the last of the debris and carried it back to the kitchen. Abigail watched him. He was a rock, as solid a man as she'd ever known. But how could she fall for him?

How could she fall for him *here*?

Mattie Young had camped out in his childhood friend's garage. Where was he now? Doyle hadn't known he was there. Lou Beeler obviously believed the chief's explanation—with Katie gone for most of the summer, he and the boys didn't use the garage on a daily basis. It wasn't as if Doyle'd had time in recent days to mow the lawn or trim the roses. He simply hadn't needed to be in the garage for anything.

As far as anyone could tell, Mattie had slipped in there for shelter. If he'd thought about knocking on Doyle's door and turning himself in, fine, but he hadn't done it.

He could have gone anywhere from Doyle's house. Into Acadia National Park, onto the ocean. He could have slipped into someone else's garage or broken into a vacant summer home, or he could have crawled under a rock somewhere.

He'd avoid the police and anyone who'd recognize him. Although news of his disappearance had hit in the media, tourists on Mt. Desert would be relatively insulated from such goings-on. Mattie could have walked past hikers and campers, and they wouldn't necessarily pay attention or recognize him as the man the police were looking for.

Abigail walked out to the porch. She and Owen had driven around, trying to spot Mattie. They'd checked his party spot in the old foundation. Nothing.

It would be a warmer, more humid night than last night, but cool for July, very cool in comparison to Boston. Far out on the water, she could see the lights of expensive yachts. Did one of them belong to Jason Cooper? Had he chucked his family's problems and gone off to enjoy his wealth, be alone?

She became aware of Owen's presence behind her, on the other side of the screen door. "I've changed in the past seven years," she said without looking around at him. "I haven't wanted to admit it. I keep thinking that if I did, I'd also have to acknowledge that Chris might not want me the way I am now."

The door creaked open and shut. Owen brushed away a mosquito floating in front of her face. "His death pulled you up off the path you were on and hurled you back down onto a different one. But you're the same Abigail."

"I don't blame Doyle Alden and the Coopers for resenting me."

"You've had every right to push for answers."

"I've done more than push for answers. Every time I come here I've reminded them of Chris. I won't let them forget him." She pushed her hands through her hair, her short curls more pronounced with the increased humidity. "I don't even have to do anything. I'm his widow. That'll never change. It's like having a circle drawn around me wherever I go that keeps people at bay, that reminds them I lost my husband on our honeymoon."

Owen placed a hand on her shoulder. "You're not keeping me at bay."

She smiled. "Maybe I should. Hell. I can't believe I'm telling you all these things about myself. I suppose if I'd remarried sooner…"

"I'm glad you didn't."

She looked back out at the dark water, the yachts gone now. "For seven years, I've thought if I'd just gone with him on those errands—if I'd taken a walk on the rocks or stopped in at Ellis's garden party—that he'd still be alive. Now, I'm not sure that's true. I'm not sure I could have done anything to keep him from getting killed."

"The break-in, the attack on you—"

"An opportunity. Something the killer could capitalize on, but not the cause of Chris's death." She kept staring into the darkness, her eyes adjusting, picking out stars, seeing outlines and silhouettes of rocks and trees. "He didn't tell me what was going on."

Owen didn't respond.

"It wasn't about who I was. If I'd been a homicide detective seven years ago, he still wouldn't have told me. He wasn't keeping secrets from me so much as just not talking. It was his personality." A firefly sparked in the trees to the side of the house, where the Alden boys had hidden just a few days ago, convinced they'd seen a ghost. "And what did I know of his relationships with the people on this island? I knew him for eighteen months. We weren't even married a week."

"Abigail…"

She seized Owen's hand, intertwined her fingers with his. "I don't want to be alone tonight."

"You don't have to be."

She raised his hand to her lips. "Not here. I can't stay with you here."

A nightmare woke her. Lying in the dark, Abigail didn't know where she was.

She heard an owl outside on a nearby tree and felt the cool breeze from an open window and the warmth of the soft blanket over her, and she remembered the slick heat of tangled limbs and thrusting bodies, hers and Owen's, as they'd made love long into the night.

She reached across the bed and touched his shoulder, thinking he was asleep. But his hand covered hers. She edged closer to him. She felt as if she'd known him forever, and yet there was so much more to find out about him, to the point that he might well have been a stranger.

"You don't know anything about my real life," she whispered. "I investigate homicides in Boston. I'm not just the widow out here on the rocks. And I know nothing about your real life."

"There's time for that." He rolled onto his side, pulling her to him. "Plenty of time."

She ran her fingertips over a scar on his shoulder and upper arm. "Where did this scar come from?" She eased her hand over his chest, unable to see, just to feel the firm flesh, another scar. "And this one…and this one…?"

"I don't remember where half my scars came from. I don't think about them."

She rolled him onto his back and climbed on top of him, straddling him. "You don't think about them, but you remember how you got them." She scraped her fingernails along his hips and sides, feeling him shudder with desire under her. "Every single one of them."

She lifted herself above him, and when she came down again, he was inside her, his arms around her as she drew down hard onto him, pulling him in as deeply as possible. She moaned, sinking her chest onto him, her orgasm instantaneous, racking her to her core.

He whispered her name, thrusting into her, shuddering with his own release.

The cold night wind gusted over their heated bodies, but neither made a move to pull the blanket back over them. Abigail laid her head on his chest and closed her eyes, hoping once she fell asleep again, there'd be no more nightmares.

CHAPTER 29

The morning was warm enough for Abigail to walk barefoot on Owen's smooth wood floors and open up the doors to the deck to let in the breeze and the sounds of the ocean. She wasn't tempted to ask Owen to build a fire in the woodstove. She made coffee, feeling the sunlight streaming in through the tall windows. Her scrapes and bruises were better, her body loose and liquid after their night of lovemaking.

When the phone rang, it didn't occur to her to answer it. Owen, seated at a bar stool at the kitchen peninsula, picked up. "Hello?" He rose, his eyes telling her everything as he handed her the receiver. "For you."

Her caller.

Owen came around the peninsula and stood next to her.

She nodded to him, then said formally into the phone, "It's Abigail Browning."

"Detective. Good morning." The voice had the familiar eerie muffle of the previous calls.

"I'm not in the mood for your games. What do you want?"

"Prickly this morning, aren't you?"

"Just tell me what you want."

"I want you to get back to Boston alive, Detective Browning." The voice on the other end remained strangely toneless, impossible to recognize. "You need to be careful in the coming days. Very careful."

"Why? What do you know?"

He ignored her. "How far will your husband's friends go to keep their secrets?"

"How far will you go to keep your secrets? Everyone has secrets. What are yours?"

"Any secrets I have are innocent ones. Your husband—"

"Chris wasn't talkative. He kept other people's secrets to himself. He was the kind of man people liked to have as a friend." Interrupting her caller had been a risk, but the status quo—being patient—hadn't gotten her anywhere. Abigail licked her lips, listening for background sounds, anything that could help her identify the person on the other end of the line. "If you're trying to make me think any less of Chris because of what he didn't tell me when he was alive, it's not working."

"I just want to help you."

"No, you don't. If you wanted to help me, you'd tell me who you are. You'd meet me."

"You don't call the shots, Detective." An edge had crept into the caller's voice, the first sign of any real emotion. "Haven't you figured that out yet?"

The coffeemaker hissed. Strong-smelling coffee dripped into the glass pot. Abigail felt a prickly sensation on the back of her neck. "Does that mean you're calling the shots?" she asked mildly.

"It means you need to be careful."

"How did you get this phone number?"

"Easy."

"How did you know I was here?"

"Even easier, Detective. You've become quite the slut, haven't you?"

She didn't let his jibe get to her. "Then you're on the island. You're watching me. We've interacted—"

"Don't waste your time trying to figure out who I am." There was no hint of worry in the eerily calm tone. "Think about the secrets people are keeping. Watch your back."

Abigail didn't move as she stood in front of the peninsula, paying careful attention to his every word.

"Promise me you'll be careful, Detective."

She could feel Owen's gaze on her and turned to him, saw his set jaw, his narrowed eyes, and knew he was thinking what she was.

"Detective?"

"You're the killer."

"Don't bother tapping your phone lines." The voice was crisp now, efficient. "I won't call again."

Once he hung up, Abigail could have smashed the telephone on the rocks. Owen put a small pad and a pen on the counter in front of her. She started to speak, but stopped herself and quickly wrote down every word of her conversation with her anonymous caller.

With her husband's killer.

Then, still without speaking, she called Lou Beeler's cell number, got through and reported what had just happened.

The senior detective didn't comment on her whereabouts. "You've got coffee on yet?"

"It'll be ready in two minutes."

"I'll be there in five."

"Five?"

"I slept on Chief Alden's couch last night."

Abigail didn't blame him. She told him she'd be waiting, and hung up, noticing Owen scanning her notes on the call. His gray eyes connected with hers. "I'm sorry," he said and walked out to his deck, leaving her alone in the kitchen.

She waited until the coffee finished brewing, then took two dark brown pottery mugs from an open shelf and set them on the counter. She filled the mugs and headed outside with them. The air was warm, but the deck was cool under her feet. She saw that Owen had gone down to the rocks. She debated leaving him alone there—at least putting on shoes before Lou arrived—but stepped off the deck and onto a sandy path, following it onto a sprawling, rounded boulder.

Mindful of her bare feet and the hot coffee, Abigail jumped to a smaller rock, making her way to Owen's chunk of granite just above the tide line. She handed him one of the mugs. "I suppose I'd be better off in the wrong shoes than barefoot."

He smiled, but she could see in his gray eyes that his mind was elsewhere. "Not necessarily."

"The rough rock's probably a good exfoliator." She paused, seeing the emotion behind his impassive face. "Owen—"

"Why the picture of Doe?" he asked quietly.

She understood his question. Of all the pieces they had of whatever was going on, the photo of his drowned sister was the one that jarred most, that didn't seem to fit. "There has to be a reason. It's not necessarily a logical reason."

"To us."

She nodded. "Exactly. This caller isn't trying to help us find Chris's killer."

"No, he's not. But we have to be sure, Abigail."

"I'm sure. This creep *is* Chris's killer."

Saying the words felt unreal to her. She tried to stand back from them emotionally and pretend she was a homicide detective working a case, not the victim's widow, not a woman who'd lived with questions and doubts about how her husband had died for seven long years. But how could she pretend she wasn't involved? With the strange voice fresh in her mind, with the photos, the cut on her leg, the memories of last night, objectivity was elusive.

"Your caller knows something about Doe's death," Owen said, staring down at a deep tide pool among the rocks. "He's talked a lot about secrets. Maybe he knows a secret about her."

"It's possible. It's also possible the picture of your sister could be a red herring designed to throw us off track, or just to upset you."

A muscle worked in his already tight jaw. He seemed to force himself to drink some of his coffee. "I want this bastard."

"I know. So do I." Abigail's voice sounded calmer than she felt. "This caller is daring and manipulative—maybe desperate, maybe at wit's end. But it's someone with a plan, even if it's not a good plan. And if it is Chris's killer, then it's also someone who's managed to go undetected for seven years, at least."

"Yes. At least."

She took a breath. "If you're thinking your sister was pushed—"

"I saw her go over the cliffs. She wasn't pushed. She was upset—more upset than her fight with Grace would account for." Owen looked up, squinting at a trio of seagulls flying out across the water from her house. "What if someone *was* in the woods that day? What if I didn't make that up?"

"Who?"

He watched the seagulls land on a finger of rocks that jutted out into the water. "It couldn't have been Will Browning or Chris—or Mattie. They were on the boat together."

"You're sure Mattie was on the boat?" Abigail asked.

"I was eleven. I'm not sure of anything."

Sean Alden's age. She remembered his wide eyes yesterday, his fear, his desire to make sense of a situation he couldn't understand. If she'd said there was a ghost in his father's garage, he would have believed her.

She asked Owen, "Did someone tell you there was no one in the woods?"

"Everyone."

"Specifically, who?"

Owen didn't answer. He sipped his coffee and watched the seagulls. It was a bright, clear day, already warm. Finally, he said, "The Coopers. My parents. Polly. They were all there."

"But who told you no one was in the woods?"

"I don't remember."

"Did anyone take a look around?"

He shook his head. "There was no time. We had to get to Doe."

Abigail didn't even want to imagine that scene, the terror and grief and shock as they'd stood out on the stunning granite cliffs and realized fourteen-year-old Dorothy Garrison was in the water.

"Understandable," she said. "Do you remember in what order people arrived?"

"My grandmother was the last to arrive. I remember that. The rest—" He shook his head, his emotions well in check. "I don't know."

"If you remember Polly was the last to get there, you might be able to remember who was first." Abigail took another swallow of coffee, the rock suddenly feeling very hard and rough under her feet. "I don't know that it'll make a difference. After everyone arrived on the cliffs, what happened? Had your sister's body been removed—or did they see her—"

"They watched Chris's grandfather pull her out of the water into his boat."

"Then what?" Abigail asked, pressing him, resisting the tug of her own emotions.

"We drove out to the harbor."

"How? Who were you with? Where were the cars?"

"The cars were up at Ellis's house. Jason Cooper and my father went to get them. The rest of us walked out to the road and met them there. I'm not sure I'd remember, but I saw an owl in a fir tree—it didn't fly away. It perched on its branch and stared at me. My sister was into birds. I thought somehow…" He shrugged, tossing the last of his coffee out into the encroaching tide. "I thought the owl was trying to reassure me that whatever had happened, wherever she was, my sister was okay."

Abigail touched his arm. "I don't know who put that picture on your doorstep or why, but it was an awful thing to do."

Owen turned to her. "If it helps find this killer, then it's worth it." He glanced out at the sparkling water. "I don't need a picture to make me remember that day."

"No. I imagine not."

"When we finish up with Lou, I'm going up to Ellis's house, then out to the cliffs. Maybe being there will jog my memory for any details I've buried all these years."

"I'll go with you."

He managed a smile. "Somehow, I knew you would."

"Unless you'd rather go alone—"

He shook his head. "No, I wouldn't."

Abigail refused Lou Beeler's suggestion that she put herself into protective custody. She was polite and appreciative of his concern, but adamant. "Not a chance, Lou," she said, refilling his mug with fresh coffee.

He didn't give up. He'd perched himself on the bar stool Owen had vacated and had listened to her recap of the call, asking few questions. "At least let me post a trooper at your side."

"That's the same thing."

"I don't like this caller. I haven't from the beginning."

"You said it was probably a crank."

"I did? Well, it still could be." He blew on his steaming coffee. "Makes you not want to answer any more phones, doesn't it?"

"No, it makes me hope he'll call again."

Lou didn't comment.

Once the state detective was finished with him, Owen had retreated to the shower, leaving Abigail to fend off Lou by herself. From the moment he'd walked in the door, it was obvious his anxiety about the situation had been ratcheted up a few notches.

Not that she blamed him.

She dumped out the last of her coffee into the sink. "Next time this bastard calls, I want to have enough caffeine in me so I can figure out a way to back him into a corner and nail him. I hate it when I get calls like that before I've had my morning coffee."

"I see you're coping," Lou said, just short of a grumble.

"I want this guy, Lou. This caller is Chris's killer. I *know* it is."

"Think he meant to give himself away?"

"Yes. I think everything he's done and said is intentional." She looked at the older man across the granite-topped peninsula. "And we're using 'he' in the rhetorical sense. It could be a woman."

"You have anyone in mind, Abigail? Any names you want to throw out there for consideration, just between us?"

She shook her head, then said, "Not Mattie Young."

"Even with the pictures, the necklace, the attack on you, the blackmail?"

"Even with."

Lou studied her a moment, nothing about him giving away what he was thinking or feeling.

"Hell, Lou, you're like a stone statue," she said with some impatience. "You could be sitting there thinking about blueberry pancakes for all I know. What's on your mind?"

"Nothing." He picked up his mug but didn't take a sip of the coffee. "Abigail—"

"I know what you're going to say. I'm not jumping to conclusions. I'm keeping an open mind."

"You're not on this case. Think for a moment what you'd do if you were in my position. Your father's the FBI director. Your deceased husband was an FBI agent. There are presently a couple of G-men in town sniffing into the secrets of a high-level State Department appointee."

"I know, Lou. It's awkward."

"Awkward? It's a damn tangled-up mess is what it is. And I haven't even gotten to the Garrisons and their history, and Owen and his work. I caught up with Doyle last night. His wife's got a big job ahead of her as director of this new field academy in Bar Harbor. Fast Rescue's not an outfit for the fainthearted. Owen has ambitious plans. He doesn't do anything by half measures—" Lou stopped suddenly, and Abigail realized she must have reddened or something, because he groaned. "Oh, hell. Damn it, Browning."

She cleared her throat. "Back to the pictures. Have your guys discovered any concrete evidence that Mattie shot them?"

Lou seemed almost relieved that she'd redirected the subject to the investigation at hand. He shook his head. "Nothing so far. Apparently he did burn a bunch of negatives, but his files are just the disaster you'd expect them to be. Maybe worse."

"If he did take the pictures, he could have given them to someone, sold them. We don't know if they've been in his sole possession all this time. He could have made copies and given them out to a half-dozen different people."

"Not likely. Someone would have come forward."

"But possible," Abigail said. She didn't wait for Lou to continue to speculate with her. "What about Linc Cooper?"

"He's home with his family. He should have told us what was going on, but now he has. The FBI was interested in what he had to say. What he did shouldn't have an impact on Grace's appointment. It's just a whiff of scandal. But what she did *herself*—lying all these years about talking to Chris at her uncle's, not saying anything about her brother—" Lou shrugged, not going on.

Abigail finished for him. "That could be more than a whiff of scandal." She pointed to his mug. "Finished?"

"Yeah. Doyle makes lousy coffee. This was better."

"How're the boys doing?"

"They seem fine. They know Mattie. They're not afraid of him, even if they should be."

She dumped out the last of his coffee and put all three mugs into the dishwasher, closing it up with a thud. "What about weapons? Did you find any guns in Mattie's house?"

"No."

"You're not going to tell me what the murder weapon was, are you, Lou?"

"I haven't in seven years. I'm not today. You know I can't."

Withholding that kind of detail was standard operating procedure, but Abigail persisted. "An automatic. There were shell casings. I didn't know what they meant at the time—"

"Abigail," he warned.

"It wasn't a lucky shot that killed Chris. The killer knows how to shoot. He likes guns. If he threw the murder weapon into the ocean, then he got himself another just like it." She walked around to Lou's side of the peninsula. "That's my guess, anyway."

The state detective ignored her completely. "What are you going to do now?"

"Owen and I thought we'd walk up to Ellis's." She smiled with feigned innocence. "I have this thing for delphinium."

"Mattie."

Mattie stirred amid the thick evergreens that grew along the cliffs where Doe Garrison drowned, listening in case he'd conjured up the voice whispering his name.

"Mattie Young."

A ghost?

Chris's ghost?

He brushed pine needles off him and stood up under the low branches of the prickly balsam firs and spruces. He'd made his way down there before dawn, after a rough night up on the ledge. A state cruiser had purred along the private road just after he crossed it and disappeared into the forest. It wasn't great timing on his part. It was luck. Pure damn luck.

He heard the rustle of dead leaves and underbrush from his own movements, and he smelled the tang of salt in the air from the ocean just below him.

It wasn't Chris.

Chris is dead. What the hell's the matter with you?

"I know you're here, Mattie."

That voice.

It wasn't Abigail, or Owen. Doyle. The people he'd betrayed but who wouldn't hurt him.

It wasn't any of them.

A cold serenity came over him. He knew what was happening now. He shut his eyes a split second and pictured himself in the ice and snow of Acadia on a soundless, frigid winter afternoon. His winter photography was some of his finest. He liked the island best on the coldest, clearest, sharpest winter days.

He'd trapped himself along the edge of thirty-foot rock cliffs.

There was nowhere to run. Behind him was the ocean. Ahead of him, a killer.

"Mattie."

He recognized the voice but refused to look to see if he was right.

He'd had his chances, and now they were done. He had nothing more to do in this life.

He would need a miracle to live out the hour.

"Mattie, what are you doing?"

I'm going to Chris.

I'm going to one of the friends I betrayed.

My best friend.

And he turned to meet his killer.

CHAPTER 30

Abigail stopped at her house to shower, change clothes and clear her head. Owen had agreed to meet her on the steps up to Ellis's. She needed a few minutes alone—a few minutes to think in the quiet rooms where the man she'd loved and married and lost had lived for most of his short life.

If only the walls could speak, she thought, heading downstairs to the entry, her hair still damp from her shower. She'd pulled on jeans, her good running shoes, a camp shirt and her gun, a .40 caliber Glock. The niceties of jurisdictions and Maine's gun laws notwithstanding, she doubted Lou Beeler would object.

She spotted Special Agents Ray Capozza and Mary Steele out on her doorstep and yanked open her front door. "What can I do for you?"

"We thought we'd stop by and see how you're doing," Capozza said.

"I'm fine. Just washed my hair. I didn't blow-dry it—"

Steele rolled her eyes. "It's a courtesy call, Detective Browning. We wanted to let you know that Grace Cooper has withdrawn her name for the State Department job. No reason stated."

Capozza stared straight at Abigail, his gaze unwavering, hard-ass. She decided she liked him. "Lying to the police in a murder investigation could have something to do with it," he said. "She told your husband at Ellis Cooper's party—the day Agent Browning died—that her brother was down here on the water. She believed that was the case. If she'd told the investigators that fact seven years ago—" He shrugged. "Who knows?"

Abigail opened the door wider. "I'm off to meet Owen Garrison in a minute, but would you two care to come inside?"

Steele shook her head. "We have some loose ends we need to tie up."

"Let us know if we can be of any assistance," Capozza said. Abigail believed his courtesy had nothing to do with who her father was. The guy just wanted to help. He winked at her. "See you around, Detective."

"Abigail," she said.

"Yeah."

She shut the door after the two federal agents left and headed for the back room, making sure the porch door was locked this time. She stood in the middle of the gutted room and heard the clatter of the tools, as if that summer afternoon so long ago were happening now. She remembered the hit on her head. The split second fear that she was going to die.

And, later, seeing Chris. That awful expression. She remembered the countless times she'd tried to describe it in her journals. He knew who'd smacked her on the head.

Mattie.

Probably, she thought. Almost certainly. But what had happened that day went beyond Mattie Young and his anger at Chris, his drinking, his sense of entitlement.

When he'd gone up to Ellis's house, Chris had asked about Linc, not because he believed the boy was responsible for the break-in, but because he wanted to make sure Linc was safe. That was all.

"Things are happening on Mt. Desert."

Her caller. The killer. Why draw her up here? Why now?

Abigail went into the kitchen and dug out her descriptions of the photos that had been left for her and Owen. She'd tried to be as precise as possible.

She read through them, pictured each shot—the people in them, the angles, the shadows, the time of day. Lou would have experts looking at them. They'd have all the right equipment.

Objectivity.

She thought of the photo of her and Owen on the rocks. She could feel his arms around her, his breath on her as he'd kept her from running to her dead husband, and she could remember how much she'd hated him. It was a visceral reaction, natural. He was the one who'd found Chris. He was the one who'd first realized there was no hope for her husband.

And he was the one who'd had to tell her.

She put her notes away and headed outside, locking her front door behind her. She saw the fat robin back up on its branch and felt a surge of hope that she couldn't describe or even understand.

Halfway up the driveway, she veered off onto the path through the woods that led to the cliffs where Doe Garrison had drowned. Chris had taken her out there once, but this had never been one of her favorite spots. The transition from woods to cliffs and ocean was too abrupt—downright scary, as far as she was concerned. She wasn't much on vertical drops unless there was a rail or a window.

Owen, she knew, wouldn't mind at all.

One of the differences between them, she thought, picking up her pace.

They'd assumed Mattie took the picture of Doe's body on the dock, after his and the Brownings' failed attempt to rescue her. But he was just seventeen then, a boy still himself.

Would a teenager snap a picture of a dead girl—a pretty fourteen-year-old he knew?

And why keep such a picture?

Why leave it for her brother?

Mattie wasn't in the shot. That suggested it was most likely his work.

Abigail paused in the shade of a massive spruce, its lower branches dead sticks poking out of its gnarled trunk. Despite the ravages of the harsh conditions of its exposed spot, the tree had survived.

The angle of the shot of Doe and her traumatized family and friends meant it must have been taken not from a boat or farther out on the dock, but from the parking lot above, perhaps from a car or truck.

She shut her eyes, seeing the horror on the faces of the Garrisons—Owen, his parents, his grandmother. And Jason Cooper, his arm around his young daughter.

Who would take such a picture?

Chris and his grandfather were there, on the sidelines, grim and sad, but not a part of the Garrison and Cooper circle.

Mattie wasn't there. Definitely. She'd remember.

And Ellis.

Abigail opened her eyes and felt a warm breeze sweep in as if from the center of the island.

Ellis Cooper wasn't in the picture.

Lou Beeler had never warmed up to Grace Cooper. People said she was nice enough. Smart. Well-connected. But she'd always struck him as a woman wrapped so tight, once she started to unravel, that'd be it. It'd be like unrolling a mummy and finding nothing inside but bits of bones and little piles of dust.

For all her success and riches, she was a woman with no center. Lou was convinced she didn't really know who she was.

He was relieved not to see any FBI agents parked in the Cooper driveway.

Grace called to him from the front porch. "Lieutenant Beeler," she said, her voice cool, collected. "I imagine you're looking for me, aren't you?"

He walked up the steps, noting that the hanging plants looked parched—missing Mattie Young, no doubt. "Mind if I have a word with you?" he asked.

"Of course not." She sat on a wicker settee with a little puff-ball of a dog in her lap. But her face was pale, her eyes distant, even as she smiled with an emotionless grace. "Please, sit down."

Lou shook his head. "I don't have that much time. I wanted to ask you, Ms. Cooper—" He paused, watching her reaction. She knew why he was there. "When Chris

Browning came up to your uncle's house after Abigail was attacked and spoke to you, why did you tell him your brother was down at the old Garrison foundation?"

"I—I—" She made a choking sound, unable to go on, and fell back against the settee. Her knees went slack, and the little dog slipped down her legs, then jumped off her lap and scampered up onto a nearby rocker.

Lou didn't relent. "Did you know your brother was on the grounds?"

"No." She recovered her poise. "I didn't know. I didn't lie to Chris."

"Ms. Cooper—Grace, why did you think your brother was down at the old Garrison place?"

But she couldn't answer, and Lou realized that she didn't have to.

He saw her answer in her eyes. The truth had hit her, and hit hard. Just as it did him.

Ellis.

Her uncle had told her.

For the first time in many years, Lou's knees buckled under him.

Oh, my God.

The two FBI agents pulled over just as Owen started up the steep steps. Special Agent Steele, in the passenger seat, rolled down her window and shouted to him. "You can't even see those steps from the road. They're amazing. I guess this island's full of hidden, amazing spots." But nothing about her manner suggested she was playing the tourist. "We just saw Detective Browning. She said she'd be along soon."

Ray Capozza leaned over from the wheel. "You shouldn't be running around out here by yourself."

"Probably good advice," Owen said.

Steele tapped her fingers on the open window. "Advice you'll ignore."

He said nothing, and the two agents went on their way. He continued up the steps. He would be able to see Abigail once she started up. He knew every inch of the stone steps, similar to, but not as dramatic as, the more famous steps up to the Thuya Gardens in Northeast Harbor, now open to the public. No such destiny awaited his great-grandfather's former property.

As he climbed a narrow section of steps, Owen imagined visiting Thuya Gardens with Abigail, hiking every trail on Mt. Desert, kayaking with her—then, with a pang of guilt, realized Chris must have had similar ideas. He shook them off and focused on the task at hand.

When he reached the top of the steps, he saw that Jason Cooper's car was in the driveway.

Owen looked down the vertical hillside, through the trees toward the road, but Abigail still hadn't turned up. He walked out to the driveway, feeling the humidity in the air.

He remembered himself charging out the front door and down the steps after his sister.

Twenty-five years ago, if anyone had said one of the Garrison kids would fall off the cliffs and drown, one-hundred percent of the people told would have guessed it would be him.

The front door of the graceful house stood open. He headed up the shaded stone walk. A hummingbird fluttered to a pot of some kind of red flowers, almost as if Doe's ghost had sent it as a reminder of her.

Owen peered through the screen door. "Hello— anyone home?"

When there was no answer, he pulled open the door and stepped onto the cool tile floor. Since his family had sold the place, he'd seldom been inside, and not just to avoid memories. Ellis was a private man who preferred small get-togethers with family and close friends. The garden party seven years ago had been an aberration, atypical of his nature.

When no one answered, Owen walked back to the kitchen.

Jason stood at the sink, staring out the window at his brother's gardens.

"Jason? What's going on?"

The older man didn't look back from the sink. He said, "Chris suspected there was something weird about Ellis—something beyond eccentric. I never wanted to listen." He lowered his head, as if in shame. "I accused him once of trailer-trash envy."

"Jason—"

"I wish I knew what was going on. I wish I'd known all along and had asked the right questions. I thought…" He gulped back a sob. "I thought selling this place made sense. I hoped it would help Ellis—help all of us."

"Where is he?"

Jason shook his head. "I don't know." He placed both his hands on the sink edge and dropped his head down between his arms. "I'm afraid he's lost in his own obsessions. I'm afraid there's no way back for him."

Owen left Jason in the kitchen and quickly checked the living room, the library, and the dining room, but saw no one. He headed down the hall toward the back bedrooms. Not since he was a child had he gone this far into the house. He pushed back memories.

He arrived at Doe's old room.

Jason came up behind him. "Ellis keeps it locked."

"Not anymore."

Owen reared back and kicked the door, splintering it away from the lock on the first try. It bounced open, and he went inside.

The room was as Doe had left it twenty-five years earlier.

The same white throw rugs, the same pink chenille bed-spread, the same simple pine furniture.

And there were differences.

Birds, Owen saw. Dozens of stuffed birds stuck up on shelves, hanging from the ceiling. Hawks, eagles, robins, bluebirds, hummingbirds, chickadees.

And guns. They were on display behind a glass cabinet. A rifle, a shotgun, two revolvers and two pistols. Ammu-nition. A stack of paper targets.

Jason staggered, falling against the doorjamb. "Dear God."

"Don't go any farther. We don't want to touch anything." Owen put a hand on the older man's shoulder and steadied him. "We need to get the police in here."

"What's he done?" Jason blinked rapidly, his face as pale as death. "My God in heaven. All these years…"

"Ellis was the one in the woods. He could have saved Doe."

"Believe me, Owen. I had no idea. I knew he was attached to her. But—you know him. He's always been quiet, intro-verted. Sensitive. He's not a predator. He keeps to himself."

"I wasn't wrong. There was someone in the woods that day. Doe was upset because of Ellis. He didn't save her because he knew he could never have her—or because he was afraid she'd expose him." Owen heard the steeliness in his own voice. "He must have come on to her. God knows what he tried to do to her—did do. And she rejected him. She wasn't upset because of Grace."

"Dear God."

"It all makes sense now. Look at this room, Jason. Your brother was twenty-five, and he was abusing the trust of a fourteen-year-old girl."

Jason looked as if he'd vomit. "I had no idea it'd gone this far. Owen, my God, what's Ellis done?" He gripped Owen's arm. "What—has—Ellis—done?"

"We need to find him. There are cops crawling all over this island looking for Mattie Young. I'll call—"

"No." Jason straightened, steadier on his feet. "I'll call."

Owen thought of Abigail out there with the man who'd killed her husband. "Do it," he said.

"Where are you going?"

"I'm going to find Abigail."

Doyle cleaned up Mattie's makeshift campsite in his garage. The lab guys had carted off what they needed and dusted for prints and scraped up anything that looked as if it might have an eyelash or some other kind of DNA in it. He figured Mattie hadn't cared about covering his tracks. He'd cared about getting through the night without freezing to death, starving, dying of thirst or getting shot.

Sean and Ian had promised to stay within earshot. Doyle could hear them bickering in the backyard. He'd kept them home and pulled himself off the investigation. He was a police chief in a small town and accustomed to knowing the people he dealt with, but this was different. This was Mattie Young sleeping in his damn garage. This was a guy he'd known since kindergarten messing up under his nose.

And it was Chris.

Doyle stuffed a half-filled trash bag into a plastic garbage can, replaced the lid and bit back something between a sob and a growl. He'd been mixed-up and out of sorts ever since Mattie—and it *was* Mattie—had come after Abigail with a drywall saw.

"Mattie—hell. What were you thinking?"

He wasn't thinking, just as he wasn't thinking when he'd broken into Chris's house seven years ago and hit his friend's wife on the head then, stolen her necklace, ran.

But he hadn't killed Chris.

Doyle just couldn't see that one. Mattie was a chronic screw-up and a whiner, but even when he was drunk, he wasn't a murderer. He wasn't someone who'd lay in wait for his target and take him out with a single shot the way Chris's killer had done.

Not his problem now. He'd promised to take the boys into Ellsworth for pizza and a movie.

Lou Beeler's car careened into his driveway.

Doyle called for his sons. They came running and stood at his side as the state detective got out of his car.

"It's Ellis Cooper," Lou said.

"Ellis?"

"We're going after him. You have a place to leave your sons?"

Sean slipped his hand into his father's and tugged on it. "We can stay next door with Mrs. Casey. Me and Ian will be fine."

Doyle looked down at his son. "Ian and I."

The boy grinned at their old refrain. "That's what I said."

They'd be okay, his boys. Doyle nodded to the state detective. "Give me a minute to get these guys settled and I'll ride out there with you."

CHAPTER 31

Ellis Cooper held a gun to his nephew's head. Linc was pale but very still, his blue eyes wide with fear but focused on Abigail as she stood three yards from the two men on the edge of the cliffs, her Glock drawn.

If she'd realized what was happening sooner, she'd have shot Ellis before he ever saw her. But she hadn't.

"Drop your weapon, Abigail." Ellis's voice was calm, just as it had been earlier that morning on the phone to her. "If you don't, Linc is dead. I'm an expert marksman."

She had no doubt he was telling the truth. "One of your many secrets."

He inhaled sharply through his nose. He liked being in charge. "Do it *now*."

"Okay, I'm putting the gun down—"

"Toss it in the water."

Hell. She nodded, opening her fingers from her grip on the weapon. "I'm tossing it now." She reached her arm out and pitched her Glock over the cliff. "Done. Now let your nephew go. You have me. That's enough for you to get away."

"So noble."

Linc sputtered in a mix of anger and terror. "Ellis… Jesus…"

"Focus on saving your own skin." Abigail kept her voice calm. Reasonable. Any vulnerability on her part would only increase Ellis's sense of control over her. He needed to see he had one option and one option only, and that was not to fire his weapon. "Go, Ellis. Disappear. Don't waste your time on these games."

"You won't stop. You won't ever stop."

"Neither will the FBI, Doyle Alden, Owen Garrison or Lou Beeler, even after he retires. The Maine State Police will keep the Browning file open. I know a couple of Boston detectives who'll hunt you."

"This is you. All you."

"It's not just me. It's never been just me. And that's not why you're out here now. If you wanted me dead, you could have shot me while I was sitting out on the rocks reading a book."

Linc licked his lips. "Ellis, you're sick. Let your family help you—"

"Shut up!" He pressed the barrel of his gun against his nephew's temple. "I don't want your help. I've lived in my brother's shadow my whole life. I've kept to myself. I've done so much for you and Grace. For *him*. And what's my thanks? He decides to sell my house. My sanctuary."

"You made it your sanctuary because you loved Doe," Abigail said.

"Because I *love* her. Present tense. I'm not a pervert who likes young girls—who goes from one girl to the next to the next. I keep Doe's memory alive every single day. I honor her."

"What if her ghost is here now, where she died, watching you?" Keep him talking, Abigail thought. If he's talking, he's not shooting. She went on, brisk but choosing her words carefully. "Everything I know about her tells me she was a kind, gentle soul. I saw the picture of her you left. The one you took. You knew that even in death, she was beautiful. Did you leave it for Owen to remind him?"

"He never appreciated her. It's his fault she died. Not mine."

An eleven-year-old boy, a little brother. Ellis's twisted expectations had poisoned him. But Abigail wanted to keep him talking. Owen would be missing her soon. All she needed was a distraction, a break.

"No one appreciated Doe as much as you did," Abigail said. "I see that now."

"She didn't understand. She was so young…so innocent…I was only eleven years older. What I felt for her wasn't unnatural."

"She was fourteen."

"I promised her I'd wait for her."

"That's not why she ran crying. That's not why she was so upset she slipped and fell to her death." Abigail paused, making sure his attention was on her and what she was saying. She saw his spark of anger, the resentment in him. "And it's not why you let her drown."

"I didn't let her drown!"

"Sure, you did. She was upset because of you. You didn't just express your love and tell her you'd wait. Your interest in her wasn't so innocent, was it?"

"The love we had was pure—"

"Did you rape her?"

His face reddened. "She died unspoiled."

"But you came on to her," Abigail persisted. "That porcelain skin, that silken hair—you wanted her, Ellis. You wanted her all to yourself. You had no intention of waiting until she was older. If you didn't rape her, what did you do? Expose yourself to her? Make her expose herself—"

"You slut! You bitch."

It was her opening. In his fury, he lowered his gun.

Abigail yelled to Linc. "Jump!"

But he needed no prodding. Knew it was his one chance. The tide was up, the water was deep—and he wasn't a frightened distraught thirteen-year-old. Linc propelled himself over the cliffs, even as Abigail dove for his uncle, grabbing his gun hand and, using a hold she'd practiced countless times, snapped his ulna in his right forearm. She heard the break. He screamed in pain, dropping his gun. It slid off the edge of the rock wall into the water. She sliced a low kick to the inside of his leg, bringing him down onto exposed rock.

"You bitch!" he yelled.

"Where's Mattie? He was here. I found a poncho—"

Ellis grinned, smug, as she held him on the ground. "Mattie's in the water, too. He's been there for a while. You needed a killer. I needed an end to your scrutiny. I needed to give my brother a reason to take my house off the market. The murderous yardman, the publicity—no way would Jason find a buyer. And Grace. It wasn't easy, Abigail, to sacrifice my own niece, but I had to. For all our sakes, we needed a killer."

And in Ellis's twisted logic, Mattie was there. Again. "How long has Mattie been in the water?"

"Too long. If he's still alive, he won't last. Linc won't

be able to save him. He's not a strong swimmer. The water's cold. The waves are brutal."

"You could have saved Doe."

"I did save her. That's what you'll never understand."

"Chris didn't go down to the water to find Mattie or Linc. He went down there to find *you*. He knew about your obsession."

"He'd seen Doe's room."

Her room. Abigail looked into the eyes of the man who'd let a fourteen-year-old girl drown. The man who'd murdered her husband.

"You make me sick."

He tried to reach for her throat with his good hand, but she smashed his head against the rock. He went slack, unconscious. She checked him for hidden weapons, then scrambled to her feet and looked over the edge of the cliffs.

A huge swell took Linc against the rocks to her left, but he grabbed one with both arms and held on.

Directly below her, she caught a glimpse of Mattie right before a wave took him under. He didn't fight it. If he was conscious, he clearly had no strength left in him.

If she didn't act now, he'd drown or smash his body on the rocks.

The water was deep. She was a good swimmer.

Owen would have missed her by now. He had to be on his way. All she had to do was get to Mattie and stabilize the situation.

Abigail couldn't just let him die.

She jumped.

No one was at the cliffs when Owen arrived. Dead branches clicked and cracked in the strong west wind that blew hot through the trees. Dark clouds had moved over the island, a storm imminent. He noticed tufts of wild grass that had been trampled.

He knelt down, saw a smear of blood on exposed ledge.

He heard a sound in the trees behind him.

Ellis staggered out from under a low fir branch on his walking stick. "There's nothing we can do. Abigail's in the water." He spoke rapidly, blood pouring down the right side of his head. "She jumped in to save Linc. Mattie—he was out of control. He pushed Linc into the water. He was about to push me, but I had my walking stick. I got to him first. They're all down there now. Abigail, Mattie, Linc."

Owen stood up. "How did you bloody your head, Ellis?"

"What? Oh, this." He wiped his fingers through the blood. "It's nothing."

"Abigail smashed your head on this rock, didn't she?"

He seemed confused. Snot dripped out of his nose. Sweat beaded on his forehead and darkened his armpits. "It's your fault. She wouldn't have slipped…"

"I don't have time for this."

Owen heard someone on the trail coming in from the road. The FBI agents, Lou, Doyle—it didn't matter. He needed to deal with Ellis and get to the people in the water.

Ellis lifted his walking stick, blood dripping into his right eye. "Move away from the cliffs. I want them to drown before you can rescue them. Just as your sister did."

In two steps, Owen was at him. He snatched the walking stick and tossed it aside, just as Doyle and Lou arrived, guns drawn.

"It's his fault," Ellis screamed. "It's all Owen's fault!"

Owen ignored him and looked at the two police officers. "I need to get in the water."

*   *   *

Abigail had never been so damn cold in her life. She huddled with Mattie in the cold water, the waves pushing them against the sheer rock face of the cliffs. His thin frame was limp from the battering it had taken from the rocks and water. His teeth chattered. He tried to speak, but his words were slurred. She recognized the signs of hypothermia and knew she'd be feeling them herself before too long.

Across the small horseshoe cove formed by the cliffs, Linc Cooper had managed to secure himself on a rectangular boulder just under water, but the waves continued to pound him. With the cold, he wouldn't be able to hold on much longer.

And Abigail knew neither would she.

Without help, they'd never last through high tide. The isolated cove wasn't easily visible to passing boats. The gusts of wind and the crash of waves would keep them from hearing any screams for help. And there'd be no kayakers out in these swells.

"Pretend you're in a hot bath," she whispered to Mattie. "Think about sitting by Owen's woodstove."

"I...deserve to die."

"You deserve to live, Mattie. Come on. Stay with me."

A huge swell engulfed them. Cold salt water went up her nose and down her mouth. Abigail coughed, spitting, trying to keep her feet under her, on the rocks. She hung on to Mattie, who barely responded anymore to the battering his body was taking. If she let go, he'd drown. She could feel his ribs under his soaked clothes. How long had it been since he'd taken care of himself?

His drooping eyelids struggled to open. "I'm sorry. I never meant to hurt you."

"You can't drink, Mattie. That's all there is to it." Abigail kept her tone cheerful, positive. "Once we get out of here, I'll make you a nice pot of hot coffee. We'll, hell, here comes another wave. Hang on."

It was too strong a swell to fight, and she went with it, holding Mattie under by his armpits as they smashed into the face of the cliffs. She felt rock claw at her back and legs but didn't fight the impact.

She swore she heard thunder.

"Great." She held Mattie close to her. "Locusts are next."

"Abigail…Chris…I didn't…"

"I know you didn't kill him. Ellis killed him." She felt him sobbing into her. "Oh, Mattie. You didn't cause Chris's death. Ellis would have found a way to kill him no matter what you did."

"I was mad…Grace."

"She was in love with Chris."

"A fantasy. I was real."

"You? Mattie…" Abigail grinned at him, trying to encourage him to keep fighting, even as she shivered, her own teeth beginning to chatter. "You and Grace? I'll be damned."

The thought of Grace seemed to help him stay a bit more alert. "She tries. She loves her brother. I just couldn't—" He slumped, his eyes closing again. "I couldn't fight a ghost."

"Chris knew about the two of you?"

Mattie didn't respond. He was too sleepy, nearly unconscious.

Another swell overtook them, inundating them and dislodging them from her wall and back into deeper water. She felt him slip out of her grasp and lost him as she pushed her way back to air.

As if she'd imagined them, Abigail felt strong arms encircle her.

Owen's arms.

"I've got you, Abigail. Let me take your weight."

"Mattie…"

"I've got him, too. You kept him alive."

"Linc—"

"He's okay. A rescue team's on the way."

"Ellis. I hit him, but he's still alive—"

"Doyle and Lou have him. You can relax now."

"Damn Maine water. I had to fight off ice cubes as well as rocks." She tried to stop her teeth from chattering. "You didn't just jump off the cliff, did you?"

His arms tightened around her. "Hell, no. Lou had a rope and some clamps."

"Batman." She smiled at him, wondering if she was delirious. "My very own Batman."

She didn't remember what happened after that.

CHAPTER 32

Bloodied and beaten, Ellis still had gone after one of Doyle Alden's officers with a rock, snatching his gun, and Lou Beeler had shot him.

It was a clean shot. Ellis had died instantly.

"Suicide by cop," Lou said.

Abigail, wrapped in a fleece blanket in front of Owen's woodstove, shook her head. "He still thought he could make it work. He didn't give up."

She edged closer to the fire. Thunderstorms were raging outside, and everyone else was in shorts and looked hot, but she thought she'd never get warm again. Mattie was in the hospital but would recover. He'd talked some to police before the paramedics took him away. Linc was fine, back with his family.

They'd survived.

"Ellis's gun. It fell in the water when I tackled him."

"We've got it."

"It'll be the weapon he used to kill Chris," Abigail said. "That's how his mind worked. He'd like the poetic justice of it. And he'd be too arrogant to get rid of it." She tightened the blanket around her. "It's like keeping Doe's swing in the backyard for everyone to see."

"I never had a clue," Lou said.

"Me, neither. Thank God he didn't kill anyone else."

"He was all about hate, not love. You know that, don't you?" Lou's look took in Owen, too. "Both of you?"

Owen nodded. "I had that clear in my head the second I kicked in the door to Doe's old room."

"He resented Jason for his money and power over him," Abigail said. "He felt like a second-class Cooper. His secret obsession with Doe allowed him to feel more power, more control."

Owen stared at the fire. "Doe never said a word. She kept what he did to her to herself."

"I know it doesn't make it any easier, but that's not uncommon," Lou said.

Abigail agreed. "Chris figured out Ellis was obsessed with Dorothy Garrison. That's why Ellis killed him. They both knew Linc was burglarizing homes, that Mattie was angry with Chris for dumping him as an informant. Ellis used and manipulated them—and Grace. Only his obsession mattered."

"Mattie never expected you to be at your house that afternoon," Owen said.

Lou nodded. "He's told us that already. Ellis said you weren't home. When you surprised Mattie, he panicked. He hit you and grabbed the necklace, knowing the burglar would be blamed. He didn't want to get caught with the necklace and dropped it in the wall."

"And Ellis seized the moment." Abigail felt a surge of respect for the man she'd married. "Chris did what he could to keep anyone else from getting hurt. Ellis knew he would—he counted on it."

"Your husband was a good man," Lou said. "I wish I'd had a chance to know him."

Abigail bit back tears. "What about Grace? Have you talked to her?"

"She lied to us after the fact. She didn't knowingly help her uncle kill your husband. She wouldn't have—" Lou stopped himself, getting to his feet. "The Coopers have a lot to sort out. I don't envy them."

If the Maine detective felt any lingering effects from having killed Ellis Cooper, he didn't show it in his stride as he headed out.

He stopped at the door. "By the way, about hypothermia—you know one of the best ways to get warm?" He grinned. "Shared body heat."

Abigail groaned. "Good night, Lou."

After her fellow detective left, Owen sat next to her by the fire. "He's right, you know."

"Tonight's a good night to be close to you."

He gathered up more blankets and pillows, laying them on the floor in front of the woodstove. He stretched out next to her. "We'll stay right here by the fire."

Linc drifted off on the couch in the library and awoke with a start, overwhelmed by a feeling of sheer terror. His heart beat wildly.

"It's okay, son," his father said, taking his hand in the near-darkness. "I'm here."

"Dad?"

"I'm not going anywhere. Don't worry."

Grace came into the room. "I thought you two were asleep. I've got chamomile tea made if either of you wants it." Her voice sounded curiously calm—shock, maybe, Linc thought. "Just let me know."

Their father sat on the floor next to Linc. "Ellis was a malevolent force in all our lives. He had secrets none of us could ever have hoped to penetrate. He was lost in them. He couldn't see his way out." Jason's voice faltered. "I didn't know how far he'd gone."

"Oh, Dad. I'm so sorry." Linc was too exhausted to cry. "He was your brother."

"He hated us."

"None of us knew," Grace said quietly. "We all loved him."

"We loved the man he wanted us to believe he was."

Grace said quietly, "Chris was the happiest man I've ever seen in those last days with Abigail. If I could ever dare to be so happy…"

"Dare it, Grace. Dare everything to be that happy."

Linc could see the shock on his sister's face at their father's words.

When Linc drifted off again, he was aware of his father stretched out on the floor next to him, and his sister sitting across the room with her little pot of chamomile tea.

Mattie didn't expect to see Doyle standing over his hospital bed when he woke up in a haze of painkillers and God knew what else the doctors had pumped into him. He was still on an IV. He tried to sit up. "Abigail? Linc? Are they all right?"

"They're okay," Doyle said, gruff as ever. "You got banged up the most. A couple broken ribs. About eight million bruises. You didn't puncture a lung, though. No internal injuries."

"I deserved to die."

"Well, you didn't. Now you have to figure out what comes next."

"I can't drink."

Doyle nodded. "But you know it's really about *not* drinking." He seemed awkward. "I talked to Katie this morning. We'll have to see what the prosecutors decide to do with you, but if you're not in jail, you can have the spare bedroom until you're back on your feet. One drop of alcohol, and you're out. And you're never to be there alone with the boys."

"Doyle, I don't deserve—"

"It's not about what you deserve, Mattie. Katie and I can and want to do this for you. We're not trying to save you. We know we can't. Only you can save yourself."

"When I was in the water," he whispered. "Before Abigail. Chris was there. He kept me going. I had to stay alive to tell people about Ellis. I could hear his voice. I swear, Doyle. He was there, telling me…I had this one last chance…."

If Doyle believed him, he'd never say. "You've got a long road ahead of you, Mattie Young. Katie and I can walk some of it with you, but if you stumble—if you screw up—you're on your own."

"I don't know what to say."

"Just say thank you."

"Thank you."

Sean and Ian Alden squatted in front of a tide pool down on the rocks by Owen's house. He sat on the deck with Doyle, watching the boys hold periwinkles up to their ears.

"You ever hear a periwinkle sing?" Doyle asked. "Because I never have. Katie says she hears them all the time."

Owen lifted his feet onto the deck rail. "I can't say I've spent a lot of time listening to periwinkles."

"You would if you lived out here on this rock year-round." Doyle grinned, and it was good to see. Forty-eight hours after Ellis Cooper's death, nothing was back to normal. "Something to be said for it, don't you think?" His grin broadened. "You'd go out of your damn mind."

"I'll be up here regularly once the field academy starts."

"Rappelling off cliffs. Hauling trainees up and down mountains. Diving off boats. You won't be listening to periwinkles sing."

"Sometimes, maybe."

"Katie's excited about being director. You should hear her." Doyle leaned back in his deck chair. "It's good. I'm happy for her. For us."

Owen shifted his gaze from the boys up the headland toward Abigail's house on the rocks. The media had descended in a whir, keeping Doyle's officers busy. Special Agents Capozza and Steele had kept vigil on Abigail's house during the worst of it. John March called his daughter from Washington. He'd wait and see her when the frenzy had died down. By last night, most of the media had departed.

Doyle nodded in the direction of her house. "Her cop buddies from Boston are there. Bob O'Reilly and that other one—Scoop Wisdom. Have you seen him? Hell. He looks like he could dig Ellis up and shoot him again just to be sure he's dead. Abigail says he's got cats, though."

"Cats?"

"She thinks anyone who has a cat can't be all that mean. I told her she should look up all the murder cases involving weird cat people. Of course, she knows there are exceptions—she's just saying this guy Scoop's not as big a bad-ass as he looks. I guess not, because he's helping her and O'Reilly nail up wallboard and paint the place."

"Doyle," Owen said. "Are you okay?"

His eyes filled with tears, but his gaze never left his sons. "I keep going back over what I could have done. I was the responding officer after the break-in seven years ago. If I'd realized it was Mattie—if I'd known Chris was on to Ellis…"

"Ellis manipulated Mattie. Seven years ago, and this past week."

"Mattie's responsible for his own decisions."

"But Ellis played on his weaknesses. Chris knew. He didn't realize Ellis was a marksman. The police had found where Ellis practiced in the woods behind his house here, and at a private shooting range near his home in Washington. He'd kept his skill to himself. Chris guessed that Ellis stood by and watched my sister die, but that's different from ambushing someone."

"If he'd asked me to come down here with him—"

"Then you'd both be dead."

Doyle was silent a moment. "Maybe so." He pointed at the cloudless sky. "Hey, a heron."

Owen saw it, a giant blue heron, ungainly looking and yet so graceful as it flew up the rockbound coast toward the cliffs.

"Herons were always one of Chris's favorites," Doyle said.

"One of Doe's, too." When the bird disappeared, Owen got to his feet. "I have to go. You and the boys are welcome to stay here as long as you like."

"Where are you off to?"

"Guatemala," he said. "There's been a massive mudslide."

"I thought you were supposed to be resting."

Owen shrugged. "I'll rest another time."

"How're you getting to Guatemala?"

"I'm flying to Austin and meeting my team there. We'll head out together."

Doyle squinted up at him. "Abigail know you fly your own plane?"

"Abigail has thick files on all of us, Doyle." Owen grinned, clapping a hand on his friend's shoulder. "She knows more about us than we know about ourselves."

Bob and Scoop were in her kitchen making dinner—boiling lobsters, which she hated to do—when Abigail saw Mattie limp up from the spruce trees down by the back porch. He looked thin and colorless, but his hair was clean, pulled back in a neat ponytail, and his bruises, the blossoms of purples and yellows on his arms, were beginning to heal.

"Don't get up," he said. "I'm not staying. I just want to leave you this." He placed a small silver gift bag on her bottom porch step. "I know I can't make up for what I've done to you."

"I haven't asked you to."

"Yeah. Anyway, I'm sorry."

He started to walk away. Abigail climbed down the steps. "Wait—stay."

Nervous, eager, he watched her open the bag and take out a white rectangular box. She lifted the lid, and inside, nestled on soft cotton, was her necklace, the chain repaired, the pearls restrung.

"I told the jeweler there was a cameo pendant," Mattie said.

"I have it."

"When I grabbed the necklace with the saw, I broke the

chain," Mattie explained. "I got a plastic bag in Doyle's garage and put all the pearls and the pieces of chain in there. It's the one okay thing I did, because if they'd been loose in my pocket when Ellis knocked me in the water…" He didn't finish the thought. "Well, I just wanted to get your necklace back to you."

"You took a huge risk, coming here to steal it. Were you afraid I'd find it when I started knocking out walls?"

"Not just that. I used it to put more pressure on Linc. I wanted more money. I wanted to believe he was responsible for what happened to Chris. Because I wouldn't have broken in if he hadn't been burglarizing. I've been mixed-up for a long time."

"What about the money Linc paid you?"

"I returned it. He says—" Mattie seemed embarrassed. "He says he'll insist it was a loan, but I was too drunk and stupid not to realize it."

Abigail stood up. "Mattie—the pictures—"

"I took the ones at Ellis's. I didn't know he had them. I snapped them with a disposable camera after I broke in here." He flushed. "I was trying to give myself an alibi."

"The police found the pictures on Ellis's computer. But the one the morning Owen found Chris's body—"

"That was Ellis," Mattie said.

"Then he was there. Watching us." She'd need time to get used to that one. "Thank you for returning the necklace."

He nodded to the bag. "There's something else in there."

She helped open the bag and lifted out a photograph in a simple black frame.

It was of Chris as a boy out with his grandfather on their lobster boat, laughing, loving life. Mattie must have been on shore, just a boy himself.

"Thank you."

But she realized he was gone.

Scoop and Bob came out onto the porch with a platter of lobsters. Bob sighed at her. "You're trying to keep the State of Maine from prosecuting him, aren't you?"

She knew he meant Mattie, and nodded.

Scoop scowled. "Someone comes after me with a drywall saw, I'd want his butt in the slammer."

"Look at it this way, Scoop," Bob said, grinning, "if not for the cut on that leg, who knows if Abigail and Batman ever would have gotten together?"

"Yeah." Scoop winked at her. "There's that."

"Forget it, guys. Owen's off to Guatemala."

Bob slung an arm around her. "Not forever."

CHAPTER 33

Abigail struck a match to her pile of charcoal and lighter fluid and stood back just in time to avoid getting her eyebrows singed from the two-foot flames.

One of these days, she'd get the knack for lighting a damn grill.

She'd been back on the job a month. The work felt good.

Being alone in her bed didn't.

But she'd needed the weeks on her own. Her routines had helped her turn the last corner on her past. She and Bob and Scoop had sat up late many nights going over the details of the case. Her housemates never tired of helping her put the pieces together, until they became like a worn puzzle that she could do blindfolded.

She had answers. Most of them, anyway. Understanding, she realized, never would come—she never wanted to live in a world where she could understand someone like Ellis Cooper.

"You shouldn't be out here barefoot. Hot coals and all."

Owen. She spun around, grinning at him, trying not to let on her surprise at seeing him—her delirious pleasure. "Yikes, man, you look even more rugged here in the city than you do up in Maine amid all that granite."

"Does that mean I'm invited to stay?"

"I'm grilling hot dogs. Normally I don't eat hot dogs, but the Red Sox are on a winning streak."

He smiled. "That's Bostonian logic."

"Bob's making potato salad. Scoop's doing up a bean salad. And we've each got a pint of Ben & Jerry's in the freezer. We're going to bring them all out at once and see who picked what." She slung her arms over his shoulders. "And, yes, you're invited."

"Good, because you're invited to a Polly Garrison function."

"Uh-oh."

"Uh-oh is right. Do you own a dress?"

"Of course—"

"A gown, I mean."

"A gown?"

"It's a formal. A fund-raiser for Fast Rescue here in Boston. She wants her rich friends to cough up big-time. She's here—"

"I don't suppose she'd like to join us for hot dogs?"

"Knowing my grandmother, she would, but I'm not telling her she's invited."

"When is this fund-raiser?"

"Tomorrow night." He slipped his arms around her. "Which gives us tonight."

"My apartment—it's not even as big as my house in Maine."

"Does it have a bed?"

"A double bed. I can't fit a queen-size mattress in my bedroom."

"Then we're all set. The rest will sort itself out."

Abigail was a hit at the fund-raiser, as Owen knew she would be. He sat with her the next morning in her tiny yard, drinking bad coffee while she strapped on gun and pager and whatever else she carried as one of Boston's finest.

"Austin, Boston, Maine, my life, your life." She grinned at him. "We'll figure it out, won't we?"

"We will."

"I love you, you know."

He winked at her. How many times had he told her he'd loved her in the past two days? Not nearly enough. "I love you."

"I like hearing that. What're you going to do while I'm off catching bad guys today?"

"Buy you a new multimedia system. The bed works fine. As you know." He sipped more of his coffee, which tasted as if it'd been boiled in her gritty grill. "But your multimedia system has to go. Your TV has rabbit ears."

"That's an exaggeration."

Bob and Scoop yelled from their balconies, "No, it's not."

Abigail started arguing with them, and Owen grinned, stretching out his long legs and feeling at home.

* * * * *

Turn the page for an exciting sneak peek at
THE ANGEL
by Carla Neggers,
available May 2008
from MIRA *Books.*

Not for the first time in his life, Simon Cahill found himself in an argument with a snob, this time in Boston, but he could as easily have been in New York, San Francisco, London or Paris. He'd been to all of them. He enjoyed a good argument—especially with someone as obnoxious and pretentious as Lloyd Adler.

Adler looked to be in his early forties and wore jeans and a rumpled black linen sport coat with a white T-shirt, his graying hair pulled back in a short ponytail. He gestured toward a watercolor painting of an Irish stone cottage across the crowded, elegant Beacon Hill drawing room. "Keira Sullivan is more Tasha Tudor and Beatrix Potter than Picasso, wouldn't you agree, Simon?"

Probably, but Simon didn't care. Keira Sullivan was supposed to have made her appearance by now. Adler had griped about that, too, but her tardiness hadn't seemed to stop people from bidding on the two paintings she'd donated to tonight's charity auction. The second was of fairies or elves or some damn things in a magical glen. Proceeds would go to support a scholarly conference on Irish-American folklore to be held next spring in Boston and Cork, Ireland.

In addition to being a popular illustrator, Keira Sullivan was also a folklorist.

Simon hadn't taken a close look at either of her paintings. A week ago he'd been in Armenia searching for survivors of a moderate but damaging earthquake. Over a hundred people had died. Men, women, children.

Mostly children.

But now he was in a suit—an expensive one—and drinking champagne in a chandeliered drawing room on the first floor of an elegant early nineteenth-century brick house overlooking Boston Common. He figured he deserved to be mistaken for an art snob.

"Beatrix Potter's the artist who drew Peter Rabbit, right?" Simon swallowed more of his champagne. It wasn't bad, but he wasn't a snob about champagne, either. He liked what he liked and didn't worry about the rest. He didn't mind if other people fussed—he just minded if they were pains in the ass about it. "When I was a kid, my mother decorated my room with cross-stitched scenes of Peter and his buddies."

"I beg your pardon?"

"Cross-stitch. You know—you count these threads and—" Simon stopped, deliberately, and shrugged. He knew he didn't look like the kind of guy who'd had Beatrix Potter rabbits on his wall as a kid, but he was telling the truth. "Now that I'm thinking about it, I wonder what happened to my little rabbits."

Adler frowned, then chuckled. "That's very funny," he said, as if he couldn't believe Simon was serious. "Keira Sullivan is good at what she does, obviously, but I hate to see her work overshadow several quite interesting pieces here tonight. A shame, really."

Simon looked at Adler, who suddenly went red and bolted into the crowd, mumbling that he needed to say hello to someone.

A lot of his arguments ended that way, Simon thought as he finished off the last of his champagne, got rid of his empty glass and grabbed a full one from another tray. The event was catered, and guests included a wide range of people—academics, graduate students, artists, musicians, folklorists, benefactors, a couple of priests and a handful of politicians. And at least two cops, but Simon steered clear of them. Most people were dressed up and having a good time.

"Lloyd Adler's not that easy to scare off," Owen Garrison said, shaking his head as he joined Simon. He was lean and good-looking, as all the Garrisons were. Simon was built like a bull. No other way to say it.

"I'm on good behavior tonight." He grinned, cheekily putting out his pinky finger as he sipped his fresh champagne. Owen just rolled his eyes. Simon decided he'd probably had enough to drink and set the glass on a side table. Too much bubbly and he'd start a fight. "I didn't say a word."

"You didn't have to. One look and he scurried."

"No way. I'm charming. Everyone says so."

"Not everyone."

Probably true, but Simon did tend to get along with people. He was at the reception as a favor to Owen, whose family, not coincidentally, owned the house where it was taking place. The Garrisons were an old-money family who'd left Boston for Texas after the death of Owen's sister, Dorothy, at fourteen. It was a hellish story. Just eleven himself, he had watched her fall off a cliff in Maine and drown. There had been nothing he could do.

Simon suspected that childhood trauma was the central reason that Owen had founded Fast Rescue, an Austin-based international rapid-response search-and-rescue organization. They could put volunteer teams in place within twenty-four hours of a disaster—man-made or natural— anywhere in the world.

Fast Rescue had arranged the Armenian mission. Simon had become one of its volunteer search-and-rescue specialists eighteen months ago, a decision that was complicating his life more than it should have.

Owen, a top SAR specialist himself, was wearing an expensive suit, too, but he still looked somewhat out of place in the house his great-grandfather had bought a century ago. The decor was in shades of cream and sage-green, apparently Dorothy Garrison's favorite colors. The first floor, where the drawing room was located, was reserved for meetings and functions, such as tonight's reception. The second and third floors comprised the offices for the Dorothy Garrison Foundation.

Owen glanced toward the door to the main entry. "Still no sign of Keira Sullivan. Her uncle's getting impatient." Her uncle was Bob O'Reilly, one of the cops there tonight. Owen's fiancée, Abigail Browning, was the other one. They were both homicide detectives with the Boston Police Department. O'Reilly was a beefy, freckle-faced redhead with a couple decades on the job. Abigail was twenty years younger, slim and dark haired, a rising star in the homicide unit.

She was also the daughter of John March, the director of the Federal Bureau of Investigation and the reason Simon's association with Fast Rescue had become complicated. He used to work for March. Sort of still did.

He'd decided to avoid Abigail and O'Reilly, because they both had a nose for liars.

"Any reason to worry about your missing artist?" he asked Owen.

"Not at this point. It's pouring rain, and the Red Sox are in town—rained out by now, I'm sure. I imagine traffic's a nightmare."

"Can you call her?"

"She doesn't own a cell phone. No phone upstairs in her apartment, either."

"Why not?"

"Just the way she is."

A flake, Simon thought. He'd learned, not that he was interested, that Keira was renting a one-bedroom apartment on the top floor of the Garrison house until she figured out whether she wanted to stay in Boston. He understood wanting to keep moving—he didn't live on a boat by accident.

"Abigail's bidding on one of Keira's pieces," Owen said.

"The fairies or the Irish cottage?"

"The cottage, I think."

They were imaginative, cheerful pieces. Keira had a flair for capturing and creating a mood—a part-real, part-imagined space where people wanted to be. Her work wasn't sentimental, but it wasn't edgy and self-involved, either. Simon didn't have much use for a painting of fairies or an Irish cottage in his life. No house to hang it in, for one thing.

Irish music kicked up, and he noticed five young musicians in the far corner, obviously enjoying themselves on their mix of traditional instruments—an Irish harp, bodhran, tin whistle, mandolin, fiddle and guitar. They'd use what a song required.

"The girl on the Irish harp is Fiona O'Reilly," Owen said. "Bob's oldest daughter."

Simon wasn't sure he wanted to know any more about Owen's friends in Boston, especially ones in, or related to people in, law enforcement. It was all too tricky. Too damn dangerous. But here he was, playing with fire.

Owen's gaze drifted back to his fiancée, who wore a simple black dress and was laughing and half dancing to the spirited music. Abigail caught his eye and waved, her smile broadening. They were working on setting a date for their wedding. Whenever it was, Simon planned to be out of the country.

"You can't tell her about me, Owen."

"I know." He broke his eye contact with Abigail and sighed at Simon. "She'll find out you're not just another Fast Rescue volunteer on her own. One way or the other, she'll figure out your relationship with her father and that I knew and didn't tell her. Then she'll hang us both by our thumbs."

"We'll deserve it, but you still can't tell her. It's classified. We shouldn't even be talking about it now."

Owen gave a curt nod.

Simon felt a measure of sympathy for his friend. "I'm sorry I put you in this position."

"You didn't. It just happened."

"I should have lied."

"You did lie. You just didn't get away with it."

The song ended, and the band transitioned right into the next one, "The Rising of the Moon," which Simon knew well enough from his days in Dublin pubs to hum. But he didn't hum, because if he'd been mistaken for an art critic—or at least an art snob—already tonight, next he'd be mistaken for a music critic. Then he'd have to rethink his entire approach to his life, or at least start a brawl.

"In some ways," he said, "my lie was more true than the truth."

Owen stared at him. "Only you could come up with a statement like that, Simon."

"There are facts, and there's truth. They're not always the same thing."

A whirl of movement by the entry drew Simon's attention, and he gave up on his explanation as he noted a woman standing in the doorway, soaking wet, water dripping off the ends of her long blond hair.

"The missing artist, I presume."

But even as he spoke, Simon saw that something was wrong. He heard Owen's breath catch and knew he saw it, too. The woman—Keira—was unnaturally pale and seemed to struggle to keep herself upright, her eyes wide as she appeared to search the crowd for someone.

Simon surged forward, Owen right behind him, and they reached her just as she rallied, straightening her spine and pushing a wet lock of hair out of her face. She was dressed for the woods, soaked and obviously shaken, but even so, she had a pretty, fairy-princess look about her with her black-lashed blue eyes and flaxen hair that hung almost to her elbows. She was slim and fine boned, and whatever had just happened, it hadn't been good.

"There's a body," she said tightly. "A man. Dead."

That Simon hadn't expected. Owen touched her wrist. "Where, Keira?"

"The Public Garden—he drowned, I think."

The Public Garden was just down Beacon Street. "Are the police there?" Simon asked.

She nodded. "I called 911. Two Boston University students found him. We all got caught in the rain, but they were ahead of me and saw him first. He was in the pond. They pulled him out—they're just kids. They were so upset. But there was nothing anyone could do at that point." Despite her obvious distress, she was composed, focused. Her eyes narrowed, searching the crowd. "My uncle's here, isn't he?"

Simon glanced back into the room. The well-dressed crowd and the sparkling room—the lively Irish music and tinkle of champagne glasses—were a contrast to the stoic, drenched woman behind him and her stark report of a dead man down the street.

Detectives Browning and O'Reilly were working their way over to Keira from different parts of the room, their intense expressions indicating they'd already found out about the body through other means. They'd have pagers, cell phones.

Abigail got there first. "Keira," she said crisply but not without sympathy. "I just heard about what happened. Let's go into the foyer where it's quiet, okay?"

Keira didn't budge. "I didn't see anything, or the patrol officers on the scene wouldn't have let me go." She wasn't combative, just firm, stubborn. "I'm not a witness, Abigail."

Abigail didn't argue, but she didn't have to because Keira suddenly whipped around and shot back into the foyer, water flying out of her hair. Simon knew better than to butt in, but he figured she'd decided she'd rather discuss the dead man with Abigail than with her uncle, who was about two seconds from getting through the last knot of people.

Simon wished he still had his champagne. "I wonder who the dead guy is."

Owen stiffened. "Simon—"

"I'm just saying."

But Owen didn't have a chance to respond before Detective O'Reilly arrived, his jaw set hard, clearly not pleased with the turn the evening had taken. "Where's Keira?"

"Talking to Abigail," Owen said quickly, as if he didn't want to give Simon a chance to open his mouth.

O'Reilly gave the unoccupied doorway a searing look. "She's okay?"

Owen nodded without hesitation. "Remarkably so. She's not the one who actually found the body."

"She called it in." Clearly, that was plenty for O'Reilly not to like. He sucked in a breath. "How the hell does someone drown in the pond in the Public Garden? It's not even a real pond. It's about two feet deep."

Good question, but Simon clearly wasn't on O'Reilly's radar and he preferred to keep it that way.

The senior detective glanced back toward his daughter. She and her ensemble had just finished a song and were taking a break. "I need to go with Abigail," he said, addressing Owen. "You'll make sure Fiona stays here until I know what's going on?"

"Sure."

"And Keira. Keep her here, too."

"She got caught in the rain. She'll want to change—"

"Yeah, good. That's fine. Just don't let her go traipsing off somewhere. She's like that. Always has been."

"There's no reason to think the drowning was anything but an accident, is there?"

"Not yet," O'Reilly said without elaboration, and stalked into the foyer.

Simon didn't mind being a fly on the wall for a change. "The uncle doesn't get along with his daughter and niece?"

"They all get along fine," Owen said, "but they're a complicated family."

"All families are complicated, even the good ones." Simon moved closer to the foyer doorway, just as Keira started up the stairs barefoot, wet socks and shoes in one hand. She was prettier than he'd expected. More or less drop-you-in-your-tracks pretty. He noticed her uncle scowling at her from the bottom of the stairs and grinned, turning back to Owen. "Maybe especially the good ones."

Ten seconds later the two BPD detectives left through the front door.

The Irish ensemble started up again, playing a quieter tune.

Owen headed for Fiona O'Reilly, who cast a worried look in his direction even as she and her ensemble launched into a new song. She had freckles, but otherwise didn't resemble her father as far as Simon could see. Her hair had reddish tints, but really was blond and long like her cousin's, and she was a lot better looking than her father. Simon thought Owen had said Fiona was nineteen. She looked younger.

People in the crowd seemed unaware of the drama over by the door. Caterers brought out trays of hot hors d'oeuvres. Mini quiches, little flaky buttery things oozing cheese, stuffed mushrooms, skewered strips of marinated chicken. Simon noticed Lloyd Adler pontificating to an older couple who looked as if they thought he was a pretentious ass, too.

Simon went in the opposite direction, making his way

to the back wall where Keira's two donated watercolors were on display.

He'd bid on the one with the cottage, just to give himself something to do.

It was a white stone cottage set against a background of wildflowers, green pastures and ocean that wasn't in any part of Ireland that he had ever visited. He supposed that was part of the point—to create a place of imagination and dreams. A beautiful, bucolic place. A place not of this world.

At least not the world in which he lived and worked.

Simon settled on a number and put in his bid, one that virtually assured him of ending up with the painting. He could give it to Abigail and Owen as a wedding present. If he was invited to the wedding, he'd make sure he was in another country that day. But he could give them a present.

He acknowledged an itch to head down to the Public Garden with the detectives, but he let it go. He'd seen enough dead bodies, enough to last him a long time. A lifetime, even. Except he knew there would be more. There always were.

Instead, he'd find another glass of champagne, maybe grab a couple of the chicken skewers and wait for a dry, calmer Keira Sullivan to make her appearance.

$2.00 OFF

A suspenseful and evocative tale from

CARLA NEGGERS

THE ANGEL

SAVE $2.00

on the purchase price of **THE ANGEL** by Carla Neggers.

Offer valid from April 29, 2008, to May 31, 2008.
Redeemable at participating retail outlets. Limit one coupon per purchase.

KILLER FOCUS

THE SECOND BOOK IN
AN EXCITING NEW TRILOGY BY
FIONA BRAND

Courtesy of a new identity in the Witness Security Program
Taylor Jones was almost enjoying her quiet new life with
a nice, normal guy. Then her next-door neighbor turns
up dead, a stray bullet barely misses her and the former
FBI agent knows she's right in the crosshairs.

She discovers a chilling connection between the
South American cocaine trade, terrorism and, amazingly, a
secretive cabal that began with the fall of Nazi Germany...
and whose influence reaches all the way to the White House.

But even more frightening, she suspects her nice, normal
guy may be at the center of it all.

> "A rare and potent mixture of adventure,
> mystery and passion that shouldn't be missed."
> —*Romantic Times BOOKreviews*
> on *Touching Midnight*

REQUEST YOUR FREE BOOKS!

2 FREE NOVELS
FROM THE ROMANCE/SUSPENSE
COLLECTION PLUS 2 FREE GIFTS!

YES! Please send me 2 FREE novels from the Romance/Suspense Collection and my 2 FREE gifts. After receiving them, if I don't wish to receive any more books, I can return the shipping statement marked "cancel." If I don't cancel, I will receive 4 brand-new novels every month and be billed just $5.49 per book in the U.S., or $5.99 per book in Canada, plus 25¢ shipping and handling per book plus applicable taxes, if any*. That's a savings of at least 20% off the cover price! I understand that accepting the 2 free books and gifts places me under no obligation to buy anything. I can always return a shipment and cancel at any time. Even if I never buy another book from the Reader Service, the two free books and gifts are mine to keep forever.

185 MDN EF5Y   385 MDN EF6C

Name	(PLEASE PRINT)	
Address		Apt. #
City	State/Prov.	Zip/Postal Code

Signature (if under 18, a parent or guardian must sign)

Mail to **The Reader Service:**
IN U.S.A.: P.O. Box 1867, Buffalo, NY 14240-1867
IN CANADA: P.O. Box 609, Fort Erie, Ontario L2A 5X3

Not valid to current subscribers to the Romance Collection,
the Suspense Collection or the Romance/Suspense Collection.

Want to try two free books from another line?
Call 1-800-873-8635 or visit www.morefreebooks.com.

* Terms and prices subject to change without notice. NY residents add applicable sales tax. Canadian residents will be charged applicable provincial taxes and GST. This offer is limited to one order per household. All orders subject to approval. Credit or debit balances in a customer's account(s) may be offset by any other outstanding balance owed by or to the customer. Please allow 4 to 6 weeks for delivery.

Your Privacy: Harlequin is committed to protecting your privacy. Our Privacy Policy is available online at www.eHarlequin.com or upon request from the Reader Service. From time to time we make our lists of customers available to reputable firms who may have a product or service of interest to you. If you would prefer we not share your name and address, please check here. ☐

BOB07

THE RIVETING DEBUT NOVEL BY
DEANNA RAYBOURN

"LET THE WICKED BE ASHAMED,
AND LET THEM BE SILENT IN THE GRAVE."

These ominous words are the last threat that Sir Edward Grey receives from his killer. Before he can show them to Nicholas Brisbane, the private inquiry agent he has retained for his protection, he collapses and dies at his London home.

When Brisbane visits Sir Edward's widow, Julia, and suggests that her husband was murdered, Julia engages him to help her investigate. Pressing forward, Julia follows a trail of clues that lead her to even more unpleasant truths, and ever closer to a killer who waits expectantly for her arrival.

SILENT IN THE GRAVE

"A perfectly executed debut."
—*Publishers Weekly*, starred review

*Available the
first week of
December 2007
wherever
paperbacks
are sold!*

CARLA NEGGERS

32455 ABANDON	___ $7.99 U.S.	___ $9.50 CAN.
32419 CUT AND RUN	___ $7.99 U.S.	___ $9.50 CAN.
32237 BREAKWATER	___ $7.99 U.S.	___ $9.50 CAN.
32205 DARK SKY	___ $7.50 U.S.	___ $8.99 CAN.
32104 THE RAPIDS	___ $6.99 U.S.	___ $8.50 CAN.
66972 THE CARRIAGE HOUSE	___ $6.50 U.S.	___ $7.99 CAN.
66970 ON FIRE	___ $6.50 U.S.	___ $7.99 CAN.
66923 STONEBROOK COTTAGE	___ $6.50 U.S.	___ $7.99 CAN.
66845 THE CABIN	___ $6.50 U.S.	___ $7.99 CAN.
66651 THE HARBOR	___ $6.99 U.S.	___ $8.50 CAN.

(limited quantities available)

TOTAL AMOUNT	$ _____
POSTAGE & HANDLING	$ _____
($1.00 FOR 1 BOOK, 50¢ for each additional)	
APPLICABLE TAXES*	$ _____
TOTAL PAYABLE	$ _____

(check or money order—please do not send cash)

To order, complete this form and send it, along with a check or money order for the total above, payable to MIRA Books, to: **In the U.S.:** 3010 Walden Avenue, P.O. Box 9077, Buffalo, NY 14269-9077; **In Canada:** P.O. Box 636, Fort Erie, Ontario, L2A 5X3.

Name: _____
Address: _____ City: _____
State/Prov.: _____ Zip/Postal Code: _____
Account Number (if applicable): _____

075 CSAS

*New York residents remit applicable sales taxes.
*Canadian residents remit applicable GST and provincial taxes.

MIRA®

www.MIRABooks.com

MCN1207BL